THIS BOOK IS TO BE RETURNED ON OR BEFORE THE
AF LAST DATE STAMPED BELOW CEN

26. AUG 17.
18. OCT 18.

WITHDRAWN

Balfron 01360 440407
Callander 01877 331544
Cowie 01786 816269
Dunblane 01786 823125
Plean 01786 816319
Bannockburn 01786 812286
Cambusbarron 01786 473873
Doune 01786 841732
Fallin 01786 812492
St Ninians 01786 472069
Library HQ 01786 237535
Bridge of Allan 01786 833680
Central 01786 237760
Drymen 01360 660751
Killin 01567 820571
Strathblane 01360 770737

Stirling Council Libraries

Published in 2017 by Ramoan Press

Copyright © Terry H. Waton 2017

Terry H. Watson has asserted her right to be identified as the author of this Work in accordance with the Copyright, Designs and Patents Act 1988

ISBN Paperback: 978-0-9956807-2-2
Ebook: 978-0-9956807-3-9

All rights reserved. No part of this publication may be reproduced, stored in a retrieval system, or transmitted in any form or by any means, electronic, mechanical, photocopying, recording or otherwise, without the prior permission of the copyright owner.

All characters and events in this publication, other than those clearly in the public domain, are fictitious and any resemblance to real persons, living or dead, is purely coincidental.

A CIP catalogue copy of this book can be found in the British Library.

Published with the help of Indie Authors World

FOR
GLENBOIG
THE PLACE, THE PEOPLE

Breathes there the man, with soul so dead,
Who never to himself hath said,
This is my own, my native land!
Sir Walter Scott

OTHER BOOKS BY THIS AUTHOR

THE LUCY TRILOGY:

Call Mama

Scamper's Find

The Leci Legacy

A Tale Or Two And A Few More

The Clock That Lost Its Tick And Other Tales

ACKNOWLEDGEMENTS

My sincere thanks to relatives and friends who have helped THE LECI LEGACY along the road to publication.

The encouragement that I received from readers, some of whom were strangers who became friends, helped THE LECI LEGACY join with CALL MAMA and SCAMPER'S FIND to form a trilogy and complete Lucy's story.

My thanks to the staff at Tesco, Coatbridge for their friendship and support in promoting my books and encouraging me to 'get on with the writing'.

To Martin Keating, I owe a debt of gratitude for his non-judgmental proofreading and dealing with my writing foibles.

Thanks too, to Kim and Sinclair Macleod of Indie Authors World for publishing THE LECI LEGACY and for their patience and friendship.

Finally, as always, my love and thanks to Drew and Rebecca.

PROLOGUE

The story so far:
CALL MAMA recounts the story of the abduction of fifteen-year-old Lucy Mears, a crime executed for obscure reasons and resulting in investigating officers travelling across several states in the USA in a desperate attempt to track down the perpetrators of the crime and bring them to justice. Have they arrived too late at the ultimate destination to rescue the traumatised child and her unknown abductors? Or, are they in time to discover the mysterious purpose behind the abduction?
SCAMPER'S FIND continues to explore and develop the consequences of Lucy's plight that resulted in the same investigating officers crossing the Atlantic to the UK and joining forces with detectives who unwittingly become involved in the now four-year-old unsolved crime. Scottish detectives investigating a heinous crime of their own, find themselves caught up in the perplexing and appalling outrage that also involves their London counterparts. Lasting friendships are made in the relentless

pursuit of justice. Officers of the law work together; twists and turns become the order of the day as they endeavour to conclude their investigations.

CHAPTER ONE

The sun began to rise as the traveller awoke from sleep. He had travelled extensively during his long career, jetlag had never been an issue for him, his body clock adjusting to the various time zones he found himself in. He was used to turbulence and was relieved that it did not disturb his travelling companions. Trying not to waken the sleeping youth seated by the window, he gently lifted the shade to watch night turn to day, light emerging slowly to the promise of a day ready to be filled with hope, excitement and wonder. He sat back, gave a sigh of contentment and looked lovingly at his young son. *A chip off the old block,* commented many friends. In looks, yes, but in nature he was quite different from his father. While the latter oozed confidence, a self-assurance that came from life's experience, the young boy portrayed a more sensitive, creative nature, quiet and unassuming, with a gentle soul so akin to that of his mother. The man smiled at the two people seated across the aisle, sleeping side by side as if two heads emerged from one pair of shoulders, so close were his wife and daughter. Pride came from every pore of his being as he looked at the duo. *Like mother, like daughter,* he thought. Both had long fair hair that curled uncontrollably at times giving a unique style of its own. With similar facial features the girl had inherited her mother's beauty, her tomboy nature coming surely from her father's genetic make-up. He smiled as he recalled past events in his life leading to this serene period. He felt blessed with a beautiful wife, son and daughter and thought too of his stepdaughter seated further back in the plane, out of sight, with her partner.

His reverie was disturbed as lights came on and cabin crew began serving breakfast. He gently tapped his son. "Wake up, Lucian, we're almost in Scotland." The lad rubbed sleep from his eyes, blinked and looked out at the clouds as the airplane took him nearer to his destination. He ran his fingers through his dark hair; dark like his father's, thick and straight, neatly shaped with tapered sides cut at an angle that suited the shape of his face. "I'll leave you to come to," he laughed as the boy struggled to keep awake. Glancing at his wife and daughter, his heart melted with pride.

"Morning, honey. You slept well."

"Hi, Tony! Yeah, I surprised myself."

"Morning, Dad," bounced lively thirteen-year-old Poppy, reaching across to give her father a high five. Once awake, she would remain so for hours on end, chatting non-stop, questioning, challenging and always getting the last word in, in any conversation.

"Hi, sweetie. We're almost there."

Breakfast brought Lucian to life. *It never fails to amaze me where he puts it,* mused Tony Harvey as he tackled the surprisingly edible airline food. The only sound in the aircraft came from passengers wrestling with cutlery packages that defied all but nimble fingers.

As the meal was cleared away and passengers chatted among themselves, a striking, elegant woman appeared at his side.

"Morning, Tony. Morning, Mom. Hi kids."

"Hey, Abigail, how are you guys? Did you sleep back there?"

"Ralph slept from the moment we left Chicago and snored most of the way," she laughed, her eyes smiling with happiness, belying the trauma of her younger days. They chatted for some time, comfortable in each other's company.

"Catch up with you when we land, honey," said her stepfather as the 'fasten seat belt' sign indicated that the descent to their destination had begun. He had promised his family a vacation in Scotland as soon as he felt they were old enough to appreciate what the country had to offer.

*

It was mid-summer. The capital, Edinburgh, was awash with tourists gathering in the city for the Festival. Tony's former work colleague, Carole Carr, had previously visited and assured him he must take his family to Edinburgh.

"Tony, your guys would love it. There's so much to see and do, even without the festival. We didn't have enough time as we'd booked to go to the Northern Islands. Ever since our working visit fifteen years ago, I promised myself I'd return and visit Shetland. It drew me in, Tony. You could feel the history of bygone people as you walked along the island among those ancient stones and stunning landscape. Ted and the kids loved it, so different from anything we've ever seen, such rugged coastlines and tradition. Jack loved the tiny Shetland ponies. They were so cute."

She and Tony often spoke of their time together in Chicago's police department, where as career partners they became so close that they knew every thought and move each would make in dealing with the criminal elements in the city. One case dominated their recollections. It had taken over their lives for many years, almost destroyed their careers and brought them to Scottish shores in search of fugitives who had frustratingly evaded justice in America.

"My only regret, Carole, was in not nailing that escapee, Alex Bryson, who gave our Scottish colleagues the run-a-round. I would have retired a contented man if we could have brought him before the court to face justice and drawn a line under the whole sordid episode."

"Yeah," said Carole. "He sure did evade justice. Do you think he will ever be found after all these years or will it be another mystery like the UK's Lord Lucan?"

"Very likely, Carole, although I heard from Brody Cameron – do you remember him, the forensic scientist who worked with us back then? He told me that a male body had been fished out of the river not many miles from where the suspect lived. It was never identified or claimed by any grieving relative. A real John Doe. As far as I'm led to believe, his remains have not been claimed and are stored in the local morgue."

"If he were our guy, there wasn't much chance of a grieving relative turning up to arrange a funeral," said Carole. "His wife Alice divorced him and made it clear that she wanted nothing to do with him, so she sure wouldn't come running to claim his body. His mother's illness sheltered her from the knowledge of all three sons' crimes. Poor lady."

"Yeah, I guess John Doe's remains are still in a morgue. There has been no funeral yet as far as I'm aware," replied Tony.

"I would have thought the local council would have the body disposed of, for hygiene reasons if nothing else."

"In the UK," continued Tony, "there's a Missing Persons website that publishes pictures of clothing and things like tattoos and other identifying items and they work closely with police to try to identify unclaimed bodies. Maybe the river man has been claimed by now. Who knows?"

Their conversation was subdued as they remembered the gruesome killing of two American fugitives wanted for their part in the death of Lucy Mears, abducted by her great-aunt Anna Leci as an act of revenge, a case that had snowballed over many years of investigation leaving a legacy of emotional heartache for those involved.

Linked to this, a subsequent encounter with three brothers from UK, intent on a revenge mission of their own, became a vendetta that wove both cases into one confusing, heart-breaking crime investigation. Peggy Bryson's three sons sought to settle a score for an attack on their mother, a revenge that got out of hand, effecting an arduous USA and UK joint operation resulting in the eldest son remaining unaccounted for, lying perhaps in a morgue freezer in Scotland. Her middle son, Joe, bore the burden of the heinous crime and would languish in a maximum-security prison for the remainder of his natural life. The youngest of the brothers, Bobby, suffering from severe mental illness and sentenced in court in his absence, was incarcerated in a high-security psychiatric hospital where his every move was monitored. The news that his mother's illness had deteriorated to the point that she did not recognise anyone, and his powerlessness to visit her, had tipped his fragile mind even further into a world of confusion and unreality, a world which no one could penetrate and few understood.

"Yeah, Carole, times sure were interesting back then. Do you miss the job?"

"At times I do, Tony. I miss the rush of adrenalin that came with every new case, every new clue that helped us bag a few crooks. Yeah, I miss that side of it, but not the long hours and mountains of paperwork."

"I guess I'm much the same as you. When I hear of crimes in the city I wonder, are they doing this? Have they thought of that? I suppose it never really leaves us, but, hey, I have other things to distract me now."

"Yeah, Tony. That was the best move of your life, marrying Gina; and look at your delightful kids! Who would have thought that grumpy old Tony Harvey could mellow and grin like a Cheshire cat when his kids are mentioned? You got it made, Tony."

"I'm blessed, Carole, I'm truly blessed."

His reminiscence over, Tony returned to the vacation in hand.

CHAPTER TWO

During their vacation, the family indulged Poppy's passion for ghostly things, an interest she had developed as a very young child from one Halloween when her inquisitive mind developed a fascination for all things ghostlike lasting long after pumpkins and skeletons were confined to cupboards and attics. At school, her stories and artwork inevitably centred on ghostly events and she never tired of watching eerie movies with phantom themes.

"Tony, I'm kind of concerned about this obsession," said Gina with a frown as she watched her daughter rewind a programme about the paranormal and settle to watch it for a second time.

"Let her be, honey. It's a phase she's going through. It's harmless and I'm sure in a month or so she'll be caught up in some other hobby horse. You know what she's like. She never lets go of an interest until she has exhausted all possible avenues of knowledge of the subject."

"Oh, I wonder who she takes that after then?" Gina laughed as she reminded her husband of several occasions when he drained the last drop of information for a specific project he was working on.

Poppy's obsession did not wane. Now, as a teenager and armed with a mass of knowledge, her interest in the paranormal was more than her mother felt was healthy. Her daughter portrayed an obstinate streak like her father, and coupled with her growing independence, she showed no intention of abandoning her hobby. She had researched many of Edinburgh's ghost walks. The girl pleaded with her parents to be taken to Mary King's Close, a 17th century underground street considered the most haunted, blood-curling tourist attraction, a place where myths, mysteries and plagues were expertly explained by enthusiastic guides. Underground streets had lain hidden for 400 years in Edinburgh's Old Town, one being the home of Mary King, a renowned businesswoman of some standing in the city in the 1630s, whose place was visited by tourists hungry for underground thrills of myths and legends.

An excited Poppy visited there with her father and Ralph, the others having opted for more ground-level tourist attractions. Engrossed in the event, Poppy's face lit up as she listened to the character guide bring to life events from bygone days. Tony, despite misgivings, found himself caught up in the history and fun of the attraction as their guide, Agnes, skilfully transported them into the world of old Edinburgh. *I wish I could meet a real ghost,* mused Poppy as she listened to strange tales of times gone by. As the tour neared its end and the group gathered around to hear one more tale, Poppy whispered to her father, "Did you see that man pass by with a long black coat and a kind of top hat?"

Neither Tony nor Ralph had seen such a character but did not wish to spoil Poppy's fun by saying so. As the group turned to leave the area, the guide spoke to them one last time.

"By the way, did any of you notice the plague doctor as he passed by back there? We know his ghost wanders about here but only those open to new experiences, especially the children among us, would have seen him; others among you may have felt a draught like a window being opened. On that note, ladies, gentlemen and children, I thank you for your attendance here today and your attention. Enjoy the rest of your stay in the capital and please, don't have nightmares!"

"I *knew* I'd seen a ghost, oh, Dad, it was *so* exciting. I can't wait to tell the others."

Tony and Ralph exchanged glances, neither of them willing to curb her enthusiasm and both holding a secret thought that, *well…perhaps.* Both men later admitted that they had indeed felt a draught.

*

Following the visit, the group met at an outside cafe, with the retired forensic scientist, Brody Cameron, known to Tony from their joint investigation more than a decade ago. An exuberant Poppy, still fired up from her experience, asked, when introduced to the retired gentleman: "Is it true that you really did light your smelly pipe and deliberately blow smoke into the faces of the reporters to get them to go away and stop asking stupid questions? My dad said you did."

Tony, embarrassed by the question, attempted to apologise for his daughter's outspoken remarks but was interrupted by the amused Brody Cameron who threw his head back in raucous laughter before replying to the girl. "Well, lass, you should never believe everything your old man tells you, but in this case, well, there might just be an element of truth in it." As he spoke, he lit his favourite pipe, as if to make a point, and blew smoke in her direction that caused great hilarity among the group.

He smiled as he was introduced to the rest of Tony's family, and over lunch regaled them with stories of interesting cases that he had worked on over his long career. Poppy, still fired up with tales of Edinburgh's haunted, pleaded with the affable Brody to tell her many more such tales.

"Now then, lass," he began, tapping his pipe as if to solemnise the occasion, "Edinburgh has the most number of haunted places in the UK. What, with its bloodthirsty monarchs, grisly grave robbers and the like, not to mention nearby Greyfriars Kirkyard where visitors are said to be left with bruises and cuts from the resident poltergeist, there's plenty of that sort of thing right here, some of it under your feet. Aye lass, right under your feet in underground passages just like the one you were in." As he spoke he looked down at the ground, the inquisitive child following his every move. "And you say you saw Doctor Plague, as we Edinburgh folk refer to him? Wee lassie, you won't be the first and I dare say you won't be the last."

"That sure is cool," she managed to say through a mouthful of pizza.

Once the inquisitive child had her fill of things that go bump in the night, the group went off to explore more of what the city had to offer, leaving Tony and Brody to reminisce about bygone times, times that brought them together in an attempt to solve two grisly murders that took place not many miles from where they were at present.

"It was a dreadful way to die, tossed into a pit shaft while still alive, albeit, barely alive," said Brody.

"Yeah, but we got our perps, two of them anyway. I guess the other guy is still on the run, or is he? I hear a body was fished out of the river near to where he lived."

"That's right, Tony, and it wasn't long after he absconded. For the life of me, I don't know why the body hasn't been identified...taking up space, that's all he's doing. But it's out of my hands now. More's the pity. I would have solved the case in no time at all, but, once you've retired, younger, more enthusiastic guys take over and soon forget the glut of experience from us oldies."

As if to emphasise his frustration, Brody tapped his pipe rigorously on the table, emitting ash which blew everywhere in the Edinburgh wind.

"And you would be too proud to offer assistance? Am I correct?" smiled Tony, sensing the hurt and loneliness of his former comrade.

Changing the subject, Brody asked, "Aye, well. When are you folks returning to Chicago?

"Not immediately. We're making this an extended holiday, a once in a lifetime trip. We go from here to New York to meet with Carole and Ted and their kids. Both their kids attend university in New York, the younger one is celebrating her 21st birthday and we're joining forces to help her celebrate. The kids plan to go on from there to do some exploring. They've hired a motorhome for the few days that they plan to be away. I'm still trying to persuade Gina to let Poppy go with them. She feels the kid is a bit young to be out of her sight. Always at the back of her mind is the horror of what happened to poor Lucy Mears, who, as you might recall, was Abigail's best friend."

"A tough call for you both to make. I hope it all goes well for the kids. Kids nowadays have much more freedom than we had in our days."

"Yeah, Brody, but weren't we much safer back then?"

"That lass of yours is a live wire. Bet she keeps you on your toes."

"She never stops, Brody; she's on the go 24/7 and we wouldn't have it any other way."

The two chatted at length until the rest of the entourage returned, ready for evening meal and laden down with shopping bags.

"Hey, guys, we have a weight limit for our return flight, remember?"

"But Dad, we can take as much as we like, you just have to pay an excess fee."

Still laughing at his daughter's reasoning, Tony turned his attention to Abigail who held a book out for him to examine. She smiled her wide smile as she said, "Tony, look what I came across in a second-hand bookshop."

She handed him a brightly coloured book that he studied for a moment before exclaiming, "Blood Cousins by Julie Sinclair. Hey, that's the author we met all those years ago. Brody, do you remember her?"

"I do indeed. That must have been the book she was working on when we met up with her. I recall talking about it with her. It's about Mary Queen of Scots and her cousin Elizabeth, and I must say, she is quite a well-known author around these parts now; she writes crime novels and does book events around the city. I hear too, that she has become a bit of a sleuth in her village, solved a few crimes, so I hear."

"That's quite a find, Abigail," said Tony. "Carole will love to read it when we catch up with her. Now, wasn't Julie the owner of the dog who found himself sharing a pit shaft with one of our wanted absconders? What was the dog's name? Skimp or something like that."

"Scamper," replied Brody. "I well remember she had a house full of rescue dogs." Brody stood up and took leave of his old friend and promised to keep in touch. "Enjoy the rest of your stay here in bonnie Scotland and give my regards to Carole when you get back home. And you, young lass," he said addressing Poppy, "keep your eyes peeled for more ghosts!"

CHAPTER THREE

Abigail and her partner Ralph did not travel to New York with the others, but returned to Chicago to continue with their business venture. Many changes had taken place over recent years. They were both tutors at the 'Lucy Mears Academy of Music and Art', which was established by Brenda Mears as a lasting tribute to her talented, musical daughter. Known fondly by its initials, 'LMAMA', it was the former home of Brenda who had moved from the palatial mausoleum of a building to a more compact and practical penthouse apartment and donated her former home and estate to the establishment of the academy. There, young students came to study, many living in the house for the duration of their studies; courses that varied in length from several weeks to an entire academic term. Tutors and students were carefully vetted by Brenda who maintained a major say in the establishment to ensure that they were aware of her need to keep Lucy's memory alive.

The academy had been extensively refurbished to accommodate students who required to live-in during their course of study and to provide spacious work areas for both art and music faculties.

"I'm going for quality," Brenda had said, as she and the young architect had toured the large house, making notes and suggestions as they went. "If this place is to be a memorial to Lucy, the standard has to be the best to reflect my daughter's extraordinary talent and skill."

Lucy's suite of rooms remained locked and untouched as they had done from the time of her death when her young life ended tragically in a sabotaged plane, following her abduction by a mad, scheming relative who sought unwarranted revenge. Toughened glass partitions replaced the walls and doors of her suite to allow students to view, but never enter. That privilege belonged to Abigail, who often, in a solemn reflective mood would sit among Lucy's belongings remembering her dearest friend. *I miss you, Lucy; miss you so much.*

In the stunning entrance hall to the academy, hung a poignant life size portrait of the gifted musician whose life and talent was cut short, denying the world of the music of a first- class cellist. The signature of the artist written in the corner, simply read, *'Abbie'*. It was an impressive portrait drawn from Abigail's memory of her closest friend.

Ralph shared Abigail's memories of Lucy. He too had been a classmate of the talented musician and shared her passion for music. Knowing that his partner still felt the loss of her friend as deeply now as in the traumatic days of Lucy's abduction, he did not encroach on her private, silent moments. When together, they would reminisce about their time at school and share memories in the hope of easing the pain; a deep-seated pain that came from the legacy of grief from Anna Leci and her mad scheme.

"Ralph, I thought that my pain would ease in time, but I guess it will always stay with me."

"Honey," said Ralph who would share his memories with Abigail to reassure her that he too missed Lucy's presence in their lives, "Lucy often helped me out when I struggled with a piece of music. She explained things so expertly, never passed judgement on my mistakes and was really encouraging. She was a star. One time when I didn't make the grade to join the school orchestra, she encouraged me to practise, practise, practise, telling me that hard work would pay off. She was genuinely happy for me when I eventually earned my place. *I knew you could do it,* she told me with that lovely smile of hers."

Ralph and Abigail shared an apartment in the grounds of the academy, an apartment that was once the home of Molly Kelly, Brenda's housekeeper, mentor and long-time friend. A smaller apartment once used by Molly's daughter Nora, was now the private studio of Abigail, where, when not involved with students, she could withdraw to unwind and indulge in her own creativity.

The academy had grown in numbers and had a reputation for quality teaching.

"I never thought for one moment that we would have to turn students away," said Brenda as she sat with

Abigail and Ralph on one of her regular visits to her former home, visits where she not only encouraged the duo in their work but spent time in her daughter's rooms finding peace as she sat among Lucy's things. "We might have to take on some more tutors if things progress as they have been. What's your take on that?"

Abigail said thoughtfully, "It's awesome that the academy has developed such a reputation, but I worry about us getting too big. More tutors would certainly help and we have loads of space to accommodate the students. I hate when we have to turn enthusiastic kids away. Ralph, what do you feel about an increase in numbers?"

The ever-thoughtful and serious man stroked his chin as he pondered the future. "Why don't we employ some tutors on a part-time basis, and see how that pans out?"

"Let's go with that," said Brenda as she gathered her notes together. "I'll draft an advertisement and run it past you guys. Ralph, that might just solve a short-term problem. It might just be the answer for the moment at least."

CHAPTER FOUR

In New York, Tess Carr's 21st birthday celebrations took place in an upmarket Manhattan hotel. The previous evening had been given over to a party for her peers from college and now the celebration centred on family and close friends – Tony, Gina and family. The children of both families had been brought up almost as blood relatives, so close were the adults and, consequently, the children. Over the meal, the adults shared experiences of recent holidays, while the younger members, sitting apart from their parents, planned their imminent camping trip.

"Mom," interrupted Poppy, "Mom, have you decided if I can join the camping trip? Please say, yes."

This gave an opening to them all to discuss the pros and cons of the impending trip and its suitability for young Poppy.

"If only Abigail and Ralph were here to join, I'd be more at ease about it."

"Please, Aunt Gina," pleaded Tess, "please let Poppy come with us. I don't want to be the solo girl."

After pleads, reassurances and promises to take care, Gina acquiesced to her daughter's request, much to the relief of the group who felt Gina was overprotective of the girl, but fully understood that the memory of Lucy's abduction and death would probably never wane. Ted reassured the fearful mother that her child would be in good hands with his older kids.

"Gina, Jack and Tess are level-headed young adults who have coped well with being away to study 800 miles from home."

"It's not as if I don't trust you guys to look after her, it's just well, she can be obstinate and demanding…and then, I worry about her taking off on one of her exploring moods," said Gina.

"Mom," replied Poppy, "I promise I will stay with the others at all times. Honest!"

"And promise me too, that if it's at all cold, you will sleep in the vehicle and not under canvas."

"Yeah, Mom, we promise," enthused Poppy who was ready to promise any demands made on her in order to be included in the trip.

Jack Carr, studying for a doctorate in veterinary medicine at New York's State College of Veterinary Medicine was a mature, intelligent young man whose love of the outdoor life had prompted the idea of the camping adventure which was enthusiastically endorsed by his fun loving sister Tess, an undergraduate at New York's Tisch School of Arts. She had a passion for photography and honed her skills on the many camping trips that she enjoyed with her elder sibling. Her three-year degree, Master of Fine Arts, would ensure she was skilled in design for stage and film. Tess was seldom seen without a camera in hand and looked forward to the impending camping trip to add to her ever growing portfolio.

While the adults retired to the lounge to enjoy cocktails, the four youngsters sat apart from them, whispering together as they discussed their plans.

"Why are we whispering?" enquired Poppy, eyes wide open in wonder.

"Shush, sis," replied her brother. "We don't want the adults to hear us. They would put a stop to our plans if they had even an inkling of what we are going to do."

"You guys have been making plans without me?" said an incredulous Poppy.

"We weren't sure if you would be allowed to come with us and didn't want you to throw a hissy fit and tell the parents of our plans."

"As if I would," retorted the offended child who was about to sulk.

Her brother quickly put paid to that and spoke sharply to her. "That's exactly what Mom is worried about, Poppy, you going off on us. Now, grow up and behave or we will leave you behind. Here's what we plan to do; keep quiet about it."

Jack took over the conversation. He was the unofficial leader and commanded respect. Poppy sat spellbound as she listened to how they planned to spend the next few days.

"Wow, that's awesome! I'm so excited! I can't wait for tomorrow; only one sleep to go! I'm so happy that Mom relented and said I could go with you guys."

*

Later that night the young people gathered in Jack's room to finalise plans.

"Okay, guys, we know what we have to do. Tess and I will share the driving; Lucian, you oversee navigation, keep your eyes peeled for our destination. I don't think it will be easy to find as it's not marked on any recent map."

"What about me?" asked the young girl ensuring they were aware of her presence and her eagerness to be involved in everything.

"You are in charge of the food supplies. Make sure the driver, whichever one of us it is, has plenty of candy bars to keep the sugar levels up as we go along, and keep an eye on dwindling supplies throughout the trip."

"Cool," replied the excited child, pleased to be given an important role.

Seeing Poppy fighting off sleep, they retired each to their own room to dream of the imminent adventure.

Unaware of the details of their children's intentions, and trusting their maturity, the adults gathered on the steps of the hotel after breakfast, waved them off on their adventure with last minute instructions to take care and keep Poppy safe.

"Check in regularly with us, please," was the echo from four anxious parents.

"Report in each evening between six and eight."

"Will do! Don't worry, we'll all be fine. Call you tonight."

*

During the journey, the youngsters sang to the music, relishing the freedom and promise of the adventure of the next exciting days. After several hours and a pit stop to eat lunch organised by Poppy, Jack said, "We can't be far from the place now. According to this old map that I picked up in the college library, we should be seeing the house right about here."

An hour or so later of turning back and forth, Jack declared they were truly lost. "We must have missed the turning. I'll call in at that gas station. We need to refuel and I'll ask for directions."

The gas station was surprisingly well stocked and cluttered with everything imaginable for the citizens of the remote area to purchase. Jack felt that he had walked back in time to another decade. He was fascinated by the array of goods on offer.

"You gonna stand there all day, kid, or are you gonna be buying. Looking for anything in particular?"

Jack, gave himself a shake and replied, "Yeah, sorry, yeah. I'm looking for this place here," he said as he opened up the old map and pointed to his destination.

"You don't want to be going there, buddy," said the proprietor. "It's not somewhere you wanna hang around. There have been some strange goings-on up there. No, you best stay away. Anyhow, there's not much to see. It's been burned to the ground. Just a few months back, it was. Folks around here were mighty pleased to see it go, it was an evil place. No, kid, you don't want to be going near there. They say it's still smouldering and the authorities have erected a high security fence around it, with plenty of danger signs to keep inquisitive folks away. There are caretakers patrolling the place to keep ghoulish folk away. Big tough guys they say. Too many strange things happened up there. No, buddy, you just keep away. What do you want to go there for anyway? It ain't no place to be hanging around."

"Just curious. Thanks anyway."

Jack returned to the others with the news that they had missed the turning and would have to retrace their steps. He related what he had been told.

"The guy was adamant that we shouldn't go there."

"That makes me even more curious to see what's going on," said Tess.

"Yeah. We've come this far, let's stick with the plan," said Lucian.

They drove on for some time discussing what Jack had learned from the proprietor.

"Try that track over there, Jack. It might just be our destination," shouted Tess as she spotted an overgrown track of sorts.

CHAPTER FIVE

Jack turned the camper onto the rough track. He could feel a hard path underneath the overgrown foliage.

"There's been a solid road here at one time. I can feel it under this rough terrain; there's evidence of a well-established vehicular road. We should be okay to drive on it. It's more than a dirt track but no one seems to have driven on this for years." He drove tentatively, trying to avoid damaging the vehicle. Several times he had to stop while the others went ahead to clear some overgrown branches and out-of-control shrubbery. Progress was slow and they had no idea how far the path would take them. They were forced to stop as a fallen tree was blocking their passage.

Lucian shook his head as he studied the fallen tree. "We'll never be able to shift that," he said. "We would need cutting equipment."

They sat on the log debating their next move and eating candy bars that Poppy produced from her pocket.

"Let's go on by foot," said the incorrigible Poppy. "We've not got far; have we, Jack?"

"I'm not sure, Poppy, but if everyone is happy with that, we'll proceed on foot. I need to stretch my legs."

They trudged on, at times knee deep in overgrown bushes that had been left to grow wild. At times the path narrowed forcing them to walk in single file. The track veered to the right, climbed a steep gradient and came to a halt at a tall, rusted iron gateway, dilapidated and overgrown and with its metal hinges firmly set in place by years of neglect. The metal gates, once shiny and ornate were not impervious to rust, the coppery brown corrosion having attacked the metal as if in revenge for what lay behind their imposing facade, as if warning of the evil beyond.

"We'll never open that or climb it. There must be layers of stuff growing over it," commented Tess as she snagged her hand on thorns. "Ouch, that's sharp," she called out as she rubbed her hand furiously to relieve the discomfort.

Not one to concede defeat, Poppy crouched down and moved along the path like an animal stalking its prey. Her hair became tangled in the overgrowth; she tugged to release it, oblivious of the pain it must have caused her. "Hey, guys, I think we have a bit of a clearing here by this wall. We might be able to pull branches from it and see what's over there."

Working together, they disentangled some foliage to reveal an old stone wall which appeared to surround the entire estate. It was a sturdy, well-built wall, built long ago by craftsmen who knew their trade. Hands, almost raw from the effort of clearing, did not stop Jack from his determination to investigate what he had brought the others to witness. Standing on Lucian's shoulders and steadied by the girls, he pulled himself up, pulled more branches aside until he had a clearer view beyond the wall.

"Wow, you have to see this. It's been a massive house at one time. I can see the outline of the building; it must have been colossal. There's not much left of it." Jack continued his commentary. "The smell of burnt timber is overpowering and the roof has completely caved in." He coughed as he tried to clear his throat of the foul taste in his mouth. "I need some water," he said, after inhaling the putrid smoke. "The smoke is lingering and caught my throat. Cover your mouths if you're going to have a look."

"We can smell it from here," said Tess as she too coughed uncontrollably.

They took it in turns to view the remains of what was once a substantial building. Tess, carefully carrying her camera, took several pictures for them to study later. The once magnificent mansion had stretched out over a vast area but lay now, a heap of smouldering rubble with desolate, creaking timbers crying in pain, as if shamed by past events and seeking absolution for their part in evil doings.

"There doesn't seem to be a way in anywhere that I can see," said Lucian, now fired with enthusiasm for the project. "And there are signs everywhere warning of danger. I can still smell smouldering timbers. It's horrid."

Treading carefully along the path, they looked for any means possible of entering the property.

"Short of vaulting over the wall. I can't see a way in," said Jack.

"We would probably land among brambles and thorn bushes," said Tess, still nursing her hand as she stumbled over a piece of concrete. "And there's no way of knowing the height at the other side of the wall. It could be dangerously steep."

Poppy, still creeping along and ignoring the overgrowth, shouted, "Hey, I've found a manhole or some kind of vault thing, with a ring attached. Could this be a way in?"

"Could be a sewer or utility chamber; who knows what's down there? It could be the access we need," said Jack.

Lucian commented, "Or it could lead straight to rats and suchlike."

"Or ghosts!" whispered Poppy.

They tried unsuccessfully to lift the rusted ring. It was firmly set in place. Finding no other means of opening the manhole, they retraced their steps to the camper van to study the pictures taken of the burnt out mansion and to make the promised phone call to reassure their parents that they were well.

"Don't tell them where we are, Poppy. They would freak out."

"We're good, Mom," said Lucian. "We're having a fun time and Poppy is behaving." He laughed as he handed his cell phone to his sibling.

"Hey, Mom, this is a cool trip and I'm in charge of the food."

"Well, don't let the others starve now, sweetie. Love you. Talk to you tomorrow."

After a quick meal distributed by Poppy with the aplomb of a maître d'hôtel, they spent the night in the motorhome, chatting well into the night, planning their next attempt to find an entrance to the intriguing estate.

*

They took off in the morning on foot with various implements which they hoped would help them prise open the rusted manhole and allow access. The task was impossible; the cover would not budge. Frustrated, Poppy gave one almighty tug, struggled to lift the cover but fell back into a jungle of brambles and thorns, screaming as she became tangled. As the others pulled her to safety, she gasped, "Wait, look, there's a tiny door over here among the bushes; looks like it goes right under the ground. It's a funny looking shape. It might lead somewhere. It's big enough for a person to creep through."

A quick clearing of loose foliage disclosed a small cellar door with peeling paint and rusted hinges. It was fastened by a bolt which surprisingly slid open after very little effort by the boys. Jack prised the door open.

"From the state of the hinges, this entrance has recently been used for something or other, look how easy it was to open."

It opened freely to reveal a deep cavern of some kind with a metal ladder partially attached to the wall. Jack lay prone, shone a torch into the deep cave-like site, tested the strength of the ladder and declared it safe to use.

"I'm going down first. Stay here until I return and keep the torch on me."

The descent took several minutes. It was steep. He dropped down, found himself on dry ground and spent several minutes examining the cavern before calling to the others to report his findings. "It's dry and spacious and from what I can see there are two tunnels going off from the main cave."

He carefully climbed out of the cellar and shone the flashlight into the cavern for the others to have their first look at what was to become for them an adventure that would remain with them for the rest of their lives. "There's no burning smell so who's up for spending the night down here and exploring those tunnels? They might give us access up into the house, or what is left of it." Excited at the prospect, they once more trudged back to the van to collect what they needed for an overnight stay and to make the promised call to their parents to assure them they were safe and well. They did not reveal their whereabouts.

"We've found a nice spot to do wild camping," was all they would say. "We're having fun."

"And, we slept in the motorhome. We haven't erected any tents yet," said Poppy to her relieved mother.

*

In the morning after Poppy had distributed food packs, they returned to the cellar and descended the ladder, assisting each other with backpacks and claiming their spot for the night's stay. Snuggled into their sleeping bags, they turned off their flashlights and took it in turns to tell ghost stories, much to the delight of the excited Poppy, who regaled them with her experience of Mary King's Close, exaggerating the tales of myths and mayhem beneath the Old Town of Edinburgh. They had heard of her claim to have seen a real ghost, backed up, it appeared by the eminent Brody Cameron. No one would dismiss Poppy's claim; neither would they condone it.

They chatted well into the night. Jack told a story about paranormal investigations by ghost hunters, interspersed with suitable sound effects to the amusement of Tess and Lucian and the delight of Poppy who begged for more such tales.

"There were objects moving around the room in front of their eyes, they tried to take pictures of it all but nothing showed up when the film was developed." Tess talked about the merits of digital cameras against traditional photography; she was on her hobby horse. One by one they all gave in to sleep. Despite the solid concrete floor under their sleeping bags, they slept. Poppy smiled in her sleep as she undoubtedly dreamt of ghostly happenings.

CHAPTER SIX

Lucian, always a light sleeper was the first to awake. The cavern had no natural light. It lit up from his powerful torch as he rummaged in his backpack for food, the rustling waking the others. "Okay, you guys, who's taken my food pack?" he said as he made even more noise emptying the contents of his luggage.

As they came to life, the others annoyed at the early rising, chided him.

"You've left it in the camper van, you idiot," snapped his sibling. "I had everything laid out, all you had to do was put it in your backpack."

Fully awake they each stretched and groaned as they clambered out of their sleeping bags.

"We'll need to bring some cushions if we plan to stay here another night. That was so uncomfortable," said Tess.

They shared their food with Lucian as Poppy berated her shamefaced brother for his carelessness.

"But I did pack it. I know I did," he protested. "It must have fallen out when I climbed over the tree."

"Let's plan how to spend the day," interrupted Jack, hoping to defuse the impending sibling row. "I vote we explore these two tunnels, two of us to each tunnel. I'll take Poppy with me, and you two guys go together. After thirty minutes, mark your position on the wall and return. We meet here in an hour. Check that you have plenty battery power for the flashlights but use them sparingly. Finish eating and synchronise watches. Now!"

*

Tess and Lucian took off to explore the left-hand tunnel. The floor was cobbled, with the occasional loose stone. They felt their way carefully by feeling along the rough wall, using their torches to light the way ahead.

"We could probably walk for miles under here, under the entire house. Wish we could find an opening into it. Look upwards and down at the floor, there could be an opening anywhere. This is a maze of tunnels that will go for miles, that's for sure," said Tess, the adventurer. "These tunnels were probably custom-built for storage. There's bound to be a way up into the house."

"Hey, I wonder how the others are doing?"

Jack and Poppy, making their way carefully through the right-hand tunnel, were no more successful than the others at finding a way into the main house.

"There's bound to be a labyrinth of tunnels down here to explore," said Jack, shining the light above and around them, looking for openings.

"I'm so excited," said Poppy. "This is real cool. I'm sure there are ghosts here. Don't you just feel their presence, Jack? Come on, ghost, show yourself!"

He laughed at her enthusiasm.

"Poppy, I'm sure we will find you a ghost or two, if only we could get into the remains of the mansion. It's frustrating."

After an hour, the group assembled in the main cave and exchanged findings.

"It's more of a man-made gigantic cellar than a natural cavern. I guess it goes right under the entire house and was probably used for storage for wine and dry stuff for the house. It's really dry," reported Jack.

"Yeah, okay, but let's eat," said Lucian. "It must be lunchtime. Oh, but I don't have anything."

"Serves you right, bro, for leaving it in the van."

"But guys, I know I had it with me. I must have dropped it when we were crawling along on all fours."

"Don't worry, we won't let you starve." Jack chimed in, "Let's eat then go back to the van to restock. We need more battery power if we are to explore some more and we have to call the parents."

"And collect some soft cushions," added Tess. "Poppy, not a word to them about our location. They will freak out."

"I know. I know the drill. But, hey, don't you think it's time you guys came clean and told me about this place? What's so secretive that we can't tell Mom and Dad?"

The others looked at each other and nodded in agreement.

"We'll tell you back at the motorhome," said Tess as she helped Poppy climb up the ladder and retrace her steps through the overgrowth.

There, they sat around curled up on comfortable cushions, ready to answer Poppy's questions. "Okay," said Jack, the leader, "I guess we can tell you the story of Leci House. The saga goes back a long time…nearly twenty years or so when our folks worked together in Chicago Police Department."

"CPD? What's that to do with here in New York? What's the connection?" interrupted Poppy.

"Hey, keep quiet, sis, and we'll tell you everything. Don't interrupt," said Lucian. They each took up the story, adding to it as they recalled what they had heard from their parents when they were growing up.

"This estate belonged to Anna Leci who was the great-aunt of Lucy Mears, Abbie's best friend," began Lucian.

"Yeah," interrupted Poppy yet again. "I've heard of her. She and Abbie were best buddies and Lucy's mom gave her gigantic house over to be the academy where Abbie and Ralph now live and work. Abbie took me through it and showed me Lucy's suite of rooms. It was so sad to think of Lucy and what she went through."

"That's correct, Poppy," said Jack. "Now let's get on with the story… Anna Leci was jealous of Lucy's mom Brenda, because her sister Francesca died not long after giving birth to Brenda. Anna blamed Brenda for Francesca's death, and sought revenge by kidnapping Lucy for weeks on end to let Brenda experience what it was like to lose someone close to her, and Lucy was brought here to this house to meet the great-aunt she never knew she had. She was meant to be flown home from here in a private plane, but tragically it crashed killing all those on board including Lucy. This house is where she spent the last days of her life. We so wanted to see it. We were fascinated by Lucy's story."

Tess took up the story from her brother. "The aunt, it turned out, was so crazy-mad that she didn't really know what was happening around her. Parts of the story are a bit vague. My mom and your dad were the investigating officers and witnessed the plane crash when they were waiting to reunite Lucy with her mom. For weeks after the crash Abbie was so distressed that your dad would call over as he was mighty worried about her."

"Yeah," said an elated Poppy, "and he fell in love with my mom Gina, they got married and me and Lucian were born… it's an awesome love story… how romantic… and we have Abbie as our stepsister. But it's so sad too."

"I was named for Lucy," piped in her brother. "If the baby had been a girl she was to be called Lucy. Abbie chose the name."

"And I was named for dad's fiancée who died from a horrible illness when she was young. Dad has a picture of her in his wallet. She was beautiful. This is all turning into a very sad tale."

Jack continued, "It turned out that two criminals working for Anna Leci sabotaged the airplane to seek revenge on the pilot who had double-crossed them way back when they ran a money lending scam in New York. Then it transpired that one of the bad guys was in collusion with a dodgy lawyer, Edward Garnett, and wanted Lucy killed so that she couldn't inherit this place. He and Anna Leci's nurse planned to stay in this mansion after the old lady's death. He changed the documents and got the sick old lady to sign them. She was unaware of what she was signing."

Lucian took over the story, "Dad and Aunt Carole were back and forwards across the Atlantic to investigate the deaths of those two criminals, who were found murdered in Scotland, dropped into mine shafts and left to die."

"Yuk, what a way to die, even if they were rotten to the core," said Poppy. "So that's how we got to meet that forensic scientist in Edinburgh. I guess he must have worked with them on the case. Now I know why Dad spoke so often of Scotland. He loved the place and wanted us to visit. Which we have done. Cool!"

"And that explains why Dad never suffers from jet lag. He seems to be immune to it by flying thousands of miles just doing his work."

"Now you know, Poppy, why we had to keep this adventure secret from the parents. They would go crazy if they thought we were here," concluded Tess. "That reminds me, we best call them to say all is well. Remember, Poppy, not a word of this..."

"I won't say anything," Poppy said indignantly, annoyed that she was still being treated as a child when she felt she had conducted herself as a responsible young person. "But who burnt the place to the ground?"

Lucian said, "We don't know the answer to that yet. Anyone up for spending our last night back in the cellar and exploring the tunnels again? Or would you prefer to sleep in the motorhome?" The others were amused at Lucian's enthusiasm, knowing how naturally reserved and cautious he was.

"Yeah, let's do it," said Tess. "We have to be back at the hotel on Friday; let's make the most of our last night and spend it in the cellar. We haven't unwrapped the tents yet, so let's leave them be and sleep in the cave place. It's creepy and eerie but, hey, I love it!"

"Right, guys," said the leader of the pack after they had finished their call, "take what you need for the night and, Lucian, remember, food!"

"But guys, I tell you, I did have my food pack with me."

"I'll pack it for you personally then you'll not drop it on the way through the undergrowth," said his sister revelling in her important job.

CHAPTER SEVEN

Once again they trudged along the overgrown path like experienced walkers and scrambled expertly over the fallen tree, unbolted the door and descended into the dark cellar.

"The plan," said Jack, as they sat around on soft cushions, "is that this time we go together into the tunnels, the right-hand tunnel first. We stay together as we don't know the length of it and we don't want to be separated. There must be a way up into what's left of the burnt shell of a house. Right, guys, let's go. Take it in turns to shine the flashlight, all around the walls, floor and roof. Look for any sign of an entrance to the house. Use only one torch at any one time to conserve battery power."

After thirty minutes or so, they found the mark on the wall left on the previous visit and continued on, feeling their way along the wall and using their flashlights sparingly. The cellar tunnel twisted around for several metres, but the group found no evidence of any other passageway which would afford them access to the house. Marking the wall for future reference they carefully retraced their steps to the main cellar, disappointed that their efforts did not yield a result.

"Let's eat something before we head to the other tunnel," suggested Lucian as he opened his new food supply.

"Hey! Mine has gone," said Tess as she emptied out the contents of her bag.

"And you thought I was kidding?" said Lucian.

"Come on," continued Tess, "fun's fun and I'm hungry, who's hidden it?"

Laughter stopped as they realised the seriousness of the situation.

"Someone has access to this chamber," said Jack. "Someone has stolen our food. They must have come from the left-hand tunnel while we were in the other one. We'll explore more in the morning if you guys feel up to it. Does anyone want to head back to the camper instead of staying here? Anyone freaking out?"

"No way," Poppy enthused. "Let's stay and catch us a thief or a ghost."

"I think we need to sleep as we can't hang around too long tomorrow," said Jack. "I'll stay awake and keep watch for a while. If anyone comes in here I'll give a shout, loud enough to waken the dead."

"Oh let me stay awake with you for company," pleaded Poppy. "If there's a ghost around I want to see it. It could be the ghost of Anna Leci, wandering around, a lost spirit, guilt-ridden and moaning like this... moaaaan, moaaaan, moaaaan, as she searches for Lucy."

"Oh Poppy, you and your ghosts. Put your imagination to sleep, sis."

Jack positioned himself where he had a view of the left-hand tunnel, listening for any untoward sounds and glad of some quiet reflective time. He reasoned that someone, a homeless person perhaps, was living there, but where? And how did he gain access to the cellar. There had to be another way into the cellar and he was determined to find it. Deep in thought, he eventually succumbed to sleep, only to be wakened several hours later by the coming to life of the others.

"Well," enthused Poppy, "did you see any ghosts? Was it the desolate, tormented spirit of Anna Leci searching for a way to atone for her past life? Did you hear any moaning sounds?"

"Poppy, give it up. Calm down. This is getting serious," said Jack becoming a bit annoyed with her.

The girl looked at the faces of the others who were looking at each other in shock, bemused at what had happened in the night. They were ignoring her questions.

Jack looked at the others. "Everything's gone! All our stuff has gone! Our backpacks have gone. Every damn thing apart from our sleeping bags, and no one heard a sound."

They were stunned into an inert silence, fearful and angry at the turn of events.

"Whoever took our stuff," he continued, "must have come from the left tunnel after we fell asleep. Sorry, guys, I've let you down. I couldn't keep awake. We must check out that tunnel. Do we have any flashlights or have they all gone?"

"I have mine here," said Lucian. "It was inside my sleeping bag."

Jack nodded and said, "Well, let's hope it has plenty of battery power, use it sparingly. We gotta find what's going on here."

With nothing left of the food or drink, the group had no option but to explore the left tunnel from where they presumed that someone or some persons has silently crept to relieve them of their possessions. More from annoyance than anything else, Jack led the intrepid group along the tunnel, keeping as close to each other as they could. They moved quietly, like a silent parade of mourners. Feeling along the wall, they passed the previous mark and walked on further into the darkness. Their footsteps appeared to echo throughout the cavern, their breathing coming in bursts of anxiety mixed with excitement. They felt their way along, hoping to find another tunnel or access door, or some indication as to where the thief had come from.

Jack whispered, "This is hopeless. We need to go back to the van and collect some more flashlights. Okay, head back, everyone. Lucian's flashlight is dimming, so hold on to each other."

"I'm hungry," moaned Lucian.

"Me too, bro. There's food in the van."

"We'll eat something when we get out of here. Thank goodness our moms packed plenty for us," commented Tess.

"Yeah," said Poppy. "I did an inventory before we left; we have five apples, seven candy bars..."

"Oh, do be quiet, you're not helping my hunger," said her brother.

Returning to the main cellar they headed for the ladder to exit by the trapdoor. Tess, who led the way shouted, "Hey, the ladder has been removed. We can't get out. Some strong people must have been here. That ladder is really heavy."

"Oh no!" shouted Lucian. "Our sleeping bags have gone now. We've been robbed of everything."

"Damn!" roared Jack. He could feel tears of frustration building and was determined to maintain his dignity. "We're trapped in here, guys."

"How the heck do we get out now? Who is doing this? Where are they?" shouted Tess.

Frustration changed to anger, then fear, fear of being trapped underground with no obvious means of escape or communication.

"Guys, we are really, truly stuck here. Someone, probably some hobos, have messed with us and I'm sure as hell going to find out who has imprisoned us. We have nothing left, not a damn thing," said a forlorn Jack as he held his head in his hands.

The others gathered around him, hugged each other in comfort.

Tess whispered, "What do we do now?"

CHAPTER EIGHT

"The kids are late calling tonight," said Gina looking at her watch. She had never fully relaxed since the road trip began, finding it hard to accept that the younger ones would eventually want to find their own way in the world. Since the trauma surrounding Lucy, she had been overprotective of her children and constantly worried about them if they were late from events at school or being out with friends. She had only recently allowed Poppy to have a sleepover at her friend's house, preferring instead to have the friends come to her home.

"But Mom," pleaded Poppy, "Chloe has been here hundreds of times, please, please let me go stay at hers, please."

Tony, while not wanting to undermine Gina's decision, had a difficult time persuading her to let go of her angst and allow the girl a bit more freedom.

"Honey, cut Poppy a bit of slack, let her try a sleepover. Chloe's folks are great guys and she'll be fine with them".

Now, with no phone call forthcoming, her nervousness increased.

"Don't be anxious, honey; they'll call when they're ready. They seem to be having a fun time."

"Tony, didn't you get the impression when we spoke to Poppy that she wanted to say more?"

"Honey, Poppy always wants to say more," he laughed. "You know she never stops talking." Keen to distract Gina from her overwrought frame of mind, he suggested they go and join Ted and Carole for a last swim. "I'll leave my cell phone by the poolside. We'll hear it ring from there."

After their swim, and with no call from their kids, the adults retired to the dining room for a last meal together. "Jack and Tess seem well settled here at college," said Tony, attempting to move the conversation away from the late phone call, and aware of his wife's increasing anxiety. "Why did they choose New York for their studies and not Chicago?"

Ted replied, "As you know, Jack has always been crazy about animals. Remember our mutt, Walt? Jack was so good with him when he got old and infirm and nursed him to the end. He was a volunteer helper at the local animal rescue centre during school holidays and, if we had let him, he would have filled our house with all sorts of animals including, at one point, a request to home a snake or two."

"I put my foot down at that," laughed Carole. "I didn't mind when he brought a dog home while it waited to be rehomed. We had a few cute dogs, but snakes, no way.

We always knew he would choose a career in the veterinary world, so it was no surprise when he decided to become a vet."

Ted took up the story. "As far as I'm aware the University of Illinois is the only centre in our state for veterinary medicine, but he wanted to branch out, leave home and pursue his chosen career elsewhere. Two of his high school friends were planning to study in New York and we gave Jack our blessing to join them."

"It worked just fine," continued Carole, "and when Tess's turn came to choose her career, she opted to join her brother in New York and was accepted at the Tisch School of Arts. They look out for each other and we see how mature the move has made them both."

"Isn't it time we heard from them?" Gina sounded worried as she looked at her watch, yet again.

"Honey, I'll call them now. I've been reluctant to call; I don't want them to think we are chasing after them, but it is getting late."

There was no reply from any of the kids' phones. Each adult tried to call and, as the evening wore on and night fell, Tony had a sick feeling in the pit of his stomach. He did not want to transfer his anxiety to his already-stressed wife.

Ted paced up and down in the hotel foyer, pushing deep on the buttons on his cell as if by rough handling it would connect him to his children.

Carole sat with Gina, attempting to reassure her that they would hear soon, but in her heart she felt a fear not experienced since events long ago when a crazed stalker terrorised her young family causing her endless days of worry about the safety of her children. She had tried to put the incident to the back of her mind, but occasionally, like now, the memory unsettled her and reawakened the nightmare of the experience. "There's probably a simple explanation for this," she said as calmly as she could muster, despite her own doubts. "Perhaps they are in a noisy restaurant or have gone to the movies where they have to switch off cells. Yes, I'm sure that's what it is. They're at a late night movie."

"Not now surely? Not now, it's far too late," blurted out a sobbing Gina. "Oh, Carole, I'm scared. I'm scared something has happened to them. They could be lying injured somewhere and we have no way of knowing where they are. Oh, why didn't we insist that they tell us exactly where they were heading? All this wild camping! It's not good."

Tony and Ted made calls to several hospitals in the area to enquire of any accidents involving kids in a camper van. Unsure of the area, it took some time to locate which hospitals to call. The hotel manager, seeing the men pace up and down, offered assistance and helped speed up the enquiry. No hospital within a hundred-mile radius had the information they required.

"No news is good news then. At least we know they are not in an ER anywhere around."

"Tony, we should call the cops. Do you still have contact here with some NYPC guys?"

"Sure, Ted, but do we have any info on the vehicle? Type, plate number, anything? Oh God, why was I so remiss about stuff like that?"

"All I know is that they hired the van from a college friend whose uncle runs a rental company. Maybe Carole will know the guy's name."

"Ted, let's not involve the girls at the moment until we are sure it's the right thing to do. Do you know anything at all about Jack's friend or where we could locate him?"

"Sorry, and shamed to say it, but no. I don't know who the guy is."

Carole, worried sick and anxious for news, joined her spouse. By now the enormity of the situation hit home increasing their fears for the safety of their children. Ted, arm around his wife, gently asked if she knew which of Jack's friends had arranged the motorhome hire.

"Think hard, sweetie, did either of them mention a name?"

"I know his flatmate is Gerry, Gerry Scanlon. The other guy who shared their apartment was Jason. Sorry, but I don't recall ever hearing his surname. Oh, honey, I'm scared for our kids."

Ted whispered, "Try not to transfer our concern to Gina any more than necessary. This is turning into a nightmare for her, what with Lucy..."

Seeing Gina approach, Carole put her finger over Ted's lips to silence him.

Tony, in detective mode, ushered them towards the lounge where the hotel manager had suggested they sit in private and discuss their plight.

"First thing first, we have to locate those friends you mentioned, Carole. Ted, can you get on to college, see if you can rouse anyone at this time of night and find out where those kids are likely to be. If we can find the guy who hired out the camper at least we'll have a make and model and licence plate before we go to the cops." His voice began to waver as he continued. "That's the first thing they will ask and we'll come across as bad parents if we can't even give them basic info."

"But we *are* bad parents," sobbed Gina. "We should have been more careful before we sent our babies off on an adventure to God knows where."

"Apollo!" cried Carole. "They are in an Apollo Eclipse van. I remember when we waved them off I thought of the Apollo space mission and our kids going off on their own exciting adventure. Yes, Apollo Eclipse, white with blue trim. I'm sure of that."

"That's a start. Don't suppose you noticed anything else, any of you?" asked Tony.

No one recalled anything of any use.

Ted eventually located a reluctant caretaker at the college, but the news was not good.

"The students are still on vacation, buddy," he was told. "The place is like a morgue, wish they would drift back and be noisy and wild, I like it that way; this quietness gets to me. Sorry, but I'm not allowed to give out student details, you would need official permission for that."

"Right," said Tony to Ted, "give me that phone. I'll be as official as I can be."

Tony spoke to the caretaker, stating he was Superintendent Harvey from CPD, omitting to say he was retired and no longer held rank. He urgently needed to locate two students, Gerry Scanlon and his roommate Jason. It was a matter of life and death and he urgently needed to contact the person whose uncle had a vehicle hire business.

"Certainly, superintendent. You should have said who you were. I know who you mean, sir. Jason Freeman. His uncle Albert owns Albert's Hire downtown, but you won't get hold of him, he's gone to Miami for vacation and the business is closed until Monday first. My wife is friendly with Albert's wife and she told me their plans. Albert never takes a vacation but it's a special wedding anniversary for him, that's why it sticks in my mind that he closed, first time in his life, sir. I can give you the office number but you'll only get on to his voice mail. Young Jason has gone home to Philly for the vacation and I don't have any way of contacting him. Gerry Scanlon is at his grandma's funeral somewhere in New Jersey and is expected back later in the semester. Sorry, detective, but I can't help you."

"There's nothing else for it but to call it in. Let's have one more try at calling the kids' cells," said Tony, "before we speak to the cops."

None of the four youngsters picked up.

"Right," said Tony, "there's nothing else for it, we have to call it in."

"Why don't we go over to the kids' apartment first, Tony, and have a look around; that's if you can persuade the caretaker to let us in. We might find some clues there as to their plans, some receipts or something. Leave Gina and Carole here in case the kids arrive back."

"Anything we can do is better than sitting here thinking the worst. Ted, I'm sure the kids will come prancing in before long with a reasonable explanation as to why they've put us through this hell."

CHAPTER NINE

Bilson Duncan was a difficult man to rouse. With the college as empty as a politician's promise, he had retired for the night after a final walk around the premises accompanied by his trusted Dobermann, whose presence alone would keep intruders at bay, and settled to sleep in his caretaker's office. TV cameras monitoring the ghost-like campus would record unwanted activity which he would study in the morning, knowing that his always alert canine would warn him before then of any intruders.

Neither man could rouse the sleeping caretaker.

"The guy's cell is off," said Tony. "The only thing we can do is vault over the gate and hammer on the main door. Are you up for a bit of vaulting Ted?"

"Let's go for it. The girls haven't called in; they promised they would call as soon as the kids turned up. I must admit, I'm scared, Tony. I have a horrid feeling in the pit of my stomach that something sinister has happened to them."

"You're not alone, Ted. I've been trying to keep things in check for the women, but I'm scared out of my mind."

After much huffing from the two out-of-condition men, they entered the grounds, banged on the door and waited. And waited. The wait became almost unbearable, until from a distance a dog was heard, a light went on, then another, until finally the door opened to reveal a paunchy man with his hand firmly gripping the Dobermann that looked as if it would welcome the opportunity to show its mettle.

"What the..." he began, but stopped when Tony Harvey introduced himself, showing a folded piece of paper, which in the semi-darkness, was indistinguishable from a cop's identity card.

They explained the purpose of their intrusion into his evening and begged to view Jack's rooms for anything that would give a clue to the kids' whereabouts.

"It's against the rules for me to open the students' apartments, but I suppose I could bend the rules seeing how you are cops."

He made no reference to the fact that both men looked well beyond working age but with a few dollar bills pressed into his hand he led the way through a labyrinth of corridors until he stopped at a room which Tony and Ted prayed would give them some answers. Several rooms led off from a long corridor: a sitting room, surprisingly tidy for students, was checked over by Tony, while Ted moved along the corridor until he located his son's room. He felt as if he were intruding on the boy's privacy, unsure of what he might find, but desperate to find some scrap of information to help locate the kids. He booted up the Mac and perused emails and various sites which Jack had visited, a chilling feeling of guilt overpowered him. He felt as if he were spying and looking into the very soul of his son.

Tony, meanwhile, checked out the room belonging to Jason Freeman, going though drawers and cupboards, being careful not to disturb anything and replacing the student's pile of pornographic magazines that he found stacked underneath the bed. *I hope this guy hasn't shared these around,* he thought as he continued his search.

Nothing turned up that had reference to Albert's motorhome rental firm. Tony copied a few phone numbers that were written on a piece of discarded, crumpled paper that he rescued from the floor under the work desk.

"Typical," he told Ted when they met in the corridor, "a list of phone numbers with no names. They could be anything from pizza shops to girlfriends. We have no way of knowing if we can locate this lad from these or not."

They both checked over the room belonging to Gerry Scanlon and found nothing of any help. A foul smell led them to locate the boy's washing from under the bed.

"He's not as tidy as the others," remarked Ted. "Reminds me of my student days." Ted, still feeling the guilt of violating his son's private domain, suggested they get out of the place and head for the police HQ, aware too, that the caretaker was hovering outside the apartment and was probably anxious to lock up and return to his sleep.

"Find anything of use, detectives?" he said.

Neither man had corrected his assumption that they were cops.

"Not a thing, but we appreciate your assistance."

A few more dollar bills changed hands as the caretaker locked up, knowing that neither they nor he would reveal their visit to apartment 43B and that he could delete any sighting of them that had been caught on camera.

"Right, Brutus, let's get us some sleep."

CHAPTER TEN

The four youngsters stood in disbelief looking up at the trapdoor, their only means of exiting the cold cavern. It appeared higher now than when they had exited on previous occasions.

"There's nothing for us to stand on to reach that door. We are well and truly trapped," said Tess.

"Why don't we try standing on each other's shoulders?" Poppy suggested. "Could we reach the door that way?" Despite her young age, she was determined to play her part as a member of the team.

"It's worth a try," replied Jack. "But are you girls strong enough to hold us? If any of us fall onto the concrete floor, we're in real trouble."

Poppy and Tess looked at each other, raised their eyes heavenwards as if ready to challenge him for questioning their strength, but thought the better of a confrontation and began positioning themselves for the task in hand, a task which would surely lead them to freedom. What could be easier?

"Hey," said an indignant Poppy, "have you guys forgotten that I'm in an athletics team? I'm fit, and up for this challenge."

Jack smiled at her. Her enthusiasm spurred the others on. "Okay then. Tess first. Put your hands firmly on the wall to anchor yourself, feet apart and keep as steady as you can. Poppy, we'll help you up onto her shoulders. Put your feet squarely on Tess and don't, for any reason, move."

With the girls in position, and sure that they were steady enough to hold their weight, Jack helped to hoist Lucian onto his sister's shoulders. A slight wobble from the girls soon waned as Lucian planted his feet as firmly as he could, his palms flat against the cold wall.

"Right, Luce, free your right hand and help pull me up. Girls, I'm going to have to put my feet on your butts until I'm up on his shoulders. Everyone, keep steady and hope and pray we are high enough to reach the trapdoor. We gotta get out of here."

Like an athlete, the young Jack hoisted himself up effortlessly, steadied the column of bodies, and exclaimed, "I can reach the door! We'll be out of here in no time. Keep steady while I push it open."

He pushed with every ounce of strength that he could muster. It seemed an eternity to the others.

"Come on, Jack, I can't hold this position much longer," said his sister. "What's going on with you up there?"

"Guys," he said in a voice devoid of emotion, "guys, the door won't open. I think it's been bolted from the outside. We are trapped in this goddammed cellar."

Careful to avoid injury, the pillar of people disentangled themselves, rubbed their strained muscles and sat on the ground, drained of energy, and filled with dread. It was some time before anyone spoke.

"What now? What can we do to get out?" Poppy held back tears as she spoke.

Tess held her close, hushing her and giving the young girl the reassurance that she herself sorely needed.

"We'll be okay, Poppy. Try not to worry, we'll come up with something."

They sat there on the cold concrete floor, each with his or her own thoughts of how such an exciting adventure had turned sour.

"All we can do," replied the downhearted leader, "is to go through the left tunnel together, holding onto each other's clothes. It will be slow and laborious and scary too, I'm not afraid to admit; what with no flashlights, we must rely on each other to keep going for as long as it takes to find some goddamn way out of here. When you feel rested enough we'll get going. Any questions anyone?"

Poppy began to sob. "I need to pee."

"Not a problem, sweetie," replied Tess. "We'll go over to the corner there. I need to go too."

The boys moved away to give them some privacy and to relieve themselves.

"Okay to go, everyone? I'll lead. Lucian take up the rear, Tess go behind me with Poppy holding onto you. Don't break rank. Any problem, or if you want to stop, just shout. We'll take it easy, guys. It might take the longest time, but we will sure as hell get out of here."

Looking not unlike a line of shackled prisoners, the group moved slowly. Jack, the only one with his hands free, felt along the wall as if willing an opening to appear to release them from their terror. The burden of responsibility fell on his young shoulders. It was, after all, his idea to search for Anna Leci's mansion, his curiosity now replaced with guilt, guilt at having put his sister and cousins in danger. He cussed himself for not keeping his cell phone on his person. Although there was no signal in the cavern he knew the authorities could trace the last calls made, day or night, by tracking cell towers. He was comforted by that thought. *Was it only a few hours since I spoke to my parents?* he mused as he let his mind wander. He hoped that their location could be traced; this was, he thought, their only hope of rescue. This reassured him somewhat as he continued to move tentatively in total darkness, aware of the silence behind him from the motley crew; the only minuscule sound was the occasional quiet sob from Poppy. *She's so young to experience this,* he mused. *I guess Aunt Gina knew best after all.*

They had walked tentatively for what seemed an age; no one had a watch on them, relying as most young people do, on their cell phone. Their phones had been in their backpacks. Jack knew that they hadn't gone as far into the tunnel as previously, but he needed the group to keep strong. Lack of food and water now became a major issue. He licked his lips as if trying to conjure up some moisture.

"Guys, let's have a breather. Sit on the floor and have a rest. Sit close together for some warmth."

No one had energy or inclination to talk. Each had their own private thoughts and fears to cope with. Tess, holding Poppy in a secure comforting way, was aware that the young girl had fallen asleep. "We have to let her rest," she said. "Why don't we all try to do likewise for a bit?"

Devoid of strength and desperately needing water, it wasn't long before four worn-out youngsters dozed off, still entwined in each other's arms, linked like an unbroken chain of determination. When they awoke, it was to a reality check that they were still in dire straits. The darkness seemed even more intense; an unspoken fear smouldered in their souls. No one wanted to voice the fear they felt. They each wanted to protect and encourage the other. It was decidedly cold. They wanted out.

"Ready to move on, guys?" questioned Jack. "Poppy, sweetie, are you good to go?"

"I'm good," she said, linking herself once more as the chain gang slowly moved off.

They walked for what felt like an intolerable length of time. Jack, still using his hands to feel the way, began to tire and, losing concentration, stumbled and fell onto something sharp. He let out a cry of pain and tried to right himself but fell once more onto a hard metal surface and realised what he had tripped on.

"It's the goddamn ladder!" he cried as he stood up, rubbing his body, the pain seeming to have reached every bone and muscle that he possessed. Finding the ladder, gave them the impetus they needed.

"Jack, where are you hurting?" exclaimed his sister.

"Hey, it's okay, only a scratch or two. How about we all help carry this ladder back to the main cave? Do you think we can manage it between us? It's as heavy as lead."

Tess, heartened by the find of the ladder said, "Maybe we could use it as a hammer to prise open the trap or at least make a hell of a noise. Someone may be searching for us by now and we have to keep banging at the door. Sure, Jack, we'll manage to carry the darn thing and we can always drag it for a bit."

"Yeah," said Lucian, "dragging it along might alert someone out there."

"Or, alert whoever is in this place," whispered Lucian. They sat for a few minutes to gather their strength, then stood up, rubbed their arms and legs to generate some heat and began retracing their steps.

They each helped to carry the ladder, the burden falling on three of them as they took most of the weight to spare Poppy the walk back to the cavern burdened by the heavy contraption. Jack again led the way with Lucian taking up the rear. It was difficult walking in total darkness. They stopped often to change over when their hands became sore.

Jack was in extreme pain, but was not going to reveal that to the others. He could feel blood running from a cut in his leg. The ladder seemed to increase in weight as they struggled to keep it evenly balanced. Poppy held onto a rung for dear life, fearful that if she let go she would lose contact with the others.

"Lucian," called Jack, "can you hold your end up a bit more? It's dragging on the ground and making it harder for me and Tess. Lucian, lift the ladder up please... Lucian?"

Tess turned and called out, "Jack, Lucian isn't here. He must have stumbled and we didn't hear him."

"Oh, no!" Jack exclaimed. "Right, guys, place the ladder carefully against the wall. Link arms. Poppy in the middle. We'll go back and fetch him."

They retraced their steps carefully in case Lucian was lying on the floor in the darkness. They called out as they went, but were met with silence.

"It's possible he fell and has knocked himself out on the stone floor," suggested Tess.

"He would have called out if he'd fallen," said a very scared Poppy. "Why didn't we hear anything?"

"Don't worry, sweetie, we'll find him soon," comforted Tess. "He must be around here."

Jack said, "We've walked back quite a bit. We didn't drag the ladder for all that distance and we haven't passed him."

Overcome with hunger, fear and tiredness, Poppy let vent to her distress, calling out, screaming for her sibling. She was inconsolable.

"It's hopeless," said Jack as he tried to calm her. "Tess, you and Poppy sit here on the ground. I'll go ahead for a bit on my own. I'll be a tad quicker. Ten minutes at the most."

He took off, covering as much ground as he could in the dark, eerie tunnel, feeling his way along the wall, spreading his feet out like shovels sweeping across the area, feeling for Lucian. His own pain was excruciating. He ignored it and kept going, calling out for his cousin. Realising that he had covered more than enough ground, he reluctantly headed back to the girls. He felt himself weaken with every step; the agonising pain in his leg almost made him call out in despair; he felt faint; he wanted to lie down and sleep, but willpower kept him upright as he struggled to retrace his steps. He had never felt so despondent, so utterly scared and helpless in his life.

Where are you, Luce? Where the hell are you? he silently thought. Tears streamed from his face, tears of pain for his own injuries, tears for the dire situation he had placed the others in, tears borne out of frustration and anger. He stopped to compose himself before joining the girls who were sitting together, holding each other, sobbing and trembling, getting a modicum of comfort from each other.

"There's no sign of him. Nothing. Lucian has vanished."

CHAPTER ELEVEN

"Right, sir. Run that past me again. You're telling me your kids are missing. You're telling me a twenty-three-year-old guy and a twenty-one-year-old gal have not returned from a student weekend away with two teenagers? Students, you say?" said a sneering, obnoxious desk officer who tapped his pen irritatingly as if reluctant to use paper on what, in his opinion, was a mundane matter. "In my book, students of that age are adult enough to look after themselves, and well, we know what students are like, probably sleeping off a drunken party somewhere and don't want to face their parents."

Tony Harvey had a short fuse when dealing with people he considered self-righteous and pompous, as any former colleague who crossed his path could attest to. Ted, knowing Tony was about to lash out verbally at the officer, spoke first. "Officer, I don't think you're taking this matter seriously. We're not talking about irresponsible, drunken students; we are talking about four highly intelligent people who have not returned from a weekend camping. They could be lying injured somewhere. We need police assistance here, not arrogance."

"Sir, I believe you, but surely those, so-called highly intelligent people would have left a detailed itinerary including precise details of their hired vehicle. Have you tried calling them? Kids nowadays all have these new gadgets. Do you have the licence number of the vehicle? Make? Model?"

Ted replied, "We know that it's an Apollo Eclipse motorhome."

"Colour, sir?" snapped the bored officer, wishing these two fathers would go off somewhere else with their problem and leave him to attend to his impending lunch break.

"Probably white, with a flash of blue," said Ted.

"Probably? Now if you don't mind me saying, 'probably' ain't much help."

Tony butted in. "We have already told you we don't have that information. Look, the more you drag this out, the worse it could be for our kids. Officer, our kids are missing. They could be in danger. What part of that don't you understand?"

"No need to take that attitude with me, sir. I suggest you come back when you have more information. You haven't given me much to go on, and if I might say, as a father myself, wasn't that remiss of you not to check things out before your kids went off into the big wide world?"

Tony Harvey, sick with worry and knowing that part of what the guy said was true, could listen no further. "Get me your superior officer. Now."

"Sorry, sir, he's out of the office. He's attending a meeting. Why don't you call back later, or make an appointment to see him? If you knew anything about the top guys in this job, you would know they don't like being disturbed over things that can be dealt with at the desk."

In any other circumstance Tony would have smiled and agreed with the desk cop, but at the present time he was focused on one thing only: finding the kids.

As he was about to dismiss the two men, the desk officer saw the taller of the two take out a phone, dial a number and ask to be put through to Superintendent Ambrose Kyle of Chicago Police Department. "Tell him that Tony Harvey wishes to speak to him on an urgent matter." Within moments his call was connected. "Hey, Ambrose, Tony here. I need a favour, a real important one. Can you contact your opposite number here in New York? I'll explain what's going on."

Tony walked away from the desk to speak privately to his former colleague, much to the amazement on the face of the desk officer whose stomach churned as he felt trouble brewing. A call came through to his desk. The officer, visibly perturbed, rose to full height, pulled his massive gut in and stood to attention, as if the person calling could see his posture. "Yes, sir. Yes. I understand. Sorry, sir, Yes, I didn't know, sorry… yes, right away, sir." The call ended. The red-faced officer came from behind the desk and attempted to apologise to the men.

"Hum. Sorry, gentlemen. I wasn't aware of who you were. I've been asked by my superintendent here in New York to escort you to my boss's office. He'll be back soon. If only you had told me, sir, I would have..." Looking at Tony Harvey as he spoke, he continued, "If you had said you were a former superintendent, I sure would have..."

Unable to control the anger that was partly due to his own guilt in not having more details to hand, and frustration that led to stomach-churning fear for his family, Tony hollered, "Regardless of who comes in through those doors, prince or pauper, you treat everyone the same, with respect and courtesy, or didn't you learn that at police training?"

The subdued officer showed them into a plush office and was about to retreat when his immediate superior officer arrived on the scene.

"Tony! Great to see you and Mr Carr, you'll be Carole's husband then? I'm Detective Leo Bruce. What a team she and Tony were. I was privileged to work with them way back in my time with CPD." Turning to the uncomfortable officer who hovered around, unsure of what to do, he said, "Haven't you offered our guests some coffee, man? Three coffees, here, promptly. "Sorry, guys, for the reception you received. He's a pompous idiot at times. Now, tell me about your missing kids. We'll pull out all the stops to find them."

Much relieved, the two fathers gave as much detail as they could muster. They were exhausted and stressed beyond belief. Tony suddenly remembered the note with telephone numbers that he had copied from Jason

Freeman's crushed and discarded paper. "I'm not sure if any of these numbers will get us to Albert from the motor-hire place or not," began Tony, "we've not had time to call." He did not disclose how the numbers had got into his possession.

The desk officer returned with coffee and was instructed to call the numbers on the paper proffered to him by his boss, to locate Albert Freeman and obtain details of the hired vehicle as soon as possible, *or even sooner,* snapped the detective, still smarting at the treatment meted out to the anxious men from his officer.

Before long he returned with information they required.

"The first three numbers, sir, appeared to be fast-food joints, the fourth a bookshop downtown. I got success from the fifth one; it was Jason Freeman's sister Carrie, who told me her uncle Albert and his wife Bette were on holiday in Miami. Here's his cell number, sir."

"And the last number?" questioned his superior, not letting up on the hapless officer. "Whose was that?"

"A former girlfriend, sir, who told me she hoped Jason Freeman would rot in hell."

"Leave us now, Cooper. We have work to do."

Albert Freeman, sitting by the poolside sipping a cool beer and snoozing on and off, was irritated when his cell rang. He did not recognise the number and chose to ignore the call. *I'm on vacation whoever you are,* he muttered to the unopened phone. After the third call, he picked up, shouting, "I hope this is important. Who are you?"

He had to admit that his wife Bette was right when she said he needed a vacation. He had been relishing the peace until his phone rang out disturbing his afternoon siesta. The detective inspector introduced himself and his visitors put the phone on speaker so that Tony and Ted could speak directly to the garage owner. Tony explained the situation with the young people, and asked for details of the motorhome.

"Oh buddy, that's bad. I know the vehicle you refer to. Have you a pen? I have the licence number and everything you need right here in my head. Are you sure the camper isn't at the kid's college? The arrangement was that they would park up there, give the key to Jason, and one of my mechanics would collect it on Monday." He concluded that he had no idea where the kids were planning to go, they seemed vague about their plans and promised to take good care of the vehicle and no, it did not have a tracking device on it.

The detective wasted no time in putting a BOLO out for all sections to hunt for the vehicle. "Without an idea as to the kids' plans, we're looking for a needle in a haystack, but, find them, we will."

The men returned to their hotel, feeling sick, exhausted and hungry, hungry more for sleep than anything else, but unwilling to give into tiredness while their children were unaccounted for.

They found Gina and Carole together in one of the rooms. Gina was asleep, having been assured by Carole that she would wake her at the first sign of news. She herself dozed in the armchair, afraid to sleep, afraid to think, afraid to let her mind wander to unimaginable thoughts. They let Gina sleep on as they updated Carole on events.

"Look," said Ted, "we will all function better if we can have some sleep. We're no use to the kids if we can't think straight. I suggest we all retire to bed for a few hours. Detective Bruce has our cell numbers and will be in touch as soon as he hears anything."

Despite their reluctance, they knew Ted was right. He and Carole returned to their room, while Tony, fully clothed, lay on the bed beside Gina and immediately fell asleep. In what seemed to him like minutes, but was in fact four hours later, his cell rang, wakening both him and Gina. Grabbing it, he almost shouted into it, "Tony Harvey speaking."

"Hi Tony, I'm just checking what time you guys arrive in O'Hare. Ralph will pick you up. You sound harassed, Pop. Have I called at a bad time?" said Abigail, who was unaware of the unfolding drama. She sensed something was amiss by her stepfather's hesitancy in replying. Tony and Gina did not want to inform Abigail of events, knowing it would reawaken in her the terror of Lucy's abduction, and they hoped the children would return before she need know anything of their plight.

"Tony, speak to me. Is something wrong? Is Mom ill?"

"No, honey, Mom's fine but we have news that we wanted to delay telling you."

As gently as he could, he told his stepdaughter of the drama that was unfolding. He could hear her intake of breath as she registered the enormity of what she was hearing.

"Oh, Tony, oh no! Is Mom there? I want to speak with her."

Tony held his wife tightly as she wept when she spoke to her daughter.

"Abbie, it's history repeating itself. We are so scared."

"Mom, I'm getting the first flight out. I need to be with you. Hang in there, Mom."

CHAPTER TWELVE

The adventure was over. The nightmare was just beginning. Lucian tried to lift his head. It pounded. It throbbed. It felt as if it was about to explode. He slowly came to. He tried to sit up. His head thumped, heavy as lead, heavy, so heavy. His mouth was dry, his throat felt like rough sandpaper scraping back and forward against a rough surface. He attempted to call out; his lips seemed to be stuck together. He desperately wanted to drink. His eyes nipped. He tried to wipe them and realised his hands were tied with some kind of rough material. The more alert he became the more aware he was of his plight. Attempting to stand up sent a shock of extreme pain throughout his body. He could not stand; his feet too, were tied by the same rough material. He fell back and was aware that he was lying, not on cold slabs as in the cavern, but on something softer. His face touched the material. He tried to focus, but in doing so, a pain shot through his head, unbearable, sharp, and making him want to vomit. He focused once more. The soft material looked familiar. Why couldn't he think straight? Face down, he slowly recognised it. He was lying on a sleeping bag, not his, but Poppy's with its unmistakable pattern of wild flowers. And the smell. His nostrils seemed to come to life. A pungent smell caught his breath. The room he lay in seemed full of it. He coughed. He couldn't identify the stench. He coughed some more. His head hurt with every move he made. Falling onto his back, he became aware that he had wet himself, and worse. The odour from his own body was not as sickly as the other foul smell. He tried to identify it. Memory returned. He became more alert. Pulling himself up as well as he could into a sitting position, his head resting on a wall, he took stock of his surroundings.

He was in a cavern-like room, like the one the group had slept in but much smaller. *The others? Where was he? Where were they?* Questions tumbled around his head. He tried to focus, to remember, to concentrate. His brain was like a kaleidoscope with images changing rapidly, tumbling, varying, floating and never settling. His memory gradually returned bit by bit, like a jig-saw puzzle, not fully functioning until the last piece was in place. He recalled carrying the ladder, finding it heavy and wanting to rest, but that was out of the question. They had to keep moving. They had to find a means of escape from the underground hellhole. The last thing he recalled was his hand being gently removed from the ladder, so gently it seemed that the others had not noticed that he was no longer bearing his share of the heavy load. Something foul had been placed over his mouth. He had been carried like a bundle of rags over someone's shoulder. Before he had lost consciousness he had been aware of a smell, a rancid odour emanating from the person who had spirited him off, so quietly, like a thief in the night. The smell. It came from the body odour of his captor. It lingered in the room in which he found himself restrained. It lingered on his own clothes where contact had been made when he had been carried, and, mixed with his own body smells, was repugnant to his nostrils.

He took stock of his surroundings. The room was narrow, tiny and cramped. It contained a mattress and a bucket, from where more stenches came. There was not much else in the room, not much else, except... except... when his eyes focussed, there, spread on the floor, were all their possessions: sleeping bags, backpacks, food containers. Everything they owned had been ransacked by whoever lived in this room.

Lucian tried to loosen his bonds. He called out for water, for help. His voice was barely audible but he knew he had to alert the others to his whereabouts. There was little more he could do. His body ached. The ropes cut into his wrists and ankles, almost cutting off the blood supply. He lay down, exhausted from the effort to free himself, and felt himself being swallowed up in a swirling fog inside his head. He slept.

In the main cellar, Jack and Tess, with Poppy in tow, manoeuvred the ladder back to the cavern and set it up to try once more to open the trapdoor. Jack pushed the door with every ounce of energy he could muster, but to no avail. With Tess's help he thumped it against the door to try to attract attention, calling out as they did so, hoping against hope that someone, a dog-walker perhaps, would hear them. It was physically exhausting. Jack climbed up and attempted once more to open the trapdoor. It would not move. Blood poured from a gash in his leg. The pain was excruciating. So engrossed were they that they failed to hear a tiny whimper from Poppy as she was being carried out of the cellar.

CHAPTER THIRTEEN

Abigail's arrival at the hotel was emotional for them all. The memory of Lucy's abduction had never faded. They each held memories of the event. Tony and Carole, the investigating officers on the case that had snowballed over many years, brought themselves and their families closer together in a friendship that strengthened with each passing year, culminating in the drama in which they were now embroiled. For Gina, the loss of Lucy challenged her emotions, strengthened her already close relationship with Abigail, and led her to find love with Tony who had called in regularly to check on the distressed mother and daughter.

Abigail, more than most, suffered deeply from the loss of her best friend and, even now in adulthood, Lucy was never far from her thoughts. She felt immensely privileged to be the custodian of Lucy's memory in the form of the academy set up in her name, where students of music and art could study in stunning surroundings that were so conducive to learning. To her, it was the only positive aspect of the legacy left by Anna Leci, without whose madness in having Lucy abducted, the academy, and all its potential for good, would not exist.

Brenda Mears, in setting up the Lucy Mears Academy of Music and Art, had employed a talented young architect to design the interior of the building making it fit for purpose. In the foyer of the academy, near a portrait of Lucy was a simple plaque stating that adaptions to the building had been designed by Sergio Bregovic of Sarajevo. At the opening ceremony, Brenda gave a short speech telling a little of Sergio's life in war-torn Sarajevo, his capture and torture by enemy factions and his escape to freedom and to America in search of his family, a family caught up in the madness of Anna Leci. Discovering his family had died in the sabotaged plane with Lucy was devastating for the young man. He was cared for by Donata and Marc Stojanovic who had befriended his relatives during their flight from Sarajevo, and, sponsored by Brenda, returned to his homeland to study architecture.

In doing so, Brenda felt she was keeping her daughter's memory alive. The official opening of the academy was yet another small step in the healing process for both Brenda and Sergio and for Abigail and Gina. Other invited guests, were Donata and Marc. Nora Kelly, Brenda's long-time friend who grew up with her, almost as a sister, and Norah's husband Peter and their nine-year-old daughter, Mollie-Rose were also in attendance.

Abigail, reunited now with her mother, held the weeping woman in her arms, comforting her in a role-reversal situation.

"Mom, they will be fine. There's a simple explanation for them being late. They are level-headed kids and will look out for each other. Have faith in them, believe that they are safe. Don't go to a dark place."

With information on the camper van now available, officers patrolled a wide area, distributing flyers, setting up road blocks to question drivers, visiting gas stations, shopping malls and fast food places, all within a hundred-mile radius. Both sets of parents provided recent photographs and contact numbers to help officers in their search.

Being out of character for the young people not to have returned when expected, and given the high profile of their parents, the search was considered under special circumstances and for immediate investigation. The local precinct, where Tony and Ted first reported their missing children, became the hub of activity. An amber alert was issued to highlight the case. Media was involved with TV appeals made and details sent to social media sites. The authorities were aware that such high profile cases often attracted time-wasters and overly helpful members of the public. Technicians were working on locating the last phone call made from the youngsters' cells.

Tony and Carole, as former detectives, were anxious to be hands-on in the search for their children but were thwarted by the insistence of the chief of police, who felt they would be of more use remaining in the hotel with their spouses in case the kids contacted them or returned on their own.

"As soon as we have any lead on the kids I'll be in touch. That I promise you."

Resigned to remain at the hotel, they attempted to eat, sleep, and prepare for what lay ahead. Tony persuaded Gina to eat. "Honey, you need to be strong and at your best for the kids' return."

Unlike his wife, Tony refused to believe that he would never see Lucian and Poppy again. Memories of Lucy's fate filled Gina's every waking moment. She feared the worst. Nothing Tony or Abigail said could console her. Ted and Carole paced the room, trying to hold their emotions together, speaking little but thinking deeply. They each remembered a previous time when a crazed stalker caused them endless days of concern for their young children, and silently prayed that the ordeal they were now experiencing would soon be resolved, uniting them once more as a family.

CHAPTER FOURTEEN

Lucian woke, aware of some movement around him. He sat up as best he could, and blinking through watering eyes, he realised that lying beside him, equally trussed up and drugged, was Poppy.

"Po…ppy," He tried to speak through the gag over his mouth and became angry at the sight of his sister, so young, so vulnerable, so innocent. He wept with frustration and wriggled as near to her as he could manage. He chewed at the rag in his mouth, spitting out minute pieces of cloth, causing his lips to bleed, until he was able to utter some semblance of speech.

"Popp…y," he whispered. "Popp…y, wake u…p."

There was no response from her almost lifeless form. Lucian rubbed his wrists together in an effort to loosen the tight bond. He succeeded only in breaking his skin. After what seemed an eternity, a disorientated Poppy woke to find her brother looking at her, mouthing something undecipherable and looking dishevelled like she had never seen him before.

"Luce..." she tried to speak but the words stuck in her throat, a dry, rough throat that hurt as she attempted to swallow. She was desperate to drink. Her eyes, blurred at first, focused and settled to give her clearer vision. She too had a rag over her mouth but it had slipped down, allowing her to attempt to speak. Her wrists and ankles, like her brother's, were tied with rough rope. She wriggled nearer and sat by Lucian, finding comfort in the closeness.

She was more alert than he, having had less sedative. The two tried to communicate in whispers but it caused discomfort with each attempt.

Lucian, facing the door, stiffened as he saw in the doorway a man, the hobo- type person who had stolen their belongings and captured them both. Poppy turned to see what had startled her brother and drew an intake of breath at the vision watching them from the doorway. He was tall; his bulk filled the doorway. He was unkempt with long, straggly hair that was filthy and matted and partially obscured his face, a face wrinkled and covered with pockmarks. He wore a grey military style overcoat that reached almost to his ankles. It was held in place by a rope around his middle, the same type of rope that was used to secure Lucian and Poppy. On his feet, and tied up with the same rope, were pieces of carpets for shoes, explaining why he was able to move silently and stealthily around the cellar. He stood in silence, watching. He turned away. Poppy snuggled closer to her brother, sobbing and shaking with fear.

"Hush, Poppy. We'll get out of here. Mom and Dad will be searching for us. Hold on to that thought; they will find us. Jack and Tess will be searching too, we have to try to call out to them." He did not feel confident in what he said. The hobo returned with two bottles of water which he held to the mouths of his captives; Poppy first. She gulped as she tried to drink the welcome liquid which ran down her chin as she tried to force the water down her parched, painful throat, trying to ignore the stench from her captor. The hobo turned to Lucian and repeated the process. He loosened the gag and held the cold bottle to the boy's lips. The liquid trickled down his raw, rough throat and chilled his stomach as it reached into the depths of his being. Contact with the bottle hurt his lips but he attempted to drink as much of the liquid as he could before the man replaced his gag. Lucian tried to question and call out but the man had slipped out of the room. The water helped revive them enough to wriggle to a sitting position where they sat side by side. Lucian attempted to free himself from the bonds that restricted him. His only success was in biting through the rag that covered his mouth, the pain was excruciating as it slipped over his swollen, bleeding mouth. They whispered together, not wanting to alert the hobo and cause more misery for themselves, Lucian taking on the role of the adult, assuring his sobbing sister that Jack and Tess would find them.

"But how can we get out of the cellar, Luce? The trap-door has been bolted from outside."

It was an effort to whisper, each word was excruciatingly painful.

"They won't abandon us, don't worry. Even now they will be searching this damn cave for us, be sure of that, and our parents will be searching too. Try and sleep, Poppy, and conserve your energy."

They both gave in to sleep.

*

Tess, with Jack holding on to her and finally admitting his pain, struggled along the cellar floor, feeling their way in the dark for any sign of the others. Each step was torture for Jack; they both were extremely weak and desperate for water. They had little energy left to call out.

"This is hopeless, Tess. I need to sit down again."

He could feel the blood pouring down his leg and knew that he must have lost a considerable amount. He became lightheaded and disorientated. Tess cradled her brother, calling gently to him through a voice that was almost inaudible, and wept as she failed to elicit a response from him.

"Don't leave me, Jack. Please, please, wake up."

Huddled together on the floor of the cellar, the siblings were unaware of the hobo as he hovered over them, planning his next move.

CHAPTER FIFTEEN

The vagrant had almost lost track of the months, the years, the days since he had come to this place. His mind went back to when, walking along the side of the vast estate, he moved stealthily around the perimeter, looking for shelter from the worsening rain. He trudged through the undergrowth; his feet were cut and bruised due to his flimsy shoes whose uppers had almost parted company from the soles. He had been drifting from one place to another for several years now, the little money he had was long gone. He slept where he could, on park benches, under bridges and shared doorways with other vagrants. Once, he settled to share a corner with a sleeping tramp, only to discover the man was dead, and had been for some time. With difficulty, he'd removed the dead man's overcoat and shoes. *You won't be wanting these again, buddy.*

He joined other itinerants at soup kitchens and other such charity places where food and warmth were always available. He spoke little, giving the impression that he did not speak English. He ate quickly and moved on with haste. He had no wish to enter into conversation with well-meaning charity workers who would try to prise his life story from him. That would remain forever a closed subject. He thought often of his past life, his family and the circumstances where he had lost everything he possessed. There was no one to care about him and in turn, he cared for no one.

Shuffling along through the overgrown bushes and shrubs, head down to shelter his face from the wind, he missed his footing, stumbled and found himself clutching a metal bolt. He cleared the immediate spot as well as he could and located the source of the bolt. It held down a trapdoor, long-forgotten and covered in dirt and shrub-growth. With an effort he thought he no longer possessed, he released the bolt and cautiously opened the trap, lay prone and looked into a vast cellar. It was light enough outside for him to see that a ladder led down into the cellar. Forgetting the misery of his situation, the man gingerly descended into the bowels of the cave-like structure. It was dry, relatively clean and totally empty. A welcome relief for him from the elements. He sat on the cold floor regained his strength, and then began a regime of exploring. Two tunnels led from the main cellar. He explored one walking deeper into darkness, feeling his way as he went along until he came to a smaller room that he decided, for the time being at least, would be his shelter.

Over the next few weeks he explored the rest of the cellar and found that it covered an immense area. Under what had probably been the kitchen, he found some discarded tins of food, long out of date but to him a treasure trove of palatable items, a rusty knife, bottles of water, some wine and other items of edible food which he took back to his corner.

He dragged an old discarded mattress to his chosen site. It became his bed. Keen to explore more, he took note of the various cellar doors which he presumed led into different areas of the main house. He carefully opened one and listened. He listened and waited. Hearing nothing, he hoisted himself up into a kitchen area, long abandoned, dusty and dank. He found nothing of interest there and moved silently around what he presumed had been servants' quarters; empty now of all but the ghosts of its previous inhabitants. Rooms once the essence of high living beckoned him. All lay desolate and silent as if not wanting to disturb the past. He moved from one room to another, amazed at the vastness of the house, the richness of which could still be seen on what remained of wallpaper and cornices. He gazed at the exquisite staircase and imagined the wealth, the opulence, the life lived by the residents of this palace, for it seemed to him to be nothing short of palatial. He thought how unfair life was, how obscene it was for a few people to possess so much while others struggled to put bread on the table. His reverie was interrupted by a laugh, a faraway laugh, but a laugh all the same. He was not alone in the building. The laughter drew nearer. He identified two voices, male voices getting closer to where he stood. Quickly he hid until the voices faded and footsteps were no longer heard. He made it back to his cellar-room, glad to have escaped from human contact. Tomorrow he would explore the upper floors of the house, but for now, sleep called.

The hobo now knew every inch of the cavern. It stretched under the vast pretentious compound, being built to hold, at one end, dried food and wine and other such household items, at the opposite end, a laundry room, and at another, a garage space for several vehicles. No expense had been spared in the building of this estate. Various doors led from the cellars to the main house. Over time, the hobo familiarised himself with them all. Undeterred, he explored every room, every corner, every inch of the main house, the out-buildings and the cellars. He decided he would cease travelling, cease wandering and settle here in this house, underneath the house, empty now since the death of its owner. He was where he wanted to be. He had found what he had come for. So, this is the place?

He gathered some discarded items including an old oil lamp, some pages of musical scores, a scrap book and a bundle of pencils and other items of stationery. These he took to his corner of the cellar and made a home for himself, out of sight and sound of any intruders. His life was now one of a solitary man; he enjoyed the solitude and wanted no company, he did not want to be discovered. His years of wandering had ceased.

The property, now in the hands of a real estate agent, was secured by high fences. It had notices warning of a dangerous site. Two caretakers, whose job it was to monitor the estate, house and grounds, lived on the premises, and were allocated a part of the house for the duration of their employment. Most of the furniture and artefacts had long been removed and sold at auction. The caretakers had the minimum of comfort. A small kitchen with basic utensils served their needs. They spent as little time as possible on duty, preferring to retire to their rooms to watch television, drink and play cards and smoke some illegal substances. No one bothered to check on them, their wages were paid into a bank and collected by them when they needed to top up with food and alcohol. Unknown to them, things would change dramatically.

They took it in turns to patrol the vast estate, and satisfied that intruders could not break through the barricades, returned to the comfort of the house. What they omitted to check was the underground, cavernous area and its many openings that allowed access to the building.

"I ain't going down there, buddy, no money in the world will take me into the bowels of the earth," said one of the watchmen. "I'm staying up here, above ground. Ain't going down there with rats and things."

On one of their alcohol-fuelled evenings, Pete, whose turn it was to do the final patrol, rushed back, breathing heavily and holding his side from the pain of exertion.

"What's wrong? Hey, you look like you've seen a ghost."

"Shane, holy shit, I have seen a ghost. It's that old dame that lived here years ago. She's haunting us, she doesn't like us living in her house. Oh Shane, I sure was scared."

"Calm down, Pete. Tell me what you saw."

"Oh hell, it sure was her, a figure gliding along, three feet up off the ground, long dress or coat thing. I didn't hang around to see more. It had its back to me and didn't hear me coming. She looked scary enough from the back. I was sure I heard something scuffling along the other night too. It's her. I know it's that dead dame."

"It was probably a rat. Hey, buddy, sit down before you fall. Have a drink and a smoke and forget it. You're letting your imagination run riot. Chill out, man."

The two men attempted to watch television but Pete could not rid the ghostly image from his troubled mind. He kept listening out for strange sounds, jumped at the least creak that the old, empty house emitted, much to the irritation of his buddy.

"Hey man, cool it. You're making me nervous. There ain't nothing there, it's the wind blowing through this old building, no such thing as ghosts. Here, have another drink."

"Shane, I did see summat; honest, man; it was that dead woman, scariest thing I've ever seen. Tomorrow I'm outta here, no money in the world will keep me in this creepy place."

Eventually they fell asleep; Pete's alcohol-fuelled dreams caused a restless night; he tossed and turned, called out in his sleep as he fought off dragons in drag. Shane put the pillow over his ears in an attempt to shut out Pete's moans and soon fell asleep, a sleep brought on by a mixture of drink and drugs. They were both unaware that a lit cigarette had ignited a pile of discarded food wrappings.

CHAPTER SIXTEEN

The fire was ferocious. It took hold rapidly, relentless in its wrath, as if eradicating past evil within its walls. Flames, fanned by strong winds, picked up momentum as the night wore on, devouring everything in its wake like a dragon intent on annihilation. Every bit of the colossal compound came under attack from violent, searing flames, blazing like Hades in the night sky. The roof caved in, bit by bit; burning timbers, dark and menacing fell inside destroying all in its wake. Flames could be seen for miles around and onlookers who witnessed it felt as if they were watching a spectacular firework show. Firefighters fought into the night and following days to douse the flames. Only when it was safe to do so did they enter the premises and find among the debris the remains of the two caretakers. They had been told that the house had lain empty for several years and that no one lived there.

The hobo, alerted by sirens, fled from his underground hideaway to observe proceedings from the safety of some bushes. The smell from burning embers caught his throat and lingered on his clothes. The savagery of the fire frightened him; he had never seen such burning, such devastation, and such speed of destruction. He spent the night outdoors, unsure if the fire would have damaged the underground area that he claimed as his own. He moved that night, some miles away, to a food shelter that he visited occasionally.He sat apart from the other unfortunate human beings, aware that his dishevelled appearance and his odour was repulsive, even to himself. The kindly people serving food made no comment, did not recoil at his appearance or that of his fellow diners. They served food, smiled at each person and wished them enjoyment of the meal. He did not speak, but nodded in appreciation of their kindness. At other times when he required food, he trudged for hours to the nearest habitation where he foraged in trash containers behind hotels and restaurants. Fearful of returning too soon to his makeshift home, he wandered from one stinking alleyway to another, until total misery forced him to retrace his steps to his underground home.

Several days later when he had nowhere else to go, he returned to observe the charred remains of the once ostentatious house and to claim his underground sanctuary. He was shocked at the destruction that faced him. A void. An empty burnt remnant of a massive building now glowed as the dying embers sparked and flickered their last vestige of life, sounding their miserable dirge-like eulogy as they crumbled to ash.

Workmen had erected signs warning of burning embers and falling timbers that the hobo hoped would keep intruders at bay. He tentatively entered the burnt-out shell from one of the underground doors. The rancid smell clung to his ragged clothes as if trying to draw him into the wreck to eradicate his past. The trapdoor led him to the main marble hall entrance. The fire had discoloured but not damaged the marble. It had burnt itself out long before reaching the main hallway. The hobo trod through the debris, careful not to scorch his carpet-covered feet and gingerly avoiding fallen timbers. He stood in amazement at the scene in front of him, taking in the devastation of the once magnificent, if overly ornate house. An open-air display of sky and clouds replaced the elaborate ceilings. Gentle rain fell onto the floor in a rhythmic, funeral-like dirge lamenting the passing of time.

*

Many months later, settled back into a routine of sedentary life, his peace was disturbed by voices emanating from people entering the cellar. He concealed himself in an alcove and listened. He listened to the excitement from four young people as they discovered the underground crypt, heard their plans to explore the tunnels and spend the night there. He smiled to himself as he heard them relate stories of ghosts and poltergeists: it seemed an eternity to him since he had cause to smile. When he was sure that they were asleep, he crept in, rummaged noiselessly in the nearest backpack and extracted a food pack that he took to his room. *Haven't eaten such good food in a long time,* he mused as he settled to devour a feast of food lovingly put together by Gina and Carole for their hungry brood.

"Do you think this will be enough, Carole?" asked Gina when they had packed a variety of foodstuffs. "Lucian can eat an amazing amount. We wonder where he puts it all."

"He's a growing boy," laughed Carole. "There won't be much of this left, that I'm sure of. Jack was the same in his teenage years but he seems to have modified his eating habits some."

The hobo kept well-hidden during the intruder's exploration of the two tunnels, grateful that they hadn't found his den. Another ten minutes would have brought them to my private suite, he thought as the group, linked together, moved relatively quietly back to the main cellar.

*

Once more, in the night when he was sure the sleeping bodies would not stir, he retrieved a food pack from the nearest backpack and decided if the opportunity arose, he would relieve the kids of their entire gear in the hope that by doing so, he would frighten them away.

He listened as the young people set off to explore the opposite tunnel from where he lived and made his move. He collected their backpacks, leaving only sleeping bags that he planned to relieve them of at the earliest opportunity. The contents of their backpacks intrigued him. Technology had moved rapidly, leaving him mystified by their state-of-the-art cell phones, so different from the basic one that he once possessed that he had tossed into the sea so many years ago. He studied them and threw them aside, knowing he had no one to call, he knew no one, and had no use for the gadgets. He devoured the remaining food, having been deprived of such basics as homemade fare. He still had a stock of bottled water and some wine that he used to wash down his feast. All that remained now was for him to remove the four sleeping bags in the hope that the visitors would leave promptly. When he heard the ladder being moved, he thought it possible that the kids might raise the alarm about their missing belongings and have the authorities trample through his cellar home; he planned to remove them from the premises. In his earlier search of the main building, he had come across lithium discarded among other pills and medication which he planned to use to drug the youngsters. He had no idea of its strength or power. He easily removed two of the kids, the lighter ones, to his cellar room and watched for an opportunity to sedate the others. He did not have long to wait.

The exhausted and injured boy was easy to sedate as was the girl huddling close to him, both sleeping from weakness. Drugging the two older children was easier than he thought. He crept up behind them as they lay exhausted on the ground, the ladder abandoned like a long lost piece of obsolete metal left to rust where it lay, and administered sedatives so quickly that neither Jack nor Tess were aware of what had happened to them. He was unaware that the young boy was not sleeping but was unconscious and in need of medical attention if he were to survive.

In one of the backpacks was a key. Exiting the cellar via one of the furthest away trapdoors, so as not to alert the young people, he trekked outside searching for a vehicle. He tramped around the perimeter of the estate for what seemed a lengthy time and eventually located a motorhome on a dirt track that led to the area of the cellar door that he himself had first stumbled upon many years previously. Inside he found more food packs and settled in comfort to eat, while going through items left by the kids. Having no use for Tess's camera, he left it there with Poppy's cell phone that she had left behind. He released the brake and manoeuvred the motorhome out of sight of the overgrown path, believing he had concealed it completely, and returned discretely to his cellar with a few more home comforts, flashlights, pillows and a few books.

All he needed now to return to his idea of a comfortable life was to be rid of the intruders. Anxious to keep his young guests alive, he poured water down their throats and decided he must act quickly to remove them all out of his cave-home as his supply of sedation was low. He waited for darkness to descend, righted the ladder and carried all four out of the cellar, one by one, over his shoulder by climbing the steep ladder and depositing them in the motorhome. It took some considerable time to accomplish the task and he was exhausted. Jack was the heaviest for him to carry. The hobo struggled with the burden over his shoulder as he tried to keep his footing on the metal ladder. He sweated and cursed to himself, hoping that he would not fall onto the concrete cellar floor. The climb up seemed unending, the lifeless boy becoming heavier with each dangerous step that he took. It was an immense challenge. Once out in the open he threw the boy onto the path and sat for a time to catch his breath. The trail to the motorhome was arduous and he began to question the wisdom of his plan. He left Jack in the vehicle, retraced his steps and repeated the process with Tess who was limp and still under sedation. Two more trips followed before he had completed his task. He left them still drugged, removed their bonds and left water nearby. He released the handbrake so that the vehicle trundled down into a deep wooded area and out of sight of human habitation. Believing that they would eventually recover from sedation and be totally disorientated and unaware of their location, he returned to cover his tracks by walking backwards, brushing the flattened path with twigs to disguise his activity. He bolted the trap from outside, covered it with shrubbery and re-entered the cellar via a door at the other end of the compound hoping that he could now continue his reclusive life in peace.

CHAPTER SEVENTEEN

Officers searching for the missing kids routinely called at shopping malls, grocery stores, public buildings and gas stations. In one such place, the proprietor clearly remembered speaking to one of the occupants of the motorhome as described to him. He searched through CCTV and located a tape showing time and date of around the visit in question.

"Lucky I've still have this copy; normally they are overwritten after a few days but I guess I never gotten around to it. Sure, I remember the driver. A young guy, student type if you know what I mean, he asked for directions to Leci House. I warned him off, told him it had been burnt to the ground several months ago and had an evil history. I told him he didn't wanna go there. I thought the guy had listened to me. So, what's the deal with those kids?"

"They haven't been seen for a few days, there's been no communication from them and their folks are mighty worried. We'll check out that house you mentioned.

Thanks, sir, for your help. Now, point me in the right direction."

"You ever heard of that house, Steve? Leci House?" enquired the cop of his partner.

"Can't say I have, Mike. I'll call it in and let HQ know what that guy said. He seems an okay guy, so let's head on up to the place, check it out, and take it from there."

"Fine by me."

The officers drove on further north, looking for Leci House and after several wrong turns they came upon the burnt-out estate. They parked up and went on foot, skirting around the vast perimeter looking for a way into the property. "It's sure a mystery as to where the entrance to this damn place is, Steve. We've been walking for ages, it's so overgrown."

"There's not much to see over that wall, Mike, just a burnt out old house. Let's head down this track and call it in. We must have covered the entire perimeter by now."

"This is a hell of a track! It's totally overgrown. Mind out for that fallen tree. We can't go much further without cutting equipment."

They retraced their steps to their vehicle and reported in that there was no sight of the missing vehicle or kids.

"We require reinforcements to do a ground search, sir. The estate is massive and the wooded area around it seems to go on for miles. It's totally overgrown with broken branches and hedges. According to the gas station proprietor, this was where the kids were heading. He tried to put them off and thought they had listened to him."

A call went through to Tony Harvey telling him that the kids had been sighted some days ago, by a gas attendant.

"They were in the vicinity of Leci House on the day they left you. They had called in to refuel and ask directions."

"What?" he screamed, causing the officer at the end of the phone to draw back. "What the hell were they doing there?"

"We have officers trawling the grounds of what's left of the estate, sir, searching for the vehicle."

"Right," said a concerned Tony, "we will join you there. Give me accurate directions."

"Sir, with respect, is that wise? Your kids might turn up back at the hotel. Best leave it to us."

"Officer, I hear you, but while my kids are out there I can't sit here pacing the floor. Once a cop, always a cop. I need to be in on the action." Tony related to the others what he had learnt from the officer.

"No!" cried Gina. "What possessed them to go there? It's an evil place." She burst into uncontrollable tears with her mind flicking back and forward with unimaginable thoughts of danger for the youngsters.

Tony took Carole aside. "Do you feel up to joining forces together and heading off to Leci House? We have to leave Ted and Abigail here with Gina in case the kids turn up. I think Gina needs to stay and rest. Abbie will see to her."

"Let's put it to the others. It sounds fine to me," replied Carole.

"Tony, take care out there and bring our babies back," exhorted a fraught Gina as she clung to him as if scared to let him go in case he would vanish out of her life like the children she believed in her heart she had lost. Abigail gently prised her mother from Tony's arms and, with Ted's help, escorted her to her room to await whatever the outcome was to be.

Tony drove at speed towards their destination.

"Hey, Tony, we ain't serving cops now and can't put blue lights on to get cars to move outta the way. Slow down. I know you're anxious to get there, I am too, but want to get there in one piece."

"Sorry, partner. I am anxious. I never thought we would be involved with this damned place again. They say it's burnt to the ground now. What possessed the kids to go there?"

"Calm down, Tony. If they had told us of their plans, we would have put a stop to it. They knew that. I guess we fired their imagination when we were caught up in the search for Lucy, and it must have been so tempting when we were together in New York, a once-in-a-lifetime chance to explore the past and see where Lucy spent her last days, when they knew they were so near."

"Guess so, Carole, guess so. But, hell, I'm scared for them; I fear for our kids and can't let Gina catch my fear. She's so fragile."

The journey seemed endless. Tony wiped the sweat from his hands that had covered the steering wheel. He felt stressed; his mind was in a turmoil as he tried to control his speed, anxiety taking over from clear thinking. Carole constantly called him to focus on the road ahead. She too was beyond being calm, blaming herself for not insisting on a clear itinerary from the kids believing them to be the sensible young adults she had reared.

"Oh God, Tony. I'm scared."

She put her head in her hands and sobbed; she, Carole, the thick-skinned woman who had seen more tragedy in her job than most, and who prided herself in her strong will when dealing with even the most harrowing of cases. "I never cry. You know that, Tony, but oh God, this is a living nightmare."

"Hey, partner, keep faith in the kids. Wanna pull over here at this rest stop?"

"Keep going. Leci House can't be far now. I just want to find my babies."

Me too, mouthed Tony as he drove with more determination than ever towards their destination, fearing what he might find there, but holding on to hope, a hope that came from deep within him, a hope that challenged every part of his being. His mood changed from frustration, to anger, anger at himself for allowing his kids to go off on a wild camping holiday without insisting on a detailed plan from them. Hindsight is wonderful, he thought, as he searched for the elusive Leci House, a house where evil lived, where hope had faded for young Lucy and where treachery had taken over from reality when a mad, scheming woman caused so much misery and where even now, her legacy of fear lingered and ate at the soul.

"Turn here, Tony, quick! It must be over there where those flashing lights are."

As they exited their vehicle they were stopped from entering the estate by a rookie cop who, full of importance, demanded they return to their vehicle.

"No sightseers allowed, sir, ma'am. This is a potential crime scene."

"Yeah, kid," replied Tony, "and if you block our way there will be trouble. Our kids are missing; we have history with this damned place."

The rookie cop called for assistance which came in the form of Detective Bruce who had previously met with Tony and Ted.

"It's okay, Proctor, I can vouch for these retired officers. Good to meet you again, detectives, but not in the circumstances. Let me bring you up to speed. We're sure the kids were here; the proprietor at the gas station identified them and their vehicle, and just fifteen minutes ago the last call made from one of the cell phones was tracked by the cell towers that operate 24/7. One of your kids made a call from the area we are in right now at 20:00 hours and the call lasted seventeen minutes."

"Yeah, that was when Jack called, we spoke to all four kids. It was the last we heard from them."

"What happens now?" asked Carole.

"Ma'am, my officers are searching this vast area. As you can see, the estate itself stretches for acres, not to mention the wooded area down there. My guys are doing a visual. I've called in the chopper to survey the area. You can hear it buzzing overhead. So far, there is no sighting of the motorhome... excuse me, guys, I've just been paged..."

Detective Bruce listened to the incoming call, nodded and called for more officers to join him. "We have visual on the motorhome," he told them, "over there in the woods. The chopper guys have said it's in a precarious position, on its side near a steep drop." He turned away momentarily from Tony and Carole and spoke to his men.

"Take it easy, guys. Don't disturb the vehicle or we'll lose it if it moves."

He turned back to the anxious parents, who strained to hear what was being instructed. "Sir, ma'am, we have located the vehicle but I have to ask you to stand down. Please return to your vehicle. I'll call you as soon I know what's happening."

As Tony was about to protest, Carole, held his arm and said, "Hey, Tony, let the guys do their job. Remember how we hated when civilians tried to become involved? Come on, partner, sit in the car."

CHAPTER EIGHTEEN

Tess Carr lifted her head, or at least attempted to do so, when a searing pain shot through her entire body. Her eyes were open but not yet focused. She blinked, rubbed them and attempted to sit up. Something was wrong. Something was very wrong. She could not fathom where she was; things looked familiar, yet unfamiliar. Her memory returned slowly, taking her back to the dreaded cellar where she remembered sitting on the cold, hard concrete floor with Jack whose leg oozed blood from a deep wound. They were searching for Poppy and Lucian... that was it, she remembered now, but something was not right here. This was no cellar, yet it had a strange familiarity about it. She wanted to call out but her parched lips appeared to be stuck together, her dry tongue cleaving to the roof of her mouth. She needed to drink, she needed to think. As her mind cleared she began to recognise where she was... the motorhome, but things were different. She realised what it was, the motorhome was lying on its side, resting among trees. Things were far from right.

As she sat up, the vehicle gave a shudder and moved slowly. *Oh, help,* she thought, *I'm trapped in this van, I can't move my legs.* She struggled to sit up; every little move resulted in another shudder from the vehicle. Her hand moved, only to touch the head of someone lying nearby "Luce..." she tried to call out but only muffled squeaks came from her mouth. Feeling someone touch his head, Lucian came to life, lifted his head and through a haze of confused images, saw Tess beside him.

"Wha...t? Wh...ere are we?"

He tried to speak but his painful lips were parched, his throat like sandpaper and his head throbbed like hell. He felt as if bullets from a Kalashnikov rifle had exploded in his head. As he turned to face Tess, the vehicle gave another shudder. Tess signalled to him not to move, pointed to the window, where trees appeared to be creeping towards them like monstrous tentacles from a zombie movie threatening to engulf them. His eyes focused. Things were not right. As his vision cleared he realised the vehicle they were in was on its side and slipping dangerously. Alerted by some unknown switch in his brain, he attempted to call out for Poppy and Jack. Mumbled sounds came from deep within his being and he stretched out and grasped Tess's hand, comforting them both as they assessed their dire situation. Poppy lay on the floor, a heavy cushion partially covered her lower limbs as if it and she had fallen together. She turned and moaned on hearing her brother's voice and attempted to move, only to cause the vehicle to shudder once more. Tess's foot touched something cold and metallic; a cell phone! The flowery cover identified it as Poppy's. Carefully, she pulled it towards her with her foot, aware that every tiny movement could cause the vehicle to move dangerously closer to the trees. It took a tremendous amount of her failing energy to grasp the phone in her hand and press it. She felt it vibrate, then die, the battery having been depleted by the call. Tears streamed down her face as she turned her attention to locating her brother.

"Jack," she attempted to call out. Lucian, too, called for him but from their position they could not see him. Poppy gave into tears that helped moisturise her lips. The three young people became more alert and very aware of their plight. Where was Jack?

*

Detective Bruce took a call that had him running towards the wooded area where his men were searching for a route to find the vehicle. "Officers, there has been a development. A call was attempted from the cell belonging to one on the kids, but the phone went dead. It has been traced to within a hundred yards of us... keep looking."

Several officers scoured the area anxiously looking for the vehicle. Two young officers, ahead of the others, stopped in their tracks. "Hey, Steve, what's that ahead? Down there."

"Mike, I think that's the vehicle. Yeah, it is! It's the one the kids hired; an Apollo Eclipse!"

They tramped down through the overgrowth, hurrying as fast as the shrubbery allowed, until they came as near to the vehicle as they deemed safe.

"Oh no! Look at the position of it, Steve; it could slip down into that gorge at any moment." Using his binoculars, he scanned the motorhome. "The kids are in there; I can see them."

"Are they alive? Can we get in?" asked Steve taking the binoculars from his colleague. "Oh God. They are slumped on the floor. I fear the worse, Mike."

"Can you see four people?" asked Mike.

"Hard to tell... I can see... three... call for help, we have to move real quick like to get them outta there. Call Detective Bruce."

Teams of searchers with Detective Bruce arrived to help rescue the youngsters.

"Get ropes, chains anything strong to wrap around the vehicle to steady it. We dare not go closer until it's secured," instructed Detective Bruce.

Working as quickly as they could, and aware of the impending dangers, ropes and chains appeared as if from nowhere and were secured around the vehicle, steadying it enough for an officer to approach and assess the situation.

"The kids are alive, sir; I can see movement, but they need help," said Steve. "I can see three kids. We need medics here asap. Only this littlest kid looks alert; they all look in a bad way; they seem to be in and out of consciousness."

Detective Bruce replied, "I can hear sirens. Help is on its way. Let's pray they get here in time. We have an officer positioned at the road end to direct them down here, it's a hellish entrance."

"Fetch the parents from their car," instructed Detective Bruce to a young officer, "they need to be here."

*

Tony and Carole raced to the rescue area, their faces telling of the strain, the worry, the fear that they experienced as they watched specialist teams secure the toppled motorhome and cut open the door. Tony held Carole, fearful that the once-stoical woman, crumbling in his arms, was about to pass out.

"Stay strong, Carole, I need you to be real strong right now, for both of us."

"I'm scared, Tony, I'm scared for my babies."

"Me too, partner, me too. We need to be strong for each other before we call Ted and Gina."

With the vehicle as steady as the rescue squad could make it, medics arrived at the scene and gently removed firstly Poppy then Tess, hooked them up to oxygen masks, checked their vital signs, and called for immediate back-up. One of the medics comforted Poppy who appeared to have rallied but was incoherent and distressed. "You're safe now, honey, everything will be fine. We'll get you to hospital with your friends right now. Your dad is right here."

Carole could not restrain herself; she rushed to her daughter, hugged Tess and was gently restrained by a medic.

"Ma'am, you have to let us attend to the casualties."

"Mommy's here, honey, Mommy's right here," she called as she allowed herself to be led to the side.

Tony, at Poppy's side, hugged his daughter and

assured her she was fine. "There gonna take you to hospital, sweetie, to be checked over. I'll be right there with you." As Tony spoke to his daughter, Lucian was being carried from the wreckage; he had lapsed once more into unconsciousness. Tony held his hand and called, "Hang in there, son, hang on, Lucian." Medics quickly removed all three to waiting ambulances where they were checked over.

Carole called out, "Where's Jack? Where is my son? She was frantic with worry and rushed as close to the motorhome as permitted by the rescuers who were inside the vehicle searching for Jack. "Where's my boy? Where's Jack?"

An officer gently removed her from the scene. "Stay back, ma'am, let the guys get him out. He seems to be trapped inside and they need all the space they can get to free him. Why don't you go to the ambulance and check on your daughter?"

Detective Bruce took her arm and led her away from the troubled spot. Others, working as a team, gently lifted Jack from the vehicle, secured him to a stretcher and stood back in horror as the vehicle tumbled into the deep gorge. Their faces were ashen as they realised how near they had been to going down with the doomed motorhome. Jack was gently moved to the ambulance where Carole sat with Tess. She was shocked at the state of her son, hugged him and whispered gently to him, "Mommy's here, Jack, hang in there, sweetie."

*

Ted Carr, pacing the hotel room, jumped when his cell phone vibrated and rang, He recognised Tony's number. "Tony, what's happening? We're frantic with worry here."

"We've found them, Ted. They are alive but in need of medical assistance. It looks like they may have lost control of the vehicle, we'll figure that out later. As we speak they are being transported to hospital. A forensic squad had been called to search the vehicle but it has fallen into a gorge. It's nightmare stuff here, Ted, just awful. I've spoken to Gina and Abigail, there's a police vehicle on its way to bring you all to hospital under police escort. We'll fill you in when you get here." Tony hesitated, "Ted, I have to tell you that Jack is in a bad way, so is Lucian, but please don't tell Gina. Not yet."

"Oh, God, Tony, what about the girls?"

"They seem to be responding to treatment; they are all seriously dehydrated. We'll get more information at the hospital. Hey, Ted, Carole wants to talk..."

"Honey," she cried into the phone. "It's our worst nightmare. Jack is pretty bad, Tess is responding."

"I'll be with you soon. The car has arrived to take us to hospital. Keep strong, babe. I'll be there real soon."

CHAPTER NINETEEN

Two anxious parents and Abigail, holding her mother closely and almost carrying the distraught woman, were driven at high speed through the city and shown to the relatives' room to be reunited with Tony and Carole. The reunion was highly charged with a mixture of emotions: concern, relief, anxiety and fear of what lay ahead. Tony held Gina closely to him, hushed her sobs and reassured her that Poppy and Lucian were in good hands.

"The medics are with them at the moment. They'll let us see them as soon as they have assessed their condition. Wipe your tears, honey, you don't want to let the kids see you upset."

Carole, sitting with Ted, held him tightly and explained the little she knew. "They are saying that Jack has a severe leg injury and has lost a massive amount of blood. When the vehicle toppled over he was thrown over and trapped with his leg elevated. The doctor said the fact that it was elevated saved him from any more blood loss. Tess is recovering well enough to sit up and talk. They had a nightmare few days, honey, and Tess only managed to talk a little before falling asleep… something about a vagrant abducting them… they didn't go off the road like we thought. No doubt we'll hear more as time goes on, but for now we have to concentrate on letting the physical wounds heal before we tackle the emotional scars." Ted hugged her and let her tears flow freely. "Best let it out, honey, and compose yourself before we see them."

They were interrupted when the doctor in charge entered the room.

"Good evening. I'm Jim Ashton one of the doctors attending to your kids," he said as he shook hands with each of the five adults. "Do you want me to talk to each set of parents individually, or are you happy for us to talk together?"

Ted and Tony looked at each other, nodded and made the decision for them all.

"We'll stick together, doctor, if you don't mind," said Tony as he introduced the group.

"Sure, that's fine by me." The anxious adults held on to every word from the doctor, who informed them that all four were severely dehydrated but were responding to treatment. "Lucian's vital signs," he said addressing Tony and Gina, "were giving cause for concern. All four appear to have been drugged, and young Lucian has reacted badly to it. His liver had been damaged but is repairable and he is having treatment right now. We've sent off some samples to the lab and should know soon what drug was used. I've asked them to treat this as priority."

"Drugged?" questioned Tony. "Our kids don't do drugs. Surely you're mistaken." For a fleeting moment Tony wondered if it were at all possible that the kids had experimented with illegal substances but dismissed the idea from his head almost as soon as it had appeared.

"No, no, sir," assured the doctor. "Whatever they were given was not self- inflicted, that I can tell from the state of their lips and mouths; something had been placed over them that contained some kind of sedative." Addressing Carole and Ted, he continued, "Your son is causing us concern too. He has a deep laceration in his leg that has gone through to the bone. He must have suffered tremendous pain. He has what we call a class three haemorrhage, a loss of about thirty per cent of his blood volume which means that his blood pressure dropped and his heart beat raced. We are controlling it as we speak. He has been given a blood transfusion and appears marginally better but will likely require a visit to the theatre for deep cleaning under anaesthetic."

"Marginally better?" questioned Carole.

"Yes, ma'am. It will be a slow process but we expect him to recover well. He's a strong, fit young man from what you tell me. His body will be able to fight this but it is going to take time"

"And our daughters? How are they?" asked Ted.

"They fared much better than the boys, but are emotionally exhausted, especially the little kid, Poppy, who cries constantly. We have them on saline drips and a glucose intravenous drug. They are extremely weak from starvation and don't have the energy to digest solid food. Wherever they were, they were deprived of food and water. That will be addressed soon. I think the best thing is for you to see your kids now. Officers are standing by to interview them later, to find out what happened to put them in such a dangerous situation. That will only happen when we feel that they are ready to be questioned. If you would like to follow me, I'll take you to them, but please, these young people are extremely weak so limit your time with them."

It was an emotional reunion of parents and children. Jack, extremely upset, attempted to apologise for keeping everyone in the dark. He hovered in and out of sleep but was aware of the adults' presence.

"This is all my fault… I knew you would be mad if we told you where we planned to go… it all went horribly wrong… and we could all have died at the hands of that hobo… it's all my fault."

"A hobo?" questioned Ted.

Jack's voice trailed off and he wept in his father's arms. His leg throbbed. He knew he was facing surgery to repair the damage.

"It's okay, Jack, it's okay. We parents are as much to blame by not taking note of the vehicle and insisting you leave an itinerary. Don't blame yourself, son, you are not at fault. Let's put it behind us and concentrate on getting well. No more talk of blame. We'll talk later, but, for now, you have to concentrate on getting better."

Gina and Tony took it in turns to sit with either Lucian or Poppy, reassuring, comforting and talking quietly to them well into the night. Abigail, too, took time with each of the young people, who found her easier to off-load to than their parents.

"Are they mad at us?" asked Tess.

"No, honey, they are more worried than mad. Any bad feelings they have are about themselves for not insisting that you to leave an itinerary."

"We knew they would forbid us to visit Leci House. We just wanted to see where Lucy had been, but it turned into a nightmare."

Abigail comforted Tess, reassuring her that they would all be well soon. "There will be plenty time to talk when we get you healthy again, sweetie, try to rest. I'm going to sit with Poppy for a time."

*

It was several days before the group could make statements to the police. Tony remained with his son as he spoke to the officers ensuring that the boy was not stressed out by their endless questions.

"Take your time, Lucian," said the officer, "just tell me what you remember and stop when you're tired. We won't rush you, buddy."

Lucian pulled himself up, adjusted his position and said, "I'm okay, sir. I want you guys to find that horrid person. I'll help all I can."

The officer switched on the recorder and listened to the boy's tale. He took his cue from a nod from Tony, as to when to give the boy a break. It was a slow process, Lucian's voice straining at times as the words came tumbling out. He was fired up with anger and determined to complete his statement. With four statements now clearly recorded, and samples taken from their clothes that had obvious contact with their assailant, investigating officers were sure they would soon identify the man who had turned an innocent adventure into an alarming nightmare. The first thing they had to do was to locate the entrance to the cellar taking note of Jack's directions and his description of the overgrown path.

"We will find this guy," said the departing officer. "Have no doubt about that; he will be brought to justice and get what he deserves."

CHAPTER TWENTY

Lucian and Jack remained in hospital while the girls were discharged to return to the hotel to recover under the care of their parents. They were allowed a short visit with their brothers before they left. It was an emotional visit for them all and was the first opportunity they had to talk together without the adults being present. Jack's eyes filled with tears as he attempted to apologise yet again for leading them all into danger. The others would have none of it.

"Jack," whispered Lucian through a hoarse voice. "Jack, you didn't force any of us to go on the trip. We were all up for it. All this," he said as he waved his hand over the hospital equipment, "was not your doing. It was the hobo's, so please stop blaming yourself, dude, you need to concentrate on getting better, we both do."

They all four hugged and wept at the plight of the young boys, and promised to return and visit as soon as the parents would allow it. Poppy clung so tightly to her brother that he had to ask her to let go as his chest hurt.

"I don't want to leave you here, Lucian," she sobbed.

"Hey, I'll be fine. I'll heal better if you stop squeezing the breath out of me," he laughed as he hugged his sister. "You go back to the hotel with Tess and leave us to talk guy stuff."

Jack's deep laceration had caused extensive bleeding and pain; the few days he was without nutrition impaired the healing process. His wound was treated in theatre, where the foul-smelling pus was drained and the wound deep cleaned. Infection had set in during his time in captivity, making healing even more difficult.

"We have to make a decision here," said the consultant to his colleagues who had gathered to hear prognosis for the young man. "Do we allow healing by natural process which may take some considerable time, or do we proceed with surgical skin grafting? My choice, given the severity of the wound and the amount of debris we removed by irrigation, is that we do the latter."

"Could we try deep-packing of the wound first," replied a doctor, "and apply either Clover or Manuka honey? If it works it would save surgery for the patient?"

"It could be extremely painful for him, but the pain would be controlled. Will we go down that road first then, colleagues? Do any of you want to contribute to this thought?"

Discussion lasted some time among the professionals as to the pros and cons of such treatment. A decision was made.

Carole and Ted, in consultation with consultant Jim Ashton, explained to the young patient the decision to allow his wound to heal naturally with help from Manuka honey.

"There has been great success, Jack, with this form of treatment, especially for hard-to-heal deep wounds like yours. We will use a high rating of grade ten and carefully monitor any pain that you experience. Shall we go ahead with the procedure and get you well again? It may be a bit uncomfortable but if it works as well as we hope it will, you won't need a theatre visit."

Jack looked at his parents for approval for the treatment and nodded his consent for the procedure.

Gina and Carole remained with their sick sons, chatting to them, reading and feeding them as they had done when they were infants. The boys shared a room, as requested by themselves, making it easier for the parents to share visiting. It gave them an opportunity to tell about their experience at the hands of the hobo and to offload their feelings. It was some weeks before Lucian showed any signs of emotional progress. It was as if he had withdrawn into himself. Having Jack for company had helped them both open up and talk about their experiences, sharing the fears they had for themselves and for their sisters.

"I was so scared, Jack, that the guy was going to harm Poppy, and I would have been helpless to do anything to save her. As it was, I think he wanted us out of his space. Mom was right; Poppy shouldn't have come with us. I guess moms know best."

"We have to concentrate on us now, Luce. Forget the 'what if's'. My mind turns over all the time with questions, but, hey, we need to try to put it behind us; it's not easy, dude, but we gotta try."

Abigail remained at the hotel with Poppy who had hardly spoken since being discharged from hospital. Physically she was well, emotionally not so. She lay in bed, quietly going over everything in her mind, remembering every detail of her trip to hell, a road trip she had embraced with enthusiasm, excited at being part of the quartet and looking forward to the adventure of a lifetime. Each time she tried to sleep she had flashbacks, causing her to call out in distress. It had all started off well with the promise of being counted as one of the adults.

Entrusted with the secret of where they were heading gave her a more mature outlook on life. She felt honoured to have been custodian of the secret trip. She, like her brother, had heard the story of the abduction of Lucy Mears, Abigail's best friend. She had been spared most of the gruesome details of the case, but was aware that Leci House played a role in the scenario. When it was whispered that the others planned to explore there, she was full of excitement and desperate to find a ghost or two roaming around the premises. The experience had matured her.

Abigail comforted her sister, letting her remain silent, letting her know she was there for her and that she understood something of her emotional pain.

"Whenever you feel like talking, Poppy, let me know, sweetie. Don't keep your emotions in for too long. It helps to share it with those who love you dearly. You know what I went through with Lucy, so I do really mean it when I say I know how you feel." Poppy turned to face her sister.

"I'm scared, Abbie. I'm scared that Lucian and Jack are going to die."

CHAPTER TWENTY-ONE

After recovering sufficiently from treatment, Jack had been transferred to a hospital nearer home in Chicago at his parents' request and spent several weeks there before being discharged into the care of his parents. They felt that Tess needed to be in familiar surroundings to help heal her emotional scars and having her brother at home could hasten healing for them both.

Lucian was bereft when Jack returned to Chicago with his family, leaving him there to continue treatment.

"Hey, buddy, it won't be long until they let you go home too, once they've got your crazy liver fixed. Keep focused, dude. Hey, you might even be home before they let me out of hospital in Chicago. You can come visit me there."

Back home, Carole and Ted tried to persuade their son to have a year off from study to regain full fitness.

"We don't want you going back to New York too soon, Jack. Why not think about a year off? You really need to focus on your stamina and well-being before you put yourself under pressure with exams and stuff."

Jack insisted on continuing with his veterinary medicine course despite his parents' anxiety. They were desperate to have their children at home with them for a reasonable period to recover from the emotional trauma and stress. Tess acquiesced to the request on condition she could resume her studies in the next semester.

Jack had been adamant. "Mom, Dad, I really want to continue with my course. I'm at a crucial stage now and have finished my assignments. I don't want to lose out now. Honestly, I'm good; my leg is healing, albeit slowly, but the doctor says it will heal completely through time."

He reddened as he continued, "I haven't told you, what with everything that's been going on, but I've met a wonderful girl. I was planning on telling you and get her to meet with you, but it's not the right time. Her name is Sue and she's in my group at vet school. We've been seeing each other for some time now… Mom, Dad, you will love her… she's…"

Aware of Jack's discomfort and embarrassment, Ted said, "That's cool, Jack, no need to be embarrassed. Mom and I are pleased for you. We were saying recently that it wouldn't be long before you made your own way in the world and found yourself a nice gal to settle down with."

Carole hugged her son. "We'll get to meet your Sue real soon; for now, though, we have to concentrate on putting our lives back together after your nightmare experience. I want Tess settled back with us at home, then we'll look to the future. Hey, why don't you invite Sue to visit here then we can all get to meet her?"

The idea appealed to the young man and, for a time at least, his parents had won the argument.

Lucian missed the company of his best friend and experienced a loneliness he had never thought possible. He longed to return home and resume his life before the wretched hobo almost destroyed it. With no one to share his nightmarish memories, his mental health took a step backwards. He experienced flashbacks and screamed out in his sleep, bringing concerned staff to his side. During his waking hours too, his mind wandered to events in the cellar. His gloom was interrupted by the arrival of some welcome faces.

"Hi, sisters," he called as Poppy and Abigail came into the room. They held each other tightly as if wanting the closeness to last forever.

"It's good to see you sitting up Lucian and looking much brighter," said Abigail as she hugged him. "The parents are with your consultant; they'll be along as soon as."

As they chatted together, they filled Abigail in with more details of their ordeal. Sharing the experience in some way acted as a buffer for them. They revealed more to Abigail than they had to their parents. Tears turned to laughter as they made light of telling ghost stories especially when Poppy declared in the most adamant of ways that she never, ever wanted to speak of such things. She pulled herself up to her full height and, with hand on hip, a pose they were well used to seeing from the incorrigible girl, tossed her hair and announced in a forceful voice, "I'm finished with ghostly things, for ever. I never want to see a ghost ever again, or hear anything about them." A cheer from the others caused more laughter than they had heard in the longest time.

Tony and Gina met with Lucian's doctor to discuss their son's progress."The good news is," began the kindly man, "we on the team feel Lucian has progressed enough for him to return home with continued care. I can refer him to a colleague of mine in Chicago who will continue monitoring him and treat his illness with medication. We can now safely say that is all he requires. I have to tell you we were concerned that there might have been underlying liver disease in your son. Sometimes in young people it lies dormant and manifests itself in later life, but blood tests and ultrasound and the biopsy have shown that not to have been the case. This young man's liver was damaged by the chemicals he was poisoned with, a mighty strong dose it was too. He was given much more than the others. The illness came on rapidly. His liver is no longer failing but he needs to be monitored regularly and probably for life, so I suggest you take him home and feed him up. He has lost his appetite, and from what you have told me, he was a good eater. The lethargy too will dissipate with good care at home. So, shall we tell your son the good news?"

Peals of laughter greeted them as they made the short walk to Lucian's room.

"Well," began the consultant, "that's surely a happy sound, young man," he said addressing his patient. "It seems like you are on the mend. Now, do you want the good news?"

Lucian was quite emotional on hearing he was free to be with his family.

The consultant assured him he would soon be back to his normal self. "Now, young man, no self-pity from you. With continued medication and a good attitude, you will be well, so, no going to a dark place. Keep positive and upbeat and all will be well." The consultant spent some time explaining to the boy exactly what had happened to his body, how his treatment had worked and what would be required in the future.

The family remained at the hotel for a few more days to relax before heading home. Knowing all was well, Abigail returned home before the others. "I'd like to get back to work, if it's okay with you guys. We have interviews pending for the next batch of students and you know that Brenda likes to sit in on them. She's a good judge of character and can spot when a student is genuine about studying at our academy. It's as if she is choosy about who will be admitted to share Lucy's memories. Ralph has interviews too for the music faculty, and we in the arts will start interviewing next week for our new landscape module. It's an exciting venture and I so want it to be a success. Now you two, behave, keep well and get fully fit as soon as you can."

Several days after Abigail's departure, the others headed for home.

"That was one vacation I would not want to repeat," said Gina as they settled down for the flight home.

There was no reply from Tony, who had an exasperating habit of falling asleep as soon as the plane was in the air, much to the amusement of his children.

"There's not much chance of an illuminating conversation with your father!"

Lucian beamed with delight as the plane touched down at O'Hare. Even the rain and dark skies could not dampen his enthusiasm.

"Home at last!" said the relieved boy who was met at home by Jack and Tess who had called around to decorate the house with bunting and welcome home banners.

All four recovered sufficiently to take up the threads of their life, lives that would never again be the same; memories of that dreadful vacation would never leave them, the scars too deep to eradicate with medication. Time, they were told, was a great healer.

CHAPTER TWENTY-TWO

Ralph had been interviewing young people over several days. The academy had organised a ten-week course on *Composers of Our Times* and places were sought after. Ralph secured a speaker from the European Composers' Association, Eric Orlov, and demand was high to hear him speak of his work and listen to some of his compositions. Brenda Mears, sitting in on the interviews, spoke little but listened well. She consulted with Ralph and advised him on selection of students.

"It is difficult, Ralph, and soul-destroying for those not selected. Perhaps we might consider rerunning the course at a later date. Meanwhile, those you have selected seem keen, just the kind of kids the academy wants to encourage and what a variety of talent they have!"

"Yeah," replied Ralph as he perused the list of candidates.

"The young flautist, Samuel, has real talent and as for the girl, Marie, what a beautiful soprano voice she has.

She's destined for a bright future and we are honoured to nurture that gifted voice. I think we've made a fair choice for this coming course, but, yeah, I agree, we need to consider more of the same. I expect Abigail will be having similar difficulties for her latest venture – too few places for the number who wish to join us."

Brenda continued the theme, "I'm sure we can come to some kind of compromise about numbers, but you know, Ralph, that I want this place to be a special source of nurturing young, enthusiastic and gifted kids. I don't ever want to push the numbers to the max. We would lose the intimacy. The ethos of the place would change if it became too big for us to get to know our students. I don't want them to pass through our doors without us getting to know them."

*

Abigail had returned to the academy after a final hospital visit, more at peace in the knowledge that everyone had recovered, at least physically, from their ordeal. She shared her concerns with Ralph who was her rock, knowing he would guide her through the dark moments that she was bound to experience.

"It will be a long time before the emotional scars are healed, honey, but with support and love they will come through," he assured her.

"I know where you're coming from, Ralph, but all the same, I can't help but worry about them… now, let's move on. I have to get my head around next week's interviews. I'm so looking forward to running the landscape painting sessions. Brenda will sit in with me and advise on the selection. Once again, we have more candidates than we have places for."

With Brenda's guidance, the selection process resulted in a group of excited youngsters embarking on their ten-week residential module. Abigail revelled in sharing her talent with them. The grounds afforded plenty of scenic spots to draw inspiration from to hone their skills. Students could choose privacy and peace to work alone, or with others if they required companionship. Their interpretation of the stunning landscape never failed to amaze Abigail whose work of advising, encouraging and helping them develop their own unique style, soothed in some way her constant concern for her siblings. She herself knew the profound effect on her own emotional well-being that came from immersing herself in painting. Without her art she would have felt the loss of Lucy more deeply and darkly than she had done, and she was keen to pass on her experience when faced with any troubled young person who found themselves on one of her courses. Art to Abigail was a life-saver, a therapeutic life-saver, a time of escape from the realities of life where she could take stock and prioritise and come to terms with life.

After supper each evening the students from both music and art faculties would gather together, and impromptu sing-song and story-telling became the norm. Inevitably with each new group, talk came around to Lucy Mears. Most students were aware of her tragic story. Abigail would gently relate the events from her memory and would show the group Lucy's suite of rooms, viewed only from a glass panel, no one having access to it but her. Keeping Lucy's memory alive was important for her and she found peace in doing so.

The academy was in full swing. Abigail's healing had commenced in earnest as she threw herself one hundred per cent into delivering what her young students had come to experience.

One morning, midway through the current course, Ralph, an early riser, headed out for his usual morning run. He tiptoed quietly from the room so as not to disturb Abigail who remained in peaceful sleep mode. Ralph's regular run took him out of the estate to a nearby park, where he timed himself to the minute, as he ran around the lake that gleamed in the morning sunlight, sparkling like beams of coloured beads on a necklace that had been caught in a beam of glorious light. He acknowledged the nods of the regular runners that he had come to know. No one spoke, no one wasted energy on small talk. A friendly nod of the head was all that was required to bond these runners into an unofficial club. Ralph relished the peace of the morning as a new day dawned over the city, a city slowly coming to life and, before many hours had passed, a city that would become a bustle of noisy commuters and impatient drivers as the entire world, it seemed, made its way to work, to begin yet another stress-filled week. His morning run gave Ralph an opportunity for clear thinking as he mulled over in his mind the best way forward for the academy, while never losing sight of the principles and values of LMAMA, and the reason for its existence.

He returned to the house, via the main door and headed towards the kitchen where he routinely had coffee with the staff who were preparing breakfast. They prided themselves on timing him to the last second and laughed as they poured out his black-no-sugar, drink on hearing the click of the main door. This morning he stopped in his tracks in the main foyer. A despicable sight met his eyes. He stared in disbelief. He placed his hands on the door as if to steady himself. His entire body shook as he tried to focus on the discovery in front of him. He turned and ran back to waken Abigail, his heart pounding in his chest, more from the shocking scene that he had witnessed, than from the exertion of his run.

"Abbie, honey, wake up, something awful has happened."

Thinking that someone was ill, she jumped out of bed, shook her long tangled hair from her face, donned a warm house coat and listened to what Ralph had to say.

"Abbie, Lucy's portrait has been damaged. I spotted it when I came back from my run. Oh, honey, it's dreadful."

They both stood in front of the slashed portrait painted by Abigail, commissioned by Brenda Mears not long after Lucy's death. It was her first major venture in painting a portrait completely from memory, and was an acclaimed success, not only because of the striking life-like image it portrayed but because it captured something of the soul of the tragic girl. Painting it was a turning point for Abigail in deciding on a career choice.

Encouraged by her mother and sponsored by Brenda, Abigail pursued a career in art, culminating in her present position of lecturer-in-charge of the academy with responsibilities heaped on her shoulders, responsibilities she could never have dreamt of had it not been for Brenda Mears fervent desire to preserve her daughter's memory.

She stood there, speechless at first, her eyes adjusting to the carnage. Her entire body began to shake, slowly at first then building up to a peak of near hysteria. Ralph prevented the distraught woman from falling to the ground. Her outburst of screaming brought students who were heading for breakfast rushing to the foyer to witness the vandalism of the well-loved painting. Gasps of horror, cries of disbelief and stunned silence mixed with sobs and distress came from some students who saw in Lucy's portrait, the essence of what the academy stood for. Housekeeping staff too came running to investigate the source of the commotion and cried out in horror at the unfolding scene. One clutched the cup of coffee in her hand that had been intended for Ralph who promptly took charge of the situation. By now almost everyone had gathered in the foyer, some rubbing sleep from their eyes having been wakened by screams and cries of distress at the destruction in front of them.

"Right, everyone, listen up. This has been a deliberate act of devastating vandalism. We will call the cops to investigate this crime, for that's what it is. No one, I repeat, no one is to leave the building. Please, have breakfast then gather in the main lecture room. Remain there until dismissed. Unfortunately, until otherwise proven, the finger is more than likely pointing at someone here in this house. If anyone knows who has done this despicable deed, please come forward and let us know."

Ralph placed the distressed Abigail in the care of the housekeeper who escorted the weeping woman to her sitting room and sent for a hot, sweet drink.

"Who could have done this? Who could be so cruel?" she sobbed in the arms of the equally upset housekeeper.

"Hush, ma'am, hush now. Mr Ralph will see to it. Don't distress yourself now, drink this, you're shaking and shivering."

While waiting for detectives to arrive, Ralph made the upsetting call to Brenda Mears to inform her of events. He could hear the deep intake of breath as she took in the enormity of what she was hearing.

"I'll be right over," she said as she finished the call. She stood with the phone in her hand looking absently at it as if searching for answers. She let out a sob, pulled herself together and headed over to the scene of the destruction.

Ralph called Tony Harvey and spoke with him at length.

Tony said, "As soon as Abbie feels up to it, please get her to call. I'll go break the news to Gina. Ralph, get the details of the officer-in-charge for me; I want to be kept in the loop on this."

Ralph stood in silence in front of the rendered painting, shook his head in disgust and, using chairs, cordoned off the area that he knew without doubt was a crime scene. He joined Abigail in the sitting room that led off from the hallway from where he could ensure no one entered the atrium.

Officers, headed by officer-in-charge Scott Wynne, arrived and quickly sealed off the scene. He spoke at length with Ralph before speaking to the now slightly calmer Abigail.

"Ma'am, have you any idea who would want to destroy this work of art? Is there anyone with a grudge, perhaps?"

Holding Ralph's hand for support, she replied that no one came to mind.

"I've been mulling it over in my mind and cannot think of why anyone would cause such upset. Staff who work here have been vetted most carefully and as far as we can tell, the students are all okay kind of kids."

"We will require a list of all persons staying here and commence interviews and take prints. Staff as well as students."

Abigail's efficient secretary soon had the information ready and showed the officers to a room that they could use. Photographs were taken of the damaged portrait and the area dusted for prints.

Brenda Mears arrived, and when shown the damage hung her head and shed silent tears. She felt as if Lucy had been violated in person. "Oh, my beautiful daughter. Who has done this dreadful deed?"

Ralph sat with her and Abigail, two women broken-hearted at the loss of Lucy, and once more, joined together in loss, a different kind of loss, but one that pierced their souls just as if the knife used to desecrate Lucy's portrait had plunged into their very being. They held each other closely, Abigail's unruly hair covering them both. Tears mingled with hair, hair with tears. In the past, Brenda Mears would seldom show emotion, being almost incapable of doing so, but since the loss of her daughter and others close to her, she had mellowed immensely. In establishing the academy, she had looked on Abigail as a surrogate daughter, not to replace her darling Lucy, that was impossible, but to provide a living link to her dead child. Abigail's hopes and dreams were closely followed by Brenda, who harboured guilt and regret at her refusal to allow her own daughter to follow her dream as a cellist and insisting that she follow her into the family business. It had caused tension which was never resolved. Lucy's tragic death had put paid to that.

Crime scene officers interviewing staff and requested those who were on time off to return for interview. They turned their attention to the students, many of whom were upset at the turn of events, in what, until then, had been an enjoyable time in their young lives. No one appeared to have any knowledge of the atrocity and were aware of the impact of it on Lucy's mother and friends.

"I wish I could help, sir," commented one student who was visibly upset, "but I slept soundly; it's the pace of life here. My room-mate as far as I'm aware, never moved. We were both exhausted from a day of intense work and the hilarity and fun in the evening."

Most of the students reported much of the same. One student whose room was nearest to the atrium said, "I'm a light sleeper, sir. The stairs leading down to the foyer where the painting is located are creaky in places and I would have heard footsteps. I'm sure of that. I didn't hear a sound."

While interviews were being conducted, Ralph and Abigail returned to their room to shower and change. Brenda headed upstairs to the inner sanctum of Lucy's shrine, the rooms where nothing had changed from the time of her abduction, and where, when she felt stressed or in the need to ponder some business matter, Brenda would come and sit in silence surrounded by her daughter's belongings. For the second time that day, an ear-piercing scream was heard as Brenda discovered more destruction. Someone had unsuccessfully attempted to break the toughened security glass and, unable to do so, succeeded in leaving obscene etchings on the impenetrable surface.

Officers conducting interviews were alerted to the area. Interviews were abandoned for the moment as the scene was cordoned off and the area photographed and dusted for prints. The officer in charge joined Ralph and Abigail in the sitting room where Brenda, inconsolable, sat between them.

"This is a harrowing time for you all. The finger points to someone with a grudge against either the academy or you personally," he said as he looked at the distressed trio, huddled together on one sofa, clinging to each other for support. "Let's start with the academy. Have you had occasion to dismiss any member of staff or student?"

Ralph spoke up, "There was one unsuitable cleaning lady," he said. "That was when we first opened several years ago. We found her stealing items that belonged to the students and she was asked to leave."

"Did you press charges, sir?"

"No. She returned the items and was duly chastised. Dismissal was enough."

"Oh, I remember the incident," said Abigail. "The lady went off to live with her daughter in New Jersey. I can't see that she would want to seek revenge after all these years, we're talking about a minor incident that happened about eight years ago."

"I can't help you there, officer," said Brenda. "I have little recollection of the incident. I'm sure, as Abigail says, it was a minor matter, long forgotten."

"And students?" continued the officer. "Have there been incidents or anything that comes to mind that might help us here?"

"We've never had to send any students away, sir," replied Abigail. "Over the years one or two have had to leave voluntarily. One I remember because of a family bereavement, and there was another guy who had been given a place at Tisch School of the Arts in New York. He left early too, but that was several years ago and there was nothing untoward about their leaving. In fact, we refunded their fees. There were no issues with them."

Ralph said, "I can reiterate what Abigail has said, we have never had to dismiss a student. Perhaps we are looking in the wrong direction."

Interviews with staff did not throw any light on the despicable crimes. Ursula, the longest-serving staff member said, "I've been here since the academy opened. In fact, my mom worked here when it was the family home before Brenda donated it to the academy. I often came at holiday time and helped Mom with the cleaning. I know every inch of the place. I love meeting the young students and seeing what creative talents they bring with them. There has never been an issue with any of them, no bad vibes at all, sir, and the present group of kids are real cool kids. It's hard to believe that any of them would do such wanton damage. It's unnerving and I hope you find the bad guy real quick so that we can settle back to some kind of peaceful life. It's so upsetting for everyone."

CHAPTER TWENTY-THREE

Later that day Officer Wynne spoke once more to the academy owners.

"Today has been harrowing for the young people. The interviews are still being conducted, but so far they have not thrown up any obvious suspects. The kids seem honest enough and are desperate to have the culprit caught and dealt with. Until that happens they are unsettled and wary of each other; there's a feeling of mistrust among them; they are unsure of who to turn to. Does anyone come to mind as a suspect? Has anyone shown any change in behaviour since the crime was committed? The guilty person surely will manifest some signs of stress."

Brenda, now more composed, said, "I've been talking to the kids to get their take on the whole thing. Some of them are fearful, others angry that their studies have been interrupted by such a devious deed and they want the person apprehended and dealt with. None of the kids appear to me to show guilt. It's a real mystery, officer, one that I hope can be solved quickly. They want to stay on and finish their course. No one has asked to leave."

"Ma'am, we are waiting for the results from fingerprints. Most of these young people have had no convictions so there will be nothing on our database. We're checking their home addresses for any discrepancies, any false names, dates of birth, etc. It will all be investigated. A few of the kids have left home and live elsewhere, but we will check out their family homes too."

Ralph spoke up, "Can we continue with our course of study? We are almost winding down now, but have a few loose ends to be sorted and we always put on a show at the end of each session, a musical and art extravaganza. The students are almost ready to present their work to family and friends of the academy. We are expecting quite a crowd for the show."

Abigail said, "We need to let the kids get back to their studies. Music and art, officer, are tremendous therapeutic activities. They all need to grab paints and brushes and musical instruments and get out there in the grounds for a time; they have been cooped up indoors since all this happened. I know I need to get outside too."

"Ma'am, I'm sure that will be fine but please advise the students to remain on campus. Also, on a more sensitive note, I must interview each of you. Do you have any objections to that? I have to do this for elimination purposes. The three looked at each other and nodded to confirm that all was in order. "We would not expect anything less of you, officer," replied Brenda. "We have to get to the bottom of this."

Ralph and Abigail left the room to attend to other duties, leaving Brenda with Officer Wynne who quickly established that Brenda, who was at home at the time of the incident, was not involved in any way with the desecration of her daughter's memorial.

"I'm sorry to put you through this, but it's part of the job to interview absolutely everyone. Can you think of anyone, even if it's a slight niggling suspicion, who would want to destroy your daughter's things?"

"Sir," said Brenda rather forcefully, "I've been wracking my brains over this. I know most of the staff, I was present when each was interviewed for positions here and sat in on interviews conducted by Abigail and Ralph for student places. Alarm bells did not ring in my head at any of these encounters, and, until now, we have had nothing but positive, pleasant young people staying at the academy. I'm sorry that I can't be more helpful. I wish I had some answers."

Officer Wynne's team continued with interviews throughout the day leaving him free to speak to Abigail who was becoming more stressed as the day went on, especially when Lucy's portrait was removed and packed up for detailed forensic analysis.

"Tell me, Abigail, the events of this morning; run them past me, from your perspective. Take your time, I know this is painful for you."

Abigail explained the scenario yet again to the patient officer who noted all she said.

"It began as a normal day, sir. Ralph left to do his run. He always brings me coffee from the kitchen when he finishes, but this morning he rushed in quite upset and told me what had happened. It was the start of a nightmare. I can't believe that someone would be so evil."

"When did you last see the portrait and visit Lucy's shrine?"

"Last evening after the kids had retired. I always check that the main door is locked, and glanced, as usual, at the portrait. It may sound crazy to you, but I always whisper 'goodnight, Lucy' before I retire. As for her room, I was last there about supper time; again, checking it out. We have one security light that shines into the room, night and day. It was on as usual. Sometimes I spend some time there after a stressful day, or when I feel the need to connect, but last evening I checked all was well and I returned to my apartment."

Officer Wynne continued, "Who has a key to the rooms?"

"There are only two. Brenda has one and I have the other. We never felt the need to cut more keys."

"So," he continued, "if someone wanted to visit the rooms, where would they find the key?"

"They wouldn't. Brenda and I never part with the keys. If anyone is visiting they are escorted there by me. We discourage curious onlookers. At the start of each new group, we give the students the history of the academy and invite them as a group to view the rooms. That is the only time they are allowed to view, from the corridor."

"And your partner, Ralph? Doesn't he have a key?"

"No, officer. Ralph respects my privacy. He knows I find solace, as does Brenda, in sitting among Lucy's things, and never intrudes. He has of course been there with me on one or two occasions, but never by himself."

"You say he left for his run at his usual time. What time was that?"

"I was asleep when he left, as I am most mornings. He is a creature of habit, doesn't vary his routine in anything he does. He rises before six and returns with coffee at seven each morning; that's my wake-up call."

"So, in fact, he could have left the room earlier than usual?"

"Uhm, well I suppose… what? What are you implying?"

"Nothing at all, ma'am; just establishing the facts and exploring every possible avenue. Is it possible then, that Ralph could have left earlier than normal for his run? The house would be silent at that early time, wouldn't it?"

"Officer, if you are implying, even remotely, that Ralph had anything to do with this destruction, you are way out of order. Hey, wait a minute, I remember now that as he closed the door I woke for a moment, checked the clock and went right back to sleep. It was 5:58 on my clock."

"Now that's a convenient memory, ma'am, if you don't mind my saying," smirked the officer who was anxious to wrap the crime up quickly and return to his precinct.

Abigail stood up, furious at the insinuation that her partner caused destruction of what she, and he, held dear. She glowered at the officer and said, "As this is an informal interview, I intend to walk out of this room. If you require to speak to me again, my lawyer will be present. Your innuendo is contemptible. Now if you will excuse me, I find your line of enquiry offensive." With a toss of her unruly hair, Abigail left the room.

Interesting! A fiery one that who intends to stand by her man, he thought as he wrote furiously.

Ralph, who was engrossed in helping a student with a piece of music, was asked to come for interview. He was unaware of what had gone during the other interviews.

"Ralph," began Officer Wynne, "run me through the events of this morning, if you will, from the moment you awoke."

"Sure," he replied. "I got up at 5:50 am was out of the apartment by six as usual and set off for my run which took me my usual forty-five minutes. I check my time to the last minute and always return via the main house where the early breakfast staff have coffee ready. I usually take coffee to Abigail, but this morning as I crossed the atrium, I saw the destruction of Lucy's portrait. I ran to the apartment to alert Abigail and we both rushed down. The rest of the day is what you know, sir."

"Did anyone see you leave or return to the house?"

"Not to my knowledge."

"Can anyone corroborate your story?"

"No, sir."

Ralph felt a sense of unease at the direction the questioning was going.

"Officer, you don't for a minute think I had anything to do with this carnage?"

"I'm just checking every avenue in order to eliminate you from our enquiries. Now, sir, did anyone see you while you were running?"

Ralph was taken aback at the thought of being a suspect, a suspect in what he considered a heinous crime against Abigail, against Brenda, the academy and against the memory of Lucy. For a moment he was lost for words but then regained his composure and said, "Well, I guess the other runners that I meet regularly in the park could vouch for my time there. We never talk, just nod an acknowledgement and continue running. We seem to be a focused group."

"Do you have contact details of these people?"

"I've already explained, sir. We are total strangers who happen to be running in the same park at the same time each morning. I know nothing about them."

Silence. Silence while Officer Wynne wrote furiously in his notebook, the only sound being the scratching of his pen on the paper and the laboured breathing from both men, Ralph's from stress and the officer's from overweight. After what seemed to Ralph an interminable time, Officer Wynne stood up, removed his reading glasses and stared hard at the uncomfortable interviewee. "If you have nothing else to add, sir, we're finished here… for the time being. Please do not go for your run tomorrow and if you think of anything else that might help this enquiry, please inform me or one of my team who will be remaining on the premises."

During Ralph's interview with Officer Wynne, Brenda and Abigail sat together in the sun lounge mulling over events of the day.

"Brenda," said Abigail in a quiet voice, "I got the feeling from that officer that he suspects Ralph of causing the damage." Brenda looked at her in total disbelief.

"That is not possible, not Ralph, he is the most honest, up-front guy I know. Are you sure of your feelings, honey?"

Ralph entered the room and heard their conversation. He was numb with rage, his knuckles clenched and chalk white.

"Answer her, Abigail, do you think I did this horrible thing? Answer her."

He sat on the sofa beside her, staring in disbelief and never taking his eyes from her face which was red and tear-stained.

"No, Ralph, I do not think such a thing. I'm upset because that pompous officer thinks you might have done so. I'm upset for you. Honey, I love you and trust you completely. We have to find the culprit and get that officer to see how wrong he is." She hugged him tightly and sobbed on his shoulder.

"Thank God, Abigail. For a minute I thought my world had crashed around me. How can we prove that I had nothing to do with this? I don't know who to turn to. This is playing havoc with our thinking process; mine is all over the place."

Brenda spoke up. "I do. I know the very person who can help with this. Abigail, call your stepfather and ask him to call over. If anyone can solve this, he can. Tony Harvey may have retired from active service in CPD, but his heart is still in solving crime. Tell him it's a special request from me."

*

Tony Harvey, fired with enthusiasm, renewed vigour and a great deal of anger, arrived at the academy, introduced himself to Officer Wynne who knew the history and reputation of the former Superintendent of CPD.

"It's an honour, sir, to meet you. I've heard so much about you; you're a legend and we hold you in high esteem. Hey, we even hold you up to our new recruits as a model for solving crime in our great city. It's a pleasure to meet you."

Tony, never one for such patronizing, got down to business.

"Officer, I am here unofficially. You have the right to send me away, but this is my stepdaughter and future son-in-law who are affected by this horrendous devastation, as is Brenda Mears who has had to witness the desecration of all that she has of her beloved daughter. I am here to support them and to help in any way you can use me, to help bring this sorry business to a quick solution."

Overcome by the imposing presence of his hero, Officer Wynne took Harvey up to speed on the investigation. "We have almost finished interviewing everyone. I'm waiting for lab results to help us identify the villain. I had an uneasy feeling about Ralph as he seemed particularly nervous during his interview. I just wondered…"

"Officer Wynne, I applaud your meticulous methods and how you have moved swiftly on this, but I have to assure you that Ralph is an honest, okay guy, and while you are pursuing him, you are letting the real criminal escape justice. Naturally he is nervous since a hellish crime has taken place, and he was the one to discover it. Tell me why you suspect him."

Tony could be patronizing too when the need arose. The gullible officer beaming from what he took as praise, opened up and said, "Sir, it was the timing of everything. The suspect, I mean the guy was the only one up early and had ample opportunity to do the deed. No one could vouch for his whereabouts before he went off for his run in the park. All I hope for is that the runners he came across can corroborate his story. I intend to send officers to speak to them in the morning and have asked Ralph to forgo his morning run."

"Good, officer. Ideal, but hey, I'd like to do a bit of jogging myself tomorrow," he said as he patted his rather rotund form. "I could do with getting back into shape and I could speak to the runners at the same time, unofficially of course, and I won't interfere with your investigating officers."

*

Next morning, Tony Harvey, kitted out in jogging gear, accompanied a young, fit officer on a run following the exact route given to them by Ralph.

"Hey, slow down man. I don't know how anyone can keep this pace for ten minutes let alone forty-five. There's our first runner, go over and speak to him while I draw breath. Show him Ralph's picture and ask if he has ever seen him around these parts."

The runner was at first reluctant to stop until shown the officer's badge.

"Sure, sir. I know the guy, don't know anything about him but I see him every morning jogging around here, we usually pass about that bench down there," he said pointing a few yards further along the path. And yeah, I saw him yesterday, same time. I haven't seen him this morning, is everything okay, sir?"

"It's routine enquiries, sir. Thank you for your observations, enjoy your run."

Details were taken and the jogger sent on his way. Others, too, reported similar sightings and showed concern for their fellow runner.

"Hey, officer. Is the guy okay? I haven't seen him today, hope he ain't in any trouble."

"No trouble, sir, he's just helping to clear up a bit of a mystery."

Tony, meanwhile, sat on a bench attempting to catch his breath and was approached by a concerned jogger.

"You okay, buddy? You sure don't look too good. Can I get some water for you?"

"I'm good, thanks. I sure am unfit. Hey, while you're here, I wonder, have you seen this guy today? I was meant to meet him, but there's no sighting of him," said Tony holding a picture out to the jogger.

"I ain't seen him this morning, he's as regular as clockwork, haven't seen him since this time yesterday. We nodded to each other as we passed by."

"Thanks, buddy. I'll hang around a bit, he might be running late."

Officer Wynne, reassured that Ralph was where he said he was on the morning of the destruction, and fully accepting that Abigail had woken as she said and had noted the time when he had left the apartment, cleared him of any wrongdoing.

"No hard feelings, sir," said Wynne as he told Ralph he was not in any way considered a suspect. "Just covering all situations, sir."

Tony remained at the academy, mainly to be a support for his stepdaughter but also to covertly investigate the scene of crime.

"I'll stay well out of your way," he told Abigail, "and do some background checks on staff and students, without interfering with Officer Wynne and his team. I'll be as discreet as possible."

"Sure, Pops," said Abigail, using her favourite name for him. "Why don't you use my apartment? We can bring whatever info you need to do your magic on. You know, since you've arrived I feel so much more secure. It's been scary as hell. Brenda too, appreciates your presence."

"I thought the poor woman had seen more than enough of me! Glad to be of assistance, honey, and it keeps the old grey matter alert. Now what I need from you is the current list of students. I'll work on that, and if nothing raises its head, I'll work back to your previous group. Officer Wynne has dismissed the idea of any current staff members being involved. Brenda convinced him of that. She has been meticulous in hiring them and can vouch for their honesty. I'll go with that for the moment.

CHAPTER TWENTY-FOUR

While investigations continued, life at the academy resumed as near normal an existence as possible: classes recommenced, lectures continued and practical work took on a flurry of activity with students keen to lose themselves in their creativity. The art students once more set up easels outside in the grounds and set to work on their landscape paintings, immersing themselves in work which helped them reconnect with the stunning scenery. Most students chose to work within sight of each other. Only two remained alone preferring their own company to that of the group. Abigail walked among them, encouraging, advising and always in awe at the talent of the young people.

Brenda often joined her and marvelled at their creative skills. Brenda spoke to the young people as she walked around, not only to encourage and praise, but to search for any clue from their body language as to who might have wanted to destroy her daughter's image. In music rehearsals too, she sat enchanted as she let the music fill her soul and remembered with sadness how she had often sat at home listening to her daughter's performance totally unaware of the unique talent that the child had. *If only...* She tried not to dwell on the past in case grief overwhelmed her already fragile being. She studied the young musicians and thought, *would anyone here be jealous of Lucy's talent? Have I done the right thing in keeping her memory alive?*

As the study sessions drew near to a close, students put the final touches to their art and musical extravaganza which was to take place on the last evening of their course. There was a frenzy of activity as paintings were mounted around the main dining area which was to double as a theatre for the evening. Final musical practices took place with Ralph who was engrossed in his work and had temporarily forgotten his recent upset. The academy took on a role of hectic activity as the time drew nearer for the event.

"My parents are bringing my grandmother," said one excited student as she claimed a place to exhibit her landscape painting.

"My mom is coming with my younger sister Ellie who wants to come to the academy next year. She plays trombone in her school orchestra and wants to improve her skills," replied another art student.

"She will have excellent tuition if she manages to get in here."

Students chattered among each other as they adjusted their work, moving it around to capture the best possible place to show off their creations, before settling on their chosen spot. A musical crescendo was heard from the makeshift stage as the students organised themselves in correct chamber-orchestral position, as requested by Ralph, to make the most of the acoustics of the room. There was a buzz of excitement and, for the moment at least, the horror of the vandalism was temporarily forgotten.

Tony Harvey, meanwhile, was studying the application forms of the current students. Something disturbed him. He joined Officer Wynne who had established a work area in a room allocated to him by Abigail.

"Officer, spare me a minute to look at this student's application."

"Sure, sir, have you found something?"

"This guy here," said Tony proffering the paper, "do you know anything of him? I can't explain it, but I have a niggling feeling that I've seen the guy somewhere, he looks kinda familiar. I may be wrong, but, hey, check him out. I go with my gut feeling and it's never let me down yet."

"I'll get on to it right now, sir. My team are working their way through checking details on these applications."

As parents and friends of the students arrived, they were greeted warmly by Abigail and Ralph and directed to the pre-drinks room where staff attended to them. Families were reunited and shown around by the students; all were aware of the reason for the police presence in the academy. Guests had been informed of the upset of the past few days and were aware of the situation as they were guided through the house and shown their offsprings' artistic work that adorned the walls of the vast room.

"Honey," said one concerned mother, "had we known about this vandalism we would have removed you immediately. I dread to think what you went through. Honey, were you frightened?"

"No, Mother, we all wanted to stay here and finish our work. No one wanted to leave. We were well looked after by the tutors. I felt real safe, Mother, and I so wanted to be part of tonight's fun. I'm good, really I am."

Parents and other guests conversed together as the scale of the destruction hit home. The babble of noise was halted when an announcement was made asking students to take their places on stage and for guests to gather in the performance hall. Excitement was mounting as the evening extravaganza began in earnest. One student, quiet and subdued, took his place with his fellow students. He did not have to search for familiar faces in the audience: he knew no one would be there to praise his work, to offer encouragement, to take him for a celebratory meal or to tell him how much he was loved. *No one will bother to come,* he thought as he opened his programme; *no one cares any more, if they ever did.*

The performance began. Guests sat in awe at the standard of music from the students; they were enraptured as the music touched their souls. At every performance, and, as a tribute to Lucy Mears, a specially chosen student stepped forward to perform what had become an iconic piece; Taube's 'Gentle Nocturne for Cello'. At the back of the hall, Brenda Mears sat alone, eyes closed and lost in a world of memories. Silence greeted the ending of the poignant piece of evocative music. For a few moments, no one moved until one proud parent called out, "Bravo! Bravo!" which was followed by rousing applause. The students stood together in recognition of the accolade. Abigail and Ralph joined them on stage, clapping loudly as they acknowledged their young students. Abigail gave an emotive speech, praising the students in what was a difficult time, after which she was presented with flowers from the appreciative students.

As guests gathered in another room where a buffet was served, Ralph and Abigail mingled with them accepting thanks and commiserations in equal measure.

"Ma'am," said one proud father, "you have brought out a talent in my daughter that I didn't know existed. Thank you, we will build on this for Emily-Jane. You have been so brave in continuing with the performance, given your own sad events of the past week."

In another part of the house, out of sight of the guests, Officer Wynne and his team continued their investigations. He almost ran to where Tony Harvey was working.

"Sir, sir!" he called as he banged on the door, sweat pouring from his brow. "I think we might have uncovered our villain. Look at this."

As the evening celebrations ended and students and parents were gathering their belongings together in readiness to leave, the officer located Brenda who was sitting in the sitting room quietly reflecting on the musical recital that meant so much to her.

"Ma'am, we may have our culprit. My officers are searching the building for him, to prevent him leaving with the others. Ma'am, we have made an interesting discovery. We intend to make an immediate arrest."

A young man, backpack at the ready, was about to leave his room and head out of the academy having done what he came to do. He was stopped in his tracks by two officers, followed by Tony Harvey.

"Hold it there, buddy. We would like a word with you before you go."

The student turned chalk white, his legs hardly holding him as he realised that somehow or other he had been detected. He was fearful of what lay ahead.

CHAPTER TWENTY-FIVE

Later that evening the senior investigating officer sat with Ralph, Brenda and Abigail in the latter's sitting room. Tony was invited to join them. They were anxious to hear what he had to say. Brenda sat upright, as if in defensive mode should anyone dare criticise the security of the academy. Abigail sat wringing her hands and fighting back tears that welled up in her eyes, eyes that held the memory of the destruction of the painting. The evil deed tore at her heart. Ralph had a protective arm around his vulnerable partner, earnestly wishing that he could take her pain away. Now that the session had ended and most students had left, she focused once more on the damage done to Lucy's portrait and, like the others, was anxious to have an explanation of the vile deed.

"We have arrested one of your students," began Officer Wynne, "a young man who gave his name as Ben Jackson. Thanks to good police work, my team checked his details when something didn't ring true with Tony here, and we discovered that the guy used a false name to obtain a place in the academy. When officers checked the info he had given, there was no such address so alarm bells rang. They challenged the young man who eventually came clean and admitted his guilt. He is in fact, Ben Witherspoon."

"But who *is* he?" asked Ralph. "I don't understand. What the heck is going on here?"

Brenda, whose face had drained of colour, spoke out. "I know. Or at least I think I do. Officer, is he who I think he is? The son of Ross S. Witherspoon?"

"Yes, ma'am. His father was once a high-flyer politician. I believe you and he…"

"Yes, officer. It is no longer a secret. Ross S. Witherspoon and I had an affair. Lucy was his daughter and the boy you have arrested would in fact be Lucy's half-sibling. Will I ever be free of the Witherspoons?"

She held her head in her hands as if attempting to rid her mind of past events, events that started a lifelong ripple effect of heartache when, as a young woman, she allowed herself to be wooed by a politician with a hunger for success, a hunger that, in his mind, required a dutiful wife by his side. Believing Brenda Mears to be that woman, he dated and fêted her until she announced her pregnancy believing it would seal their love, but he discarded her like a piece of trash, and looked elsewhere for a suitable lifelong partner. His rejection stunned her like a nettle piercing her soul, his caustic talk shocked her as she realised he was not the man she had believed him to be. Through time, shock turned to anger, an anger not just for herself but for her child. She could never bring herself to forgive his cowardice. The abduction of her daughter Lucy by her aunt, Anna Leci, led to the public revelation that the politician was the girl's father, the child he had demanded she abort.

On hearing the name of the person who caused even more hurt, Brenda shook her head in disgust, and a fierce anger mixed with frustration brought on quiet sobbing that sounded like a painful cry from a puppy, from the woman whose life had been changed by her liaison with the politician.

Abigail, looking bemused asked, "But why did he destroy Lucy's portrait?"

"That, ma'am, we intend to find out when we question him further. He has admitted vandalising the portrait and attempting to destroy Lucy's special rooms, and when he couldn't enter, he etched the toughened glass in frustration. He has said nothing more. He had his rights read to him and was then cuffed and led away. He is nineteen years of age and will be held over to appear before the court later. Hopefully some light will be spread on the sorry saga."

After the departure of the officer, the trio sat silently at first then tried to come to terms with what they had heard.

"That kid," began Abigail, "when I think of it, he never mixed much with the others. He painted by himself and didn't contribute much at recreational time when the other students let their hair down. I didn't think anything of it; some kids are quiet and like to be alone."

"I remember him at his interview," said Brenda, now more composed. "He seemed desperately keen to join the academy and showed us his portfolio. I didn't think he was a particularly talented artist, but he was so keen to improve his skills. I was taken in by his charm… just like… oh…"

"Yeah, Brenda, he told us at interview that he wanted to be a better artist but he knew he had to work hard to improve his lot. I too fell for the charming, eager young man. We have been truly duped. But why?"

Tony Harvey spoke up, "I was checking through the students' applications and something jumped out at me as I looked at his picture. Call it a cop's instinct if you like, but when I stared at that picture it suddenly came to me that I was looking at a very young version of Ross S. Witherspoon. Officer Wynne had his team check out his details and as we now know, they were false."

Ralph, who had been quiet until now, asked if they could think of any reason why he would want to destroy the painting.

"Jealousy, perhaps, or revenge. Who knows the mind of someone who would do such a callous, destructive, hurtful deed?" replied Tony.

Brenda said, "Oh I hope his father hasn't put him up to this. Surely not!"

"Well," said Ralph, "we won't know until he goes before the judge. Hopefully some light will be shed on this and we can get on with our lives."

"Yes," said Abigail, "we have had one of the best end-of-session- extravaganzas. Let's get busy preparing for the next batch of courses and put that guy out of our minds. Brenda, what do you want me to do about the portrait? I could try to repair it or make a copy of it, whatever you think is best. That is, when forensics say we can have it back."

Deep in thought, Brenda held up her hand, shook her head as if to say *'I can't face making a decision'*. Life for her was a never-ending reminder of tragedy, regret and loneliness. No sooner had she attempted to put the past behind her and move on, than something turned up to stir up memories, memories that were destined never to leave her. *A horrid legacy of hatred from my crazed aunt Anna… will I ever be free of her?*

CHAPTER TWENTY-SIX

Sitting in a sparse cell underneath the courtroom, Ben Witherspoon felt sorry for himself. He was dishevelled, cold and unkempt and the little facial growth that came with youth looked unclean and only added to his sad image. He was no longer the brave Ben Jackson, who had brought such sadness and anger into the academy by his irresponsible behaviour, but the troubled youth, Ben Witherspoon, awaiting his fate at the hands of the justice system. He had called his mother who was understandably furious with her younger son.

"Ben, I thought when you said you were going on a taster course for art that you were serious about something for once in your life. What possessed you to destroy a painting? And etch obscenities on glass? You will suffer the consequences of this Ben. I can hardly believe what you have done. Explain yourself."

"Mom, I've been stupid and I'm scared. Can you be here in court for me, please, Mom?"

"Ben, you know I can't leave your father and travel to court. He needs twenty-four-hour care as you well know, and you do very little to help with his needs. Jake is out of town on business, and anyway, I won't trouble your brother with your problems. You've made your bed, so go lie on it. And, Ben, I hope you learn from this. Thankfully your father is now beyond understanding your crazy actions. His illness has spared him that at least. He has deteriorated rapidly since you left and I can't possibly leave him. I'll call our lawyer, although I doubt if he will be thrilled to represent you again. The fire-raising incident last year that you stupidly caused was unpleasant for our family. And once again we're to have our name dragged through the courts. It's time to man-up, Ben."

Linda-Mae Witherspoon had not had an easy life since the exposé of her husband's affair which brought to an end his political dream. She had been the dutiful wife, always by his side at political events, smiling, encouraging and extremely proud of her handsome husband. Like the rest of the political world, she had been shocked by the revelation that he had fathered Lucy Mears, whose disappearance had stunned the nation. That he could have been remotely involved in any way was abhorrent to her, and relief was palpable when he assured her that he had no knowledge of the child's abduction, and until that fateful night, had no knowledge of her existence, believing his lover had followed his demand to end her pregnancy.

"What? You told her to abort her child? I can't believe what I am hearing from your lips."

Her shamefaced husband, unable to offer a reply, put his head in his hands and wept tears, not for his misdeeds, but for his own selfish loss of face.

The comfortable life that Linda-Mae had been accustomed to was thrown into turmoil when the family had to run the gauntlet of media attention which would have put them in the forefront of news bulletins for all the wrong reasons. Ross S. Witherspoon had no option but to decant his young family to the safety of his in-law's holiday chalet where they remained until pressure died down and they could set up a home far from prying eyes. Life was difficult. The young boys suffered torment at the hands of school bullies, who, on discovering their identity, goaded them unmercifully and made their lives miserable. The older boy, Jake, a strong character with his father's superior bearing and attitude, coped well in fending off his assailants. Ben, the younger boy, a pampered, spoilt child developed a sullen mistrust of people which resulted in a deep loathing of the human race. He became a loner who depended on his parents to fight his corner for him when he found himself in trouble of any kind. He fostered a hatred of his half-sibling and, in spite of never having known Lucy Mears, blamed her for his father's situation and ill health. Ben often wondered what it would have been like to have been brought up in the White House, fêted by everyone, his every wish catered for, and felt it had been stolen from him by a girl he had never encountered. He had researched every detail of Mears Empire and was aware of the founding of the LMAMA academy. He had planned his revenge. He had an ulterior motive which he would never reveal to anyone.

A morose kid, he did not endear himself to his peers who generally ignored him. Disappointed at her son's lack of academic interest in spite of being highly intelligent, Linda-Mae agreed that he could leave school at the earliest opportunity when he turned seventeen, on condition that he gained suitable employment. The latter did not materialise. Unwilling to work, the sullen youth did not engage himself at interviews and blamed his lack of finding work on everyone but himself. On hearing that he intended to apply for a short term taster course in art, and believing that he intended to follow an art career, she gave him her blessing as he set off for an interview. She was unaware of his ulterior motive or his devious plan in enrolling at LMAMA.

Armed with his portfolio, he attended his interview with the slyness of a fox who knows how to get what it wants. He arrived for interview confident that he would be granted a place. He had dabbled in art at school but had no real interest in putting effort into his work. He oozed charm when he wanted to and, on hearing that two women would be conducting his interview, used his best manners to enchant his prey into his lair. He was introduced firstly to Abigail Garcia, director in charge of the academy, and then to Brenda Mears, owner and patron of the academy. Unaware that Brenda was to be present he was momentarily shocked, but soon regained his composure. He had not expected to come face to face with his father's mistress, the cause of everything, as he thought, that had been taken from him and his family. His phoney charming manner won them over; his boyish looks and captivating smile secured him a place in the academy for the forthcoming landscape session.

"Thank you so much," he drooled. "I'm so looking forward to learning about landscape painting and I'll work my socks off to learn. I appreciate you giving me this chance to improve my skills. I assure you, you won't regret selecting me for this course in this amazing building. Thank you."

He smiled a fake smile as he left the building.

That kid looks kind of familiar, thought Brenda, as she moved on to the next application.

It was a lonely, anxious time for Ben Witherspoon when he appeared in court before Judge Follett who was well known for her strictness in running her kingdom. Her court ran like a conveyor belt, a well-oiled machine that depended on everyone involved with her giving one hundred per cent. She did not tolerate slackness, lateness or stroppy prisoners like the young man standing in the dock before her.

"All rise," exhorted the court official.

Everyone stood as one as if mechanically controlled by some unseen robot, all, that is, but the belligerent accused who stood up slowly, defiantly confronting authority as was his way, as if challenging any woman to dictate to him. The irrepressible Ben Witherspoon, the boy who should have been idolized as the son of America's president but for a woman, a woman whose daughter in death was honoured more than he ever is in life, was not one to be ordered about by any woman. Ben Witherspoon was a misogynist.

Judge Follett glowered at the accused, her eyes never leaving his face as she waited for him to conduct himself in a manner befitting the occasion. He attempted to outstare the judge. The court collectively held its breath as it waited for the showdown, knowing full well that the youth was on a sure-fire course to hell. Her superiority and total control in her courtroom soon made its mark on the over confident youth who, lowering his eyes, had to admit defeat.

No woman gets the better of me, he thought as his brief whispered to him to stand up straight and respect the authority of the court.

The charges were read out, the accused smirking as he pleaded guilty, defiance oozing from his being. Believing himself to be indestructible he fully expected a lenient sentence. *After all,* he had told his brief, *it was no big deal, just a horrid kid's equally horrid portrait.*

His brief was horrified at his client's apparent lack of understanding of the seriousness of the charge that he faced, and no amount of counselling had the desired effect.

"Don't, for goodness' sake, let anyone hear you say that. You're in trouble up to your neck. Am I not getting through to you, Ben?"

In his defence, his brief explained that his client, the son of a former presidential nominee, lived his live in the knowledge that greatness had been stolen from his family by what he felt was the treachery of the Mears family. In his naivety he sought revenge in the only way he could, by slashing a portrait of his half-sister. He was ashamed of his behaviour and asked the court to accept his remorse. Judge Follett, an expert in dealing with the so-called remorseful accused, who, thinking they could feign guilt and expect a lenient sentence, looked sternly at him as she made her deliberation.

"You seem to think lightly of your actions and have no concept of the damage caused, not only to a painting but to people to whom it meant a great deal. Your actions were intentional and malicious, an act of violence to property that was not your own. You are guilty of a Class E, third degree felony. This criminal mischief felony carries a custodial sentence and a fine for repair to the damaged property. You will serve three years in prison and pay a fine that will be determined when the value of the painting has been assessed, and the cost too of replacing toughened glass. I hope you will use your time in custody to consider how your behaviour has affected so many people. Perhaps you may even feel *true* remorse. Officers, take him away."

Ben Witherspoon's demeanour changed, the colour drained from his face, his legs almost gave way from under him as he wiped a tear from his eye and looked pleadingly at the judge who, gathering her papers together, left the room without as much as a glance at the distressed youth. As he was taken away to begin his sentence he glanced at the public gallery in the hope of seeing his mother or brother, only to see Brenda Mears glower at him. The enormity of his act of vandalism was beginning to strike home. Why had he agreed to this? Why did he allow himself to be sweet-talked into this?

Brenda ate lunch with Abigail and Ralph and discussed the verdict.

Brenda said, "Now we know how he managed to do such damage. He admitted that he had been watching Ralph's morning routine and knew when it was safe to slash Lucy's portrait. He had taken a sharp knife from the art room and concealed it on his person. It wasn't found until the arresting cops checked his backpack. He used it too, to etch the glass after he failed to break into the room. Goodness knows what damage he would have done then."

Ralph spoke, "How did he get into that area? Our security is as tight as can be."

"He's a sly, slippery character, Ralph. When the students first arrived and were shown around, he noted the skylight window in the corridor adjacent to Lucy's suite. All he had to do was work out how to access it and he spent his free time pursuing that aim. In the early hours of the morning he put his plan into action, but was thwarted by not being able to force open the door of her room, so decided to leave his calling card instead, in the form of obscenities."

"Well," said Abigail, "he should have plenty time on his hands to mull over his misdeeds. I hope he feels genuine remorse and comes out a better person."

"I wouldn't hold my breath on that," replied Brenda. "From what I hear he has been a troublesome boy all his life."

"And to think," said Ralph, "that he blamed it all on Lucy. Pure, downright jealousy."

Brenda gathered her belongings together ready to leave when a final thought struck her.

"My aunt, Anna Leci, has sure left a miserable legacy; even in death she haunts us, even into the next generation and to people who have never known her. Will the venom never end?"

CHAPTER TWENTY-SEVEN

The search for the elusive homeless man continued. Ongoing investigations into the crime against the four young adventurers took on a frenzy of activity as officers, determined to locate and arrest the vagrant described by the kids, scoured the vast estate.

After depositing them safely in the camper vehicle, the hobo believed he was safe now from the interfering kids who had invaded his privacy, and settled back to his nomadic lifestyle. On occasion, he would venture out, making the arduous long trek to the nearest habitation, to forage for food in restaurant trash containers and join other homeless people at charity food centres. It was the winter holiday season; he took advantage of a homeless scheme set up by joint churches to provide food and gifts to the itinerant community, as well as an opportunity to shower, shave and have a change of clothes. Feeling refreshed and cleaner than he had done for some time, he retraced his steps towards his makeshift home, carefully avoiding open spaces and trudging the well-known path to the concealed trapdoor. He was unaware of the impending chaos.

As he neared the estate, flashing lights in the vicinity of his shelter caused him to panic and seek a hiding place behind the wall where he cowered down and crept into a space that afforded him a view of the burnt out mansion. There, several police cars with powerful floodlights lit the area like a football stadium ready to host an important event. He looked in horror as officers, wielding batons, battering rams and crowbars, assembled as if ready to quell an impending riot and ready to break into as many trapdoors as they could locate. They were studying a large plan of the estate spread out on the top of one of the vehicles.

"Right, team, spread out around this massive estate and search for any drains, trapdoors and anything that looks like an entrance to the underground of this burnt-out shell. From what the kids have told us, there appears to be a labyrinth of tunnels running the entire perimeter of the building. We need access and we need to find this guy. The dog squad will join us if we need their assistance. Go to it."

Cops, collars turned up against the icy wind and armed with batons, crowbars

and powerful flashlights, set off as instructed to search various areas of the estate. They spread out as if setting up a cordon around the grounds.

The hobo lowered his head and sighed as he realised his makeshift home, his haven, his security for many years was about to be discovered by the authorities.

He had planned for the winter by making his room as comfortable as he could with blankets and discarded curtains that he had found during his foraging. Having amassed a reasonable amount of tinned food and bottled water, he was prepared yet again to sit out the worst of the winter. His collection of books and magazines would help pass the time as would his pencil drawings. The oil lantern he had scavenged would give him all the light he required. He continued to observe the officers' activities, wiped his brow with his sleeve and rubbed his hands together to generate some heat. The evening had turned cold. He pulled the sleeves of his coat down to cover his hands. The sky, heavy with snow, was ready to drop its cargo onto the waiting city. Aware now that he had no option but to move on, he was grateful for the recent change of clothes and shoes. Huddled into the long grey coat that had served him well, he pulled the collar up to protect his neck, donned a woollen hat and silently moved out of the immediate area. His priority was to find shelter from the impending snowstorm, obtain money from wherever he could, and leave the area.

He walked aimlessly at first, his mind agitated and in turmoil as he considered his plan of action, a plan that had begun many years ago, so long ago that he had almost lost track of the years and the reason for his long journey that had brought him to Leci House, and for what? To satisfy his curiosity? To find a safe haven where he could live his life in solitude? He no longer knew, nor cared. With the passing years his memory of the intensity of his desire to find Leci House had diminished somewhat, leaving him questioning his actions to flee to this place, a place where evil lived, where his hated foe spent time in comparative luxury, and from where his foe amassed a considerable number of dollars before returning to his homeland only to meet the hobo and his nemesis. The hobo walked for two days and spent the night in an abandoned warehouse before reaching habitation far from Leci House. He headed for the bus depot, a busy hub of activity where passengers, desperate to complete their journeys before an impending storm bit, hustled and pushed each other to catch what might be the last vehicles to leave the area, such was the threat of the storm forecast. The hobo, shivering from the cold air, studied timetables and fares and looked for an unsuspecting, careless traveller to rob. He spotted a harassed mother struggling to control a suitcase and pushing a child's stroller and with a distressed toddler whimpering by her side.

"Need a hand, ma'am?" he enquired in a soft, polite voice.

"Bless you, sir. Yeah, could you carry my suitcase to the cab rank? I've missed my connection. I'm gonna take a cab ride. I sure appreciate your help."

He helped the fraught mother to the cab and waved her off. It was only when she arrived at her destination that the woman realised she had been relieved of her cash.

He boarded the first long haul bus that came along and settled himself in the back seat, ready to sleep, hopefully for several hours. Another phase in his troubled life was about to begin.

*

At Leci House, officers scoured the vast grounds for any means possible to gain entry. They were hampered by overgrown shrubs and out of control bushes and trees. They walked among head high foliage and attacked it with batons and bare hands.

"This is gonna take forever," moaned one officer, tired of having to disentangle himself from jagged bushes. "I sure hope some of the others have found a way into the dungeon. Who the heck wants to live underground anyway?"

"The guy who drugged those youngsters, for a start; he must live here. Man, they could have died from the chemicals he drugged them with. We gotta find him and put him behind bars. One of the kids was in a bad way, touch and go, I heard, and the others were in a serious state."

"Yeah, and I heard the two of the kids belonged to a retired Superintendent from Chicago, that'll be why we have to pull all the stops out to get this pervert. Ouch! Hell, these things sure sting, and now the snow has started."

Other officers were facing the same discomfort in the search for a way into the cellar.

"According to the kids, the trapdoor was a fifteen-minute walk from where they had parked up," said one determined officer. "We must be near it by now."

He had hardly finished speaking when his colleague stubbed his foot on a concrete block, yelling in pain and shouted, "Hey, this might be the entrance; there's some kind of manhole here."

They cleared as much as they could while fighting off hanging branches and snow flurries that hindered their vision, and at times almost blinded them, making the task even more difficult. Eventually, a drain-type opening, with a solidly-stuck rusty ring that proved impossible to move, was discovered. It proved impossible to shift even with a crowbar.

"This thing has been stuck like this for years. We would have to use dynamite to shift it. Leave it, buddy, and we'll walk on a bit further. I don't think this was the opening the kids used."

Battling the increasing snowstorm, the officers involved in searching for an opening to the tunnel were becoming more frustrated with each difficult step they took. The overgrown vegetation, tentacles reaching out as if to hinder progress and claim domination over the searchers, was proving more difficult than expected. A shout was heard, faint at first in the increasing wind, but audible nonetheless.

"Over here, sir," called a relieved officer. "We've found a way into the cellar." He released a flare to indicate his position and while he waited for other officers to gather, an officer working with him, lay on the snow-covered ground and peered into the deep, dark cavern.

"There's been a ladder here at some point, but heck it's lying on the ground now. It's mighty deep down there. How are we going to get into the darn place?"

Other officers arrived at the scene looking like a chain gang of white, dejected men with snow-like rough cotton wool covering them from head to foot. The senior officer took charge and suggested they have one man abseil down into the cavern and place the ladder in situ. The officers shuffled their feet, lowered their eyes, not wanting to be chosen for the task and hoping that their boss would ignore them.

"Clark, you're the man for the job. Let's get going."

It took some time to complete the task with officers holding a rope and lowering the unfortunate rookie to the ground. With difficulty, and hampered by icy cold hands, he righted the heavy ladder for his fellow officers to use. Eventually everyone was safely in the cellar, lighting it up with their powerful head lamps. They were all exhausted from struggling through the overgrowth, battling the snowstorm, clambering into a deep cavern, and were glad of a respite.

"Well done, team. Have a sit down while we discuss the next stage. It's freezing in here, so we won't hang around any longer than necessary. The weather had almost beaten us, but, you guys are great. Okay, this is what I propose. The kids reckon the guy came from the direction of the left tunnel. That is, if we're in the right place, and I guess we are. Clark, Elson, with me on that; Blake, Curtis and Smith take the right-hand one. Lester and O'Bryan, stay here in case he tries to make off. Use your chalk block to mark the walls as you go along in case we have to come looking for you. Everyone has a whistle, use it when necessary."

They set off, the snow from their clothes dripping in puddles as they began their onerous task.

"I'm sure glad we got to stay here, don't think I could have walked another step. My face is ripped with those wild bushes," said O'Bryan as he shook the worst of the snow from his hair and settled to position himself where he could see both exits from the tunnel. "Lester, do you think the guy is living down in this hellhole? It's the last place on earth I'd wanna be. It's hellish cold down here."

"He must be an escapee or wanted for something. No sane person would live here. If he comes our way I hope to hell he ain't armed. We'll have to keep alert. Hell, it's so cold."

Blake and Curtis, walking quickly each concentrated on lighting up a wall each and applying occasional chalk marks while Smith looked for openings on the floor.

"No sign of anything here so far. There must be an opening somewhere, guys.

It's so creepy down here, and cold," commented Blake.

"How far are we expected to walk," asked Smith, "before we can turn back?"

"Probably until we find what we're looking for or hear a whistle from the others said Curtis as he flapped his arms across his body to generate some heat.

In the left tunnel, the three officers continued to rigorously search every inch of the area.

"The kids said they walked for about thirty minutes

along here and found nothing," began the officer in charge, "they said..."

"Boss, look at this!" yelled Clark, as he stumbled on an opening tucked in a corner of an archway.

There, in a small recess they found the hobo's hide-out, a small cave-like area with a mattress covered with several sleeping bags, and on the floor beside the make-shift bed, some books, a sketch pad and an oil lamp. A shrill whistle called the others, who, after retracing their steps to the main cavern and following the direction of the whistle, gathered outside the alcove in utter amazement that someone was using such a place as their home.

"This is a crime scene, so no one goes into the room. We gotta get our forensic guys here asap. It looks like there will be plenty of prints to be lifted. They sure as hell won't like that descent; it's like the descent into hell. There's no sign of our guy and I doubt he will return here, not if he sees our vehicles littering the place. We'll check out the rest of the tunnel but I reckon he's long gone."

CHAPTER TWENTY-EIGHT

The fugitive slept undisturbed for the entire four-hour bus journey, the rhythm of the moving vehicle soothing him. He was warmer now than he had been for some time. As the bus glided to a halt and passengers began gathering their belongings, he awoke with a start, unsure at first of his surroundings. Realisation dawned on him that he was once again having to rely on his wits for survival. He had arrived in Newton, Boston.

If the hobo thought that New York was cold, he found Boston even colder. He shuddered as he huddled into his coat. The contrast of the warm bus and the biting wind hit him hard. He had to find shelter. He had to find warmth. Darkness was closing in. The blinding snow made it difficult for him to see. Each time he lifted his head, his face was completely covered in cold, white biting blasts of snow, rock hard and sharp as it struck his face like piercing needles.

Not many people walked the streets that evening. It was still early enough for shoppers to finish their tasks and head for bars and restaurants to escape the intensity of the hostile winter. Shopping malls were busy with those taking advantage of late opening. He followed a group of people not knowing where he was heading and entered a market hall where he blended in, glad that he looked more presentable than he did several weeks ago. *I must have scared the wits out of those kids, looking like I did.* He had long discarded the rope belt that held his shabby coat together for a leather one that he acquired from his scavenging; a woollen scarf completed his ensemble and concealed the worn collar. He feasted on hot food and drink, carefully counting out the few dollars he had left from his ill-gotten gains and sat as long as he could in the warmth. He merged in with the late shoppers, stopping to admire, but not to purchase anything. When the marketplace closed for the night, he had no option but to brave the elements. Shutters creaked and groaned as they were lowered and locked; the market hall took on an eerie look of abandonment and fitted well with the hobo's demeanour. Unwilling to resort to sleeping in a miserable doorway he headed for a homeless centre that he had seen advertised on a poster. Unsure of his whereabouts, he trundled on, chilled and shivering as the cold night air turned down its thermostat by several degrees. A huge increase in demand from homeless people for night shelters meant that such places were quickly filled with people who had queued for several hours to ensure a warm meal and a bed. Latecomers were seldom successful in finding refuge on nights like this and the hobo was turned away from not one, but two shelters.

"Sorry, sir," said a sympathetic worker, "we fill up rapidly especially on cold nights like this, but I'll direct you to another place but can't guarantee they will have space."

After what seemed like hours of trudging around the city with cold penetrating his bones, the hobo finally found a shelter of sorts. Some emergency shelters had been set up in church halls to cope with the extreme weather, and in one of these he was given a nourishing meal and makeshift camp bed. Such shelters provide temporary respite for people who, for whatever reason, required a place of safety for one night. Economic cutbacks, family and marriage breakdowns and emotional and mental health problems increase the pressure on social services. Such refuges, as well as offering food and warm, also offer support and advice. Many itinerants, however, prefer not to use rescue centres knowing them to be crowded and somewhat dangerous places where those in charge can be obsessed with documentation that many vagabonds and wanderers do not possess. Some prefer the freedom and privacy and their own encampment which was the case with the hobo. As he settled to attempt to sleep in the midst of noise and brawling he wished, how he wished, he could return to his haven under Leci House.

He spent an uncomfortable night in the emergency shelter that was overcrowded and noisy and harboured some disturbed clients who spent the entire night shouting abuse at anyone who attempted to invade their limited space. The vagrant, used to solitude for so long, found the transition difficult from the hermit style of life that he had chosen. After a quick breakfast of coffee and bagels, he took himself out of the centre vowing to avoid such places if it were at all possible. Despite the weather, he walked for hours, seeking shelter where he could pass a few hours in warmth. A library afforded him some respite for a time, until aware that a staff member was watching his every move, he returned to the cold of Boston's streets. A museum too offered a few hours of warmth.

Following a discarded map that he had come across, he made his way to Beantown's transport hub, the bus and train terminal where millions of travellers passed through in the course of a year. There he spent several hours enjoying the heat of the hub and watching people arrive and depart from the hundred-year-old station. *I wonder where everyone is rushing to,* he mused as he drank the remains of coffee and leftover food abandoned by a passenger who had rushed off for his connection.

As night came, and with less people in the area, his presence was more noticeable. There was an increase too in security to rid the area of homeless people who hoped to spend the night there. He was unwilling to spend another night in a homeless shelter, he trudged through the wintery evening looking for cover, when a welcome sight, a church haven beckoned. The light from it cheered his spirit and he increased his pace, longing to be out of the miserable weather and hoping there would be room for him. It was quieter than his previous refuge and he settled to sleep in a quiet corner of the church hall, after partaking of a welcome meal and shower.

Next morning clients were sent off into the winter day as the shelter only allowed overnight stays and did not have facilities to home people for longer periods. In his search for shelter he walked fifteen minutes or so to Logan International Airport where he spent the entire day moving from terminal to terminal, studying the arrivals board and making himself appear like any other traveller awaiting a loved one. He removed his warm, shabby grey coat, folded it carefully over his arm and felt more respectable. It would be donned again when he moved on. He feasted on left-over meals, collected dropped coins, purchased a warm drink and settled to read a discarded newspaper.

Before 9/11 Logan Airport was home to many of the itinerant community, mainly women, who claimed their space and bonded together as an unofficial family. They were known to airport security patrol who turned a blind eye to the lonely group of vagrants. Since the atrocity of 9/11 security had been heightened. State troopers enforced the zero tolerance policy with regard to policing the vast terminals, and gently but firmly moved the itinerant community on.

"Okay, Susie and Mo," said one security guy who knew the people who spent their days at Logan. "Come on now, ladies, you know you can't stay here. Off you go."

"You're a tough guy," laughed Mo as she gathered her meagre belongings. "Imagine putting us old folk out in the cold, you've got no heart, man," she said as she playfully patted his chest.

"Be off with you, ladies, before I have to show my nasty side!"

Such were the friendly showdowns that the security guards had with the homeless night after night that the iterant community moved on without protest, allowing the staff to comply with regulations.

*

The hobo continued to exist in challenging conditions. He was weary now from days of wandering around searching for new places in which to shelter. Nights were stressful for him; accommodation was becoming more difficult to find; his appearance and odour worried him as he did not have access to showers; his clothes showed signs of wear; people avoided him in public places and several times he was asked to move on. He was miserable. Unable to walk much further as night closed in, he settled to sleep in a doorway where a warm air vent from a pizza shop gave him a modicum of comfort.

"Hey, dude, move off my patch, get outta here, go find your own place. Everyone knows this is my spot, Boxer by name and boxer by nature, now, clear off."

Hobo found himself facing a large homeless man whom he had seen in one of the shelters, a man who demanded respect and was given a wide berth by those who knew him, and a beating by those who challenged his authority to be king of the road. As the hobo wearily stood up ready to move on to avoid confrontation, his foe grabbed the lapels of the old grey coat

"Hey, give me that coat, buddy. Boxer here needs a warm coat and this looks a mighty fine one. You wouldn't want poor Boxer here to go cold, would you, dude?"

"Hey, that's mine. Go get your own."

"You refusing a polite request from Boxer are you? That ain't a good move, best reconsider your response."

Hobo struggled to keep his footing. He was unbearably cold and weak from hunger. He pushed his assailant's massive hands from his shoulders but in his weakness he was no match for the younger, stronger man who prised the ragged coat from him resulting in the hobo losing his footing and falling to the ground with a crack that made even Boxer shudder as his victim's head hit off a concrete slab.

"Oh dude," said the bully as he donned the grey coat, "you should always listen to Boxer. Now look at the state you're in and all that blood… man, I'm outta here… can't stand blood and now I've gotta find myself a new place to sleep. You've messed with mine."

With a final kick at his downtrodden opponent, Boxer took off into the night.

CHAPTER TWENTY-NINE

Activity in the underground cellar of Leci House was hectic. Reinforcements had been called in to search every inch of the cavernous area in an attempt to gather as much evidence as possible to prove the presence of the wanted man and his involvement with the young explorers, and to protect the crime scene from contamination. Every item was removed from the living quarters for testing; the old mattress, the kids' sleeping bags, bedding and sketch pads. All these were carefully tagged and lifted out of the cellar to be sent to the forensic scientists who were trained to lift latent fingerprints, blood and body fluids from material and other items such as that collected from the cellar.

In an area of the lab, the items were laid out for inspection and carefully scrutinised by experts. A tear in the mattress caught the eye of a lab technician, who, on investigating the ripped cloth, revealed a treasure.

"Look, sir," called out the enthusiastic young lab technician, "it's an old passport."

The worn and out-of-date document was a find of immense value. A call was put to Evan Grant, the senior officer in charge of the investigation, who arrived breathless but excited at the discovery which would surely identify the man who brought fear and terror into the lives of four young people. The passport was crumpled and stained, the picture smudged and faded, but the lab technician assured his superior officer that he would restore it as well as he could, enough, he was sure, to reveal important details from the document.

"I'll get to it right away, sir. The naked eye can't detect the faded writing, but by using infrared radiation directly onto the document we'll be able to see glowing letters and hopefully retrieve the information we need to nail the perp."

Officers meanwhile searched for information about staff who had formerly worked at the palatial compound of Leci House.

"Our absconder could well be a former staff member who knew these cellars inside out and, for some ungodly reason, opted to stay here," commented one officer. "Or, possibly he was an illegal who had nowhere else to go, but hey, who would choose to live in a cold cellar like this?"

"There are plenty of crazy folks around who would do just that," replied his colleague. "The guy seemed to have made a comfortable corner for himself. Meanwhile, we have to wait until you guys work your magic and come up with answers."

Enquires in the locality of Leci House turned up little success for the investigating officers. One frail, elderly gentleman, Karl, who had worked for some time as a gardener was keen to talk about the place. He lent on his stick as he conversed with the officers, his deformed hands showing evidence of a hard worker; his tanned face bore witness to years of outdoor labour.

"It sure was a weird place to work, sir. I kept myself to myself, kept busy I did, out in the grounds 'cos that damn house sure had an evil atmosphere. I worked there as did my father before me, tending to the grounds and keeping them nice. It broke my spirit to see the grounds turn into a jungle through sheer neglect when the owner passed away and no one took charge any more. I use to walk my old dog and we'd wander around the outside, but it sure gave me a shudder to look at that gruesome mansion... why one person wanted to live there sure beats me."

"So you would know most of the folks who worked there?" enquired a cop.

"Yeah, I guess you could say that. Saw lots of folk come to work the place, some stayed a while, others got the hell out, sure was an evil place."

"Do you know anything about the cellars under the house?"

"Them cellars? They sure were mighty big. I had occasion to go there with one of the guys who needed a hand to shift a load of boxes for storage. Never seen such a massive underground area, never knew until then just how mighty big it was, ran the whole length of that house, it did."

"Ever heard of anyone living down there, Karl?"

"Hell no, down in that dark hole?" questioned the elderly man, scratching his head as if totally bemused by the question. "No siree, no one lived there that I ever heard about… who would want to live in that place, it was a cold, cold place, great for keeping food cool and wine and stuff like that, but to live there, no sir, not to my knowledge."

"Did you ever come across a guy, Barclay Jones, while you were there?"

"Let me think about that, sir… Barclay… kind of English name… yeah, I think I do… seemed kind of close to the crazy woman who lived here… yeah, sure, it's coming back to me… a nasty kind of guy if I remember rightly… he was here around the time when the kid lived here, you know the one who was killed in a crash with some of the staff… must be fourteen, fifteen years ago. Hey you don't think he lived in the creepy cellar, do you?"

"No. It was a name that one of the cops mentioned… I just kinda wondered…"

"Didn't he come to a sticky end in some far-off place?" replied Karl. "I'm kinda sure I heard about that, long time ago though."

"Do you know if there is anyone else around here that worked in Leci House? We'd sure like to talk to them."

"Ain't nobody left, officer, but old Karl here," he said pointing to himself. "I outlived them all, they've all gone, well the old regular ones that is, my generation… can't say much about the folks that came and went, like the domestic staff them that worked in that huge house and couldn't take to it, they didn't last long so I never got to know them. What's all these questions about, sir?"

"I'm just trying to clear up a few loose ends here and see if there was anyone around that time who might have chosen to stay on in the old house after the owner died, and decanted to the cellar for whatever reason, but thanks for your help, sir."

No other former workers from Leci House could be located. Many years had gone by and people's diminished memories coupled with exaggerated tales of past events, proved an unreliable source of information for the officers who abandoned further plans to locate and talk with former staff.

The team studying the contents of the cellar were amazed at the intrinsic work in the sketch books. Each page was dated, giving the officers an almost complete history of the occupant's life underneath Leci House.

"Look at this, sir. It's a documentary, almost, of the fire that destroyed the building."

The sketches showed firefighters, high up on ladders using aerial devices to pump water onto the roof of the building.

"Here's another one showing the roof cave-in and flames devouring the entire mansion. It's like a series of still pictures."

"We should get DNA from this without much trouble and fingerprints too. They will be all over the book."

*

While the authorities continued to determine the identity of the illusive occupant of the cellar, Salvation Army personnel were patrolling their regular beat, talking to the homeless, distributing food and encouraging them to come to their shelter for the night. They knew the people by name and had established a friendly relationship with them. Few were willing to leave their patch for fear of losing their spot.

"Good evening, Mason, and how are you tonight? Would you like some warm soup?"

"Yes, ma'am, thank you kindly. I'm good, ma'am. God bless you, ma'am."

The kind ladies going along the group of vagrants came across a gruesome find.

"Oh! What's happened here to this poor man?"

"This is Boxer's spot. Is it he?"

They witnessed a homeless man lying in a pool of blood, his almost lifeless eyes were half closed and his face, covered in congealed blood, was unrecognisable as one of their regular clients.

"No. It's not our friend Boxer, although this person is lying in his pitch. He is still alive, but I fear only just. He has lost so much blood. Poor man. We need to call for help."

The paramedics arrived and treated the man who was clinging to life. Like most of the itinerant community, he had no means of identification on his person. Others there did not know him and turned away from the gruesome sight being unable or unwilling to become involved in what was a regular sight in the large city.

He was transferred to the nearest trauma centre where medics fought to save his life. He hovered between life and death. It was not unusual for them to deal with such situations where homeless, unknown people needed medical assistance.

"This guy has lost a vast amount of blood. Line please, give him one unit immediately."

*

Weeks stretched into months. The unknown patient was still not identified. A medic had chalked the name of 'John Doe' above his bed and staff treating him referred to him as John. John did not respond.

"This patient has not responded to stimuli," said a consultant to a colleague as they examined the sick man. "We used the Rancho Los Amigo scale to assess him. One of our medics trained in observational techniques carried out the test. His brain function is at the lower stage of alertness and we had to perform emergency surgery to remove a blood clot. Brain oedema was causing pressure on his brain and he is now in a medically induced coma to allow the brain to rest and help recovery. However, at this stage I'm not hopeful that this poor man will survive."

"Do we have any identification?"

"Not yet, but I believe detectives are asking among the itinerant community if anyone knows his name or anything about him. Meanwhile, all we can do is give him the best possible care and hope he pulls through."

"The authorities tell me that they may never be able to discover his identity," said a senior medic. "They say they have a team working relentlessly, sifting through lists of missing persons, contacting families, some of whom have visited the patient, but left disappointed that their loved one had not been found."

"Doctor," said one distressed man, "my family live in hope that our boy will be found. He left home after an argument and has never been seen since. When we heard about the unknown homeless man we hoped it would be our William, and were disappointed to visit and realise it was not our son. I hope you find this man's family, sir."

CHAPTER THIRTY

Tony Harvey, sitting in his den at home, was writing his memoirs. His time with Chicago Police Department spanned most of his working life, a time that saw him rise to the position of superintendent of CPD, a time when one case above all others caused him heartache and tested his confidence in his own ability to do the job. The abduction and consequent death of Lucy Mears had a profound effect on him. Even now, many years later, he was reluctant to discuss his deep feelings with his family or former work partner Carole Carr. While Lucy would never be forgotten, he had no wish to reawaken memories in them as he felt that they had moved on with their lives much better than he had done. By writing his memoirs and organising his thoughts, he reflected on events that affected him deeply. Thinking on past issues was a therapeutic exercise for him. As he wrote, the cell phone on his desk rang.

"Honey," called his wife who was sitting at the kitchen table helping Poppy with home-school work and annoyed at the interruption as Poppy had just got to grips with a maths problem, "are you going to answer that darn phone? It's been ringing for an age."

Tony, aware now of the irritating ring, reluctantly answered the call.

"Tony Harvey here."

"Sir, Detective Leo Bruce. We met during the search for your kids"

"Sure, I do remember you, detective. What can I help you with?"

"We have news of the guy who terrorised you kids. We have a name for you."

Tony, now alert and totally focused, sat upright, his hand grasping the instrument as if for support and almost shouted down the receiver:

"Tell me all. I want to know the name and whereabouts of the bummer who abducted my kids. Who is he?"

"You will be shocked by this. DNA from items in the cellar and fingerprints lifted from stuff there identified the guy, and the reconstruction of the guy's passport confirmed his identity. His name is Alex Bryson."

"WHAT?!" hollered Tony, shouting so loudly that it brought Gina rushing into the room. "I thought he had been fished out of a river back in Scotland and was lying in a morgue there."

Detective Bruce replied, "From what we've gleaned from the passport, he sailed from Scotland to Ireland, flew on to New York and was in our city before international agencies had even been informed about an escaped prisoner from the UK. Seems like the cops over there were concentrating on local areas, fully expecting him to give himself up or be apprehended, or turn up to visit his ailing mother, and they didn't inform international agencies until it was too late. The guy had given them the slip."

"That sounds a bit far-fetched if you don't mind me saying. Every cop here and over the pond had been alerted to find this guy. No one could hide himself away for that length of time. Are you sure you have this right? So, where is he? Is he in custody?"

"Sorry to give you the down side of this. The absconder is still on the run, sir. He probably took off when our guys arrived to search the ruined Leci House. They went there in force after locating where the kids had holed up. He must have taken off, but we are searching the city for him. I'm hopeful we will apprehend him before long. There's a BOLO out for him. He's probably hanging around the Big Apple."

Tony held his head as if in total disbelief and tried hard to assimilate the information that had been thrown at him. His mind, for once, was crazily mixed up and he could not come to terms with what he had just been told.

"This is astonishing. You mean to say he has been over here for more than a decade, living rough somewhere and ending up in a cellar? Unreal. It's hard to believe. Are your guys sure they've got this right?"

"If the information we have gleaned from his passport is true, he did enter our country fifteen years back. The document is torn and dog-eared but our guys in the lab have managed to rescue some details from it. Where he has been all this time is anyone's guess, although from the state of his corner in the cellar, it looks as if he's cozied up there for a lengthy time. My guys are asking around. Someone must have seen him. He had to eat somewhere. They are checking out soup kitchens and the like. The problem is that we don't have a decent picture of him. His passport shot is almost indecipherable as photos go. The sketch our guy did from your kids' description is the best we have and we're showing it around the area."

"Have the Carrs been told of this development?"

"I'm about to do that now, sir. I wanted you to have the news first. I'll get back at you with any development as it comes in."

As Detective Bruce was relaying the news to Carole and Ted, Gina voiced her fears.

"Tony, if that man is still on the run, he could come after the kids. Honey, I'm scared for them."

"Gina, honey, you are overreacting. The guy is probably in hiding. He won't show his face around here, he won't travel from New York to Chicago. For starters, I reckon he won't have dollars for that, and if he's been living as a homeless person he won't want to show face anywhere, he must know the authorities are after him. He's holed up somewhere in New York, that's for sure. Now try and relax. I'm going to call Carole and get her take on this. I'll wait a bit as Bruce will be giving them the news. God, I can't believe the guy has been over here all those years. There must be some mistake. No one can hide for that length of time."

*

Carole Carr, on hearing the name of their adversary, fumed as she paced around the family room.

"More than a decade! Fifteen years they say that he's been over here and all the time we were led to believe he had drowned. This is unbelievable. I'm going to call Tony."

"Carole," said her husband, "I didn't expect anything less of you. You and Tony have never really retired, have you?" He smiled as he handed her the cell phone.

The two former partners spoke at length at the incredulous turn of events.

"This is the most unbelievable thing I've heard," said Carole as she walked the floor. "How did that guy survive all those years without being smoked out?"

Tony replied, "I can't get my head around this either. It's too far-fetched that he evaded UK cops and got here undetected. So much for security."

"Yeah, Tony, but I guess he slipped in before our guys were alerted to a missing UK con. I guess the cops in UK weren't expecting him to cross the pond. They would be searching for him the length and breadth of Britain. And how much of a coincidence is that, our kids finding his hiding place? This is like something from a TV drama."

"The kids were so fired up on hearing our tales of Lucy and her aunt," replied Tony, "that they wanted to find the place where she spent her last days. We talked with Lucian and he said they knew we would forbid them to go exploring there, that's why they were evasive about their plans. But, hey, yes, it's so far-fetched about the guy, but the evidence points to him being in the USA all those years. But where? He could have been anywhere. Why did he come to Leci House? Was it to see where his adversary Barry Jones lived in luxury? It held no interest for him surely? And where the hell is he now? That guy is the master of evasion."

"Tony, don't you just wish we could get out there and find the asshole? Retirement doesn't suit me. I'm itching to go."

Tony laughed at her exasperation.

"I feel the same, Carole, but Gina would be mad at me if I even hinted at wanting to go find the guy. She's gotten herself into a state about the bad guy coming after the kids. Hey, maybe you need to call around and talk some with her. She listens to you."

"Yeah, let's have dinner together. We haven't seen much of each other since the kids settled back to normal life. Jack and Tess will be home next week from college, so why don't we get together at ours. The kids will love to be together again."

"As long as they don't plan another road trip."

"I reckon it will be a long time before they think of going off again," said Carole.

"Over my dead body," replied an indignant Tony.

CHAPTER THIRTY-ONE

Silence was something the patient was used to. For many years he lived an almost silent existence, a silence he embraced after the chaos of his past life, a silence that was self-imposed and a silence broken now only by the buzz and whirr of the machines that kept him alive. He felt as if he were cocooned in a bubble, a bubble where echoes infiltrated his very being. His brain tried to clarify the world outside of the bubble in which he believed himself to exist. Memories appeared in his brain like still pictures that faded before he could make sense of them, the ebb and flow setting off alerts in the machinery attached to his being, and bringing medics to his bedside to monitor their patient. He could feel someone touching his arm. His attempt at communication frustrated him. He wanted to call out but the fog in his brain prevented him from doing so. He remained trapped in an intermediate state between death and recovery. He could hear voices, voices nearby, voices far off, but voices that seemed to fade like an echo as he attempted to respond. He tried to open his eyes,came to nothing. He could not connect to the outside world.

The neurologist examining him discussed the patient with other medics who had been alerted when monitors keeping his patient alive, showed signs of activity.

"There appears to be some minimal brain activity, but he is unresponsive to the normal tests. His eyes remain closed, although a nurse noticed a slight flicker from them. This man has a long way to go to recover, if he ever does."

I hear voices, getting closer, fading now, empty voices… I'm calling out, my voice is still, it doesn't work right… I lift my arm, it stays by my side… I'm sure I lifted it, my eyes don't open, someone is nearby… I can feel sweet breath as someone touches my arm and whispers to me… open your eyes the voice tells me, and I think I have opened them, but there's only darkness, darkness and floating objects. Open your eyes, John, says the voice… is it a voice in my head? Who is John? Am I John? Someone is washing my face… have I fallen into dirt… Mum is washing my face… you do get into such scrapes, she says… she is laughing.

Now I see pictures in my mind… my brothers, what are their names? Joe, yes, Joe, but the other one, I can't get his name clear… I see Mum, she's hurt, she's in hospital, she's distressed to see her boys… me, Joe and Bobby, yes, Bobby's his name. Why is she sad? What's wrong Mum? Don't cry, Mum… we'll get him… we'll find him if we have to go to the ends of the earth to find him… don't be sad. More images flash across my mind… there's a deep hole in the ground, someone is in there, it's dark and filled with water… there's a splash.

Now someone is by my side… a male voice, fading, touching my head… touching my eyes with something cold… open your eyes, John… lift your arm, John, the voice tells me I am John. I think I lift my arm… it moves, or does it? The voice says, no change, no change…

I run from a vehicle, I hide. It's dark, very dark and I run now, away now from a house. Is it my house? I see Alice… my wife… she is angry… don't be angry, Alice… don't go… don't leave me, Alice.

I'm on a boat. The water is calm but my soul is troubled… what have I done… am I bad? … Why am I fearful? I sleep… the boat stops… where am I? … There's an airplane. I'm sitting by the window… I'm sad… restless sleep comes, then fades. I'm in a strange place… tall, tall buildings… I look up, my neck stretches like the buildings, right to the sky… I'm enthralled…

I look for shelter… I've walked and walked for a long time… I have to find something… what is it… where is it that I need to get to? It's a long way, I'm tired. I'm hungry. I must rest… I stumble. It's a trapdoor… it opens… deep, deep down in a cellar… Is this my home? I see a big house… who lives there? Is this my house? I smell burning. Flames reach high into the night, smell is bad… so, so tired… Who are those people in my cellar? I need to send them away from here… my place… my home now… where he hid from Mum… long time ago… I'll find you, Barry Jones… it's my home now… kids get out… cops surround my place… got to run… my head aches. I want to sit up. I need to drink. The bus is warm. I sleep. This town is cold, cold as ice. My home has gone. I find a place to sleep.

Why is that guy taking my coat? Blood in my mouth, in my head. I sleep.

*

In a prison cell, thousands of miles from where the injured man fought to live, Joe Bryson, serving life for heinous crimes, was summoned by a warden to the visitors' room.

"Get a move on, Bryson, your esteemed visitor doesn't have all day to spend with the likes of you."

The prisoner disliked most of the wardens who, unable to resist goading him for being the fall guy for his crimes, only added to the misery he endured.

"Thought you were clever then, Bryson? Thought you'd get away with killing? Not as smart as your brothers, are you?" said one of the officers who was meant to care for the inmates.

Another picked up the thread. "Your brothers outsmarted you, didn't they? Pulled it off, both of them. Baby brother comfortably settled into our prison hospital, warm and cosy, being attended to hand and foot, pretending to be off his rocker, he should be given an Oscar, and big brother... now, where did you say he was? Ah, yes, I remember, he scarpered. You don't know where he is... been gone long time, man. Almost fifteen years or so, they tell me. I hear he was fished out of the river and no one has claimed his disgusting body. Shame they left you to carry the can. Well, that's brotherly love for you."

Joe Bryson felt his hackles rise, but resisted the urge to retaliate having learned from earlier incidents that to do so only enticed the warden to goad him even more. To retaliate in such a hostile environment was not something a prisoner would do twice. Joe had, on an earlier occasion, responded violently when a warden made a disparaging remark about his mother and had suffered for it for days to come. Thinking that Joe's refusal to take the bait came from weakness, the bully man revelled in tormenting his prisoner. As much as he could, Joe Bryson kept himself to himself, but even in isolation some cruel staff pursued him mercilessly to break his spirit, a spirit already broken beyond repair. His main adversary, Lou Skelton, was a particularly nasty person and it was he who escorted the prisoner to the visitors' room.

Joe had resigned himself to being the only one of the three brothers to face prison; he believed Bobby's mental state had worsened over the years and that he was not faking any illness. But Alex? Alex disgusted him; Alex, the family macho man who put in place the plan to dispose of Barry Jones and his unfortunate companion in revenge for an attack on their mother; Alex, the absconder, probably living the high life somewhere in Europe; Alex, with no intention of facing up to his crime or attempting to visit their mother; Alex, the coward.

"Get a move on, Bryson, get going."

In his fifteen years of incarceration, Joe Bryson never had any visitors apart from his lawyer. He lived in hope that someday his brother Bobby would be well enough to be brought from the nearby hospital prison to visit him, but Bobby's mental state was so fragile that it was not deemed advantageous to have him meet with his elder brother for fear of a serious relapse into a world of confusion and chaos. Joe had longed for the day when Alex would be found, face trial and join him in London's Belmarsh prison. His initial fury at his elder brother's escape from police custody while en route to face charges had disgusted him, but had mellowed slightly over the years to be replaced with genuine concern for his welfare. As he walked behind the officer he prayed that his wish would come true and that he would be reunited with his brothers, but it was not to be. He was faced once more with the lawyer who had been his only contact with the outside world.

"Good afternoon, Joe. How are you bearing up to life behind bars?"

"As well as I can, sir."

"You must be wondering why I'm here?"

"Yes, it crossed my mind that you have word of Alex."

"Sorry, it's not that kind of news. Your brother is a master of escapism. He hasn't been sighted in all these years. However, the news I've come to impart is quite painful. Your mother Peggy passed away in her sleep. She was found this morning by staff bringing her morning tea. She had not been suffering from any illness apart from her dementia and simply slept away. I'm sorry for your loss."

Joe lowered his eyes and held his head in his hands trying to take in the news he had known would come someday, but the unexpectedness of her passing caught him unprepared.

"Joe," continued the concerned lawyer who had represented him at trial and felt sorry that he had been left to face court alone, his brothers having as yet not had to face the ordeal of a court appearance. "I know it's a shock for you. I've spoken to the governor regarding allowing you to attend her funeral. It's not normally granted to lifers like yourself, but the man is human and feels like I do, that you've had a raw deal carrying the burden by yourself. He will make a decision and get back to me asap. Meanwhile, accept my condolences."

The quiet, subdued prisoner was led back to his cell and the normally heartless warden who accompanied him was not without feeling.

"Sorry, Bryson, for your loss. I lost my mum six months ago and it ain't easy. Look, maybe I've been a bit hard on you lately, but hey man, how about I ask the prison chaplain to call over to see you."

"Thanks. That would be good," replied the downcast prisoner.

Prisoner Bryson spent an uncomfortable night alone in his cell where tears flowed freely. He was glad that he did not have to share his cell with anyone else and was free to grieve in the quietness of his room. In his mind he relived his life at home with his loving mother and siblings. His father had died in a rail accident when he and his brothers were young, leaving Peggy Bryson to bring up her brood single-handed. While serving in a mini-market near her home she had been attacked and robbed by a local tearaway Barry Jones, and, as a result, had suffered a massive stroke which changed her quality of life forever. She later developed dementia, and spent her remaining years in care. Her sons, determined to pursue her attacker, located the hoodlum and inflicted a horrific death as revenge, resulting in Joe's present incarceration, his brother Bobby's internment in prison hospital, and brother Alex's whereabouts still unknown. Authorities had scaled down the search for him, believing that he had ended his life although there was no proof to back up that theory.

The prison chaplain, an elderly, kindly man whose calm persona endeared him to the inmates who found him non-judgmental and trustworthy in his dealing with them, visited Joe in his prison cell and spent time with the distraught man who poured out his heart and his life story to the compassionate cleric. He felt that a lifetime's burden of guilt had been lifted by the simple act of sharing with the pastor.

"You poor fellow," said the chaplain as he listened to Joe's outpouring of grief. "I am not here to judge you, Joe. The court has already done that and your fate is now in the hands of your maker, a merciful judge, and I implore you to turn to him in prayer where you will find some peace. I have been asked by the governor to give you the news that you will be granted special compassionate leave to attend your dear mother's funeral accompanied by myself and two officers. Unfortunately, you will be handcuffed throughout, at the discretion of the officers, but it will be a small price to pay. Now, I must go across to the prison hospital to impart the news of your mother's passing to your younger brother. He has been too unwell these past days to have such sad news given to him, but his doctor feels he may be amenable now to receiving the news. He won't be attending the funeral I'm afraid."

That night, Joe Bryson slept sounder than he had for some time. Sharing his grief with the chaplain had lifted his burden of guilt and dispelled any anger he still harboured in his soul. He had aged considerably since his incarceration, not just in years but in appearance; his once thick, healthy hair was now grey and matted, its lustre long gone. His skin too, had lost its rugged outdoor colour befitting his years of outdoor activities, where he fished and camped with his siblings; his pinched face showed an unhealthy weight loss; he exercised less as the months and years slowly eroded the life he once knew. He spent most of his time reading, but that too was becoming uninteresting as he felt he had read all there was on offer in the prison library. He carried out prison work with monotonous regularity; he had little interest in computer courses or other classes that were meant to rehabilitate prisoners and prepare them for life outside, knowing that he was destined to endure prison for the remainder of his life. There were too few jobs for the growing prison population, and he often spent longer in his cell than that recommended by H.M.I. of Prisons Joe chose not to mix with the various ethnic groups, where tension could build up and violence could flare like a spark igniting a waiting powder keg. As upsetting as it was, he looked forward in a strange way to a few hours out of prison to say his farewell to his beloved mother.

Peggy Bryson's funeral was attended by few people: some care assistants from the Strand Bay Care Home were present, as was a representative from her previous home, GWR, from where she had been abducted by her sons several years previously when they refused to allow her to be transferred from her settled life to a large hospital ward for patients with dementia. The removal from the care home had a snowball effect on the life of her sons, resulting in them being tracked down, identified as killers, captured and sent for trial. It was a bitter-sweet move for Peggy Bryson who, due to her frailty of mind, was unaware of her sons' heinous crimes to revenge her attacker Barry Jones. Also present at the crematorium was elderly Liam Norris, who had been head gardener during Peggy's time at GWR, and who foolishly aided her sons in furtively snatching her from the care home. Reggie Allison, Peggy's former boss at the mini-market where she had worked until the unprovoked attack, was now housebound and unable to attend the funeral but sent a rather expensive floral wreath. It was he who had funded Peggy's stay while in care, feeling, as he did, a lifelong guilt at leaving the woman alone in his shop while he attended to other business.

Joe Bryson, flanked by two officers, took his seat at the front of the crematorium where the service was to take place. The hospital chaplain who had been asked to lead the service noticed that Joe never took his eyes from his mother's coffin. Unknown to the prisoner, some undercover officers were patrolling the area in the unlikely event that Alex Bryson would put in an appearance. Peggy's death notice had been deliberately inserted in several newspapers in an attempt to draw the missing killer out into the open. It was not to be.

During the service, the chaplain called Joe forward.

"Peggy's son has asked to say a few words about his mother."

There was a hush as his handcuffs were released by ever watchful officers, and Joe took his place at the side of his mother's coffin, his hand gently stroking it as he spoke.

"My mother was a kind, gentle woman who had a difficult life after my father was killed along with several others in a train derailment. She was left to bring up the three of us by herself. She worked hard. Our home was spotless, we were well fed and cared for. She was always cleaning and mending and making ends meet. My fondest memory is coming home from school to a house filled with the smell of home cooking. She would wrap her arms around us and laugh and chuckle when us macho boys struggled to free ourselves from her embrace pretending we were too old for such things, but secretly loving it. Mum, I wish you could hold me one more time."

Joe took a deep breath and continued, "At night after supper, we would sit beside her as she read stories to us and sang to us with the most beautiful voice I have ever heard. She saw that our homework was always completed, and encouraged us to be the best we could be in life. She chided us when necessary and guided us through our growing years. She did not deserve what happened to her when she was violently attacked and left seriously ill, nor did she deserve to spend the rest of her life in care, away from the home she loved, and she did not deserve to lose her mind to that awful illness that stole her from us, but most of all, she did not deserve to have her sons turn killers to avenge her attack."

Joe bent forward to plant a kiss on her coffin, and in a voice filled with remorse, whispered, "Sorry, Mum. Sorry from the three of us. Love you, Mum."

As he returned to his seat, a hush descended on the small gathering, broken only by the click of the handcuffs being attached to the bereft man. At the end of the service he was led away by a side door to a waiting car to return to his misery of prison. The grim-faced chaplain stood at the main door and thanked each person for coming and explained that, no, they would not be able to speak to Joe, and that he would pass on their condolences.

CHAPTER THIRTY-TWO

THOUSANDS OF MILES FROM WHERE Peggy Bryson was laid to rest, life at LMAMA academy took on a near-normal existence with art and music lessons in full flow. The reputation of the academy had not suffered from the adverse publicity from Ben Witherspoon's vile actions, but, if anything, it had bought its existence to the attention of potential students who clamoured to enrol there.

Those who had witnessed the distress of that time left with a sense of pride in how they continued with their work amid the investigation and chaos that followed. The students left too, with new improved skills and friendships that would last some of them throughout their lives; they left with a sadness at witnessing a vile crime by one of their peers, and left with a more mature understanding of human nature with all its faults and failings. As they said goodbye to Abigail and Ralph, their sincere thanks and good wishes were genuine. No one had been left untouched by events of the past months.

The college was now quiet. Silence took over from the cacophony of the past few weeks. Abigail sat in her private wing of the house working on the restoration of Lucy's portrait which had been carefully transported there by Ralph when forensics had released it back into her care. She methodically repaired, restored and worked on the precious painting over many weeks. She was determined to restore it to its former and rightful place in the atrium of the academy.

Life moved on for those affected, as Brenda pointed out as she prepared to leave for her penthouse condo, by the legacy of Anna Leci. "So many people have been affected by her actions; even to this day people are feeling the effect of her behaviour," she said as she hugged Abigail and Ralph who were seeing her off.

The horror of Ben Witherspoon's actions had brought them even closer, each being aware of the other's pain, at times unspoken, at times vocalised.

As Brenda called in at the grocery store near her home to pick up provisions, a headline jumped out at her from the Tribune: *Death of Former Politician.* At home, she settled to read about the death of her former lover, a man who caused so much hurt to her and her family, a man whose selfish ambitions were thwarted by the revelation in public that he was Lucy's father, a disclosure that ended his political career and almost ended his marriage. Brenda Mears felt no emotion as she read the short notice announcing the death of Ross S. Witherspoon:*The death is announced of Ross S. Witherspoon, former resident of Cook County, beloved husband of Linda-*

Mae Sheringham-Witherspoon, devoted father to Jake Samuel Witherspoon and Benjamin Simon Witherspoon, now of Shelbyville, Illinois. Funeral took place in private with only close family in attendance.

Another victim of my aunt's actions, thought Brenda as she tossed the newspaper in the trash.

Not far from her residence, Tony Harvey had spotted the brief death notice and called Carole Carr to inform her of the death of their former adversary, but was directed to her voice mail service.

"Hey, Carole, have you a copy of the Tribune? Check out page forty-three. Catch you later."

Tony called his stepdaughter, Abigail, who, on hearing the news had little to say on the demise of the man who had fathered and neglected her best friend.

"I guess not many people will miss that guy, judging from the few attendees at his funeral. I for one won't be extending my sympathy to his widow."

Carole returned Tony's call. "Hi, Tony, sorry to miss your call, we were next door for a barbeque meal with new neighbours. Ted popped out and got me a newspaper. There's not much in it about a one-time possible President of the United States, is there? Ted's older sister lives in Shelby County, he's going to call her to find out more information, not that I'm too bothered but it will make for interesting reading."

The Shelby News carried the following article on Ross S. Witherspoon:

The death has been announced of Ross S. Witherspoon, former resident of Cook County and resident here in Shelby

County for the past nineteen years since his fall from grace following a scandal in his private life. The once ambitious politician, tipped for high office, and on the verge of becoming his party's nomination for President of United States, was unveiled as the father of Lucy Mears, daughter of Brenda Mears, President of Mears Empire, at a time when the fifteen-year-old had been abducted and had been missing for several weeks. The politician at first denied all knowledge of the girl, but, under pressure from his aides, and on the advice of his lawyer, admitted that in his youth he had had a brief affair with the girl's mother but was unaware of the child's existence, believing her mother had 'dealt with the problem'. There was outrage among his supporters at his indifference to a young girl's plight, and he and his family had to leave the area. They settled here in Shelbyville. He never returned to politics and spent his time writing his memoirs. His wife, Linda-Mae Witherspoon refused an interview with our reporter and would say only that her husband was at peace now, having suffered a debilitating illness for the past five years. Their elder son Jake, an I.T. trainee consultant, spends time in Europe pursuing his career, while the younger son Ben, is currently in a correction facility in Chicago for malicious destruction of property, a crime believed to have taken place at the former home of Brenda Mears, which is now a renowned academy in Lincoln Park, Chicago. When contacted by this newspaper, Brenda Mears refused to comment on the death of Ross S. Witherspoon.

*

Jake Witherspoon returned home from Europe for his father's funeral, more to support his mother than to grieve for a father to whom he had difficulty relating, and took charge of decisions which were painful for his mother to cope with. It was known among the family that Jake was his mother's favourite while Ben related more to his father. During his early childhood Jake saw little of his father who spent most of his time on the political circuit, building his career in politics. After the family fled from the disgrace of his father's downfall and settled in Shelbyville, Jake found the transition difficult. At school he was bullied mercilessly when his peers discovered his true identity, but they soon lost interest when the young boy began to retaliate with force.

"You have to fight your corner, Jake," exhorted his disgraced father. "Don't let them get the upper hand or wear you down. Fight, boy, fight them."

Such was the only advice that Jake ever remembered receiving from his father who was so caught up in his own miserable existence to recognise that his elder son was growing away from him emotionally. As Jake grew to adulthood he withdrew even further from his father and seldom entered the dark library where the former politician spent most of his morose existence in writing his memoirs and leaving the rearing of his elder boy to his long-suffering wife.

Jake sat holding his mother's hand, comforting her as best he could.

"Mom, why don't you come back with me to Europe? I'll be in France for at least two months, then Germany for possibly three months. It would give you a complete break... let's face it, you have never had a vacation in years... in fact, Mom, I don't remember you ever having a holiday. Will you give it some thought? The company have an apartment that we could stay in and it would be cool to come home from work to..."

"Ah, so there's a hidden agenda," laughed Linda-Mae. "You want someone to cook and clean?"

"Mom, it's so good to see you laugh! No, there's no hidden agenda, but if you insist... well... how could a guy refuse?"

The sound of her laughter caught Linda-Mae by surprise. It was as if an alien sound had come from somewhere deep within her as she realised how long it had been since she last laughed aloud, if in fact she ever had.

"I'll give it some thought, Jake, but for now I have to visit Ben; you know how close he was to his father and he is bound to be suffering. Will you come with me, Jake?"

Jake had little time for the sibling who had caused nothing but heartache to his mother, and had vowed to disown him after his disgraceful behaviour at the LMAMA academy that resulted in a jail sentence that brought even more humiliation to the already scandal-hit family. Putting his feelings aside, he determined to be a support for his mother in what he knew would be a harrowing visit.

"Sure, Mom. I'll drive over with you."

Sometime later, Ben Witherspoon was called to the visitors' room at the prison where he had been held since his court appearance. Apart from visits from his lawyer, the last one being to impart the news of his father's death, he had had no other visitors. His father's demise had hit him badly. He was the favoured son and had spent hours in his company, mostly in the dark library where Ross S. Witherspoon, more at ease with the boy who was so like him in nature, shared family secrets known to no one else.

"This information, Ben, is sacrosanct, never to be divulged. Do you understand?"

"Sure, Dad, I really do understand."

The young boy listened, eyes wide in astonishment like a rabbit caught in car headlights as his father spoke quietly to him and shared a part of his life that had long faded into the dark recess of his mind, surfacing now like a memory that had emerged from a long sleep, a supressed memory, a memory that continued to haunt him, a memory that reappeared, perhaps from guilt or perhaps from an awareness that his illness now forced him to face his destiny.

"Wow, Dad. You can trust me to keep this between us. How cool to share such a secret!"

"Now, Ben, look at this picture."

"Wow! Tell me about it. This is awesome."

Ben Witherspoon, custodian of information that would rock the political world, his family and many others, and now an inmate in a Chicago correction centre, entered the visitors' room to be greeted by his mother and brother. He had changed in the short time of his imprisonment; gone was his baby-faced looks that had allowed him to pretend to be younger and more innocent than he was, to be replaced by a hardness that shocked his mother. His attempt to grow a beard resulted only in adding to his unkempt appearance, his cold eyes reflecting the coldness of his heart. He was genuinely pleased to see them, having thought that he had deservedly been abandoned by his family. His bearing mellowed at the sight of familiar faces.

"Mom. Jake. How are you? Heh, I'm so glad to see you. Tell me about Dad; hell, I miss him so much and was mad that the governor wouldn't let me attend his funeral, they do it for some inmates."

As he rambled on, Linda-Mae did not disclose that she had requested that the governor refuse her son's request to attend the funeral, believing that her action was for the best, knowing that Ben could be a disturbing influence and do himself no great favours with the authorities if he made a scene.

The three spoke at length, Jake describing the short funeral service, Linda-Mae contributing where necessary, aware that her younger son was vulnerable in spite of his brave facade and macho stance.

"I loved him, Mom. You have to know that."

"I do, honey. I do. You were always close to your father and this has hit you hard, but Ben, he's at peace now and that dreadful suffering is over for him and we must get on with our lives. It was painful for me to watch the man I love suffer so much and I was glad you two boys were spared that towards the end. Try to remember the good times, Ben. It will help with grieving."

The hardness that had so long been in his soul slowly softened a little and he wiped a tear from his eye as he looked around furtively to make sure his weakness hadn't been noticed by any of the wardens.

"Yeah, Mom, you're right. There ain't no point in me grieving and hey, I do have happy memories of Dad."

"Ben, sweetie, I'm pleased about that. Hold on to your memories."

Jake, who had been watching his brother intently, felt that the moment was right to tell him of their plans. He nodded to Linda-Mae, indicating that she should speak to Ben.

"Ben," she began, "we have something to tell you."

She wiped a tear from her eye as if in sympathy with her younger son and, relieved to see something of the good boy surfacing once more, continued.

"I've made a decision, Ben, a big one. I'm selling up. I never did like where we lived, it was forced upon us, and I can count on one hand the number of friends I have there, so, I'm going firstly to Europe with Jake for a few months, and when I get back I'll move away from the area. We can discuss it with you later, but I guess I'd like to settle in Florida."

"What?" screamed the prisoner whose shout alerted wardens who were nearby, waiting to diffuse any situation that arose between visitors and inmates. They were well used to confrontations at visit times when tensions rose and tempers got out of hand.

"You're going off and leaving me here in this shit hole?"

"It's only temporary, sweetie. When I come back in a few months' time I want us to make a fresh start somewhere far from here, far from memories, perhaps, like I say, Florida or somewhere around that area."

Linda-Mae looked at her son's face and saw anger; she saw a face contorted with rage, a face she had seen so often on her husband. *He has become so like his father,* she thought.

"But what about me? What's to happen to me? And all my stuff back at the house? You gonna dump it just like you're gonna dump me?"

"Ben, we can put your things in safe storage until you are out of here, but you know, sweetie, you need to stand on your own feet when you are released. You can't return to the life you've had and I can't support you. You have to grow up, you'll be twenty in a few weeks, you have to act like an adult. I am not abandoning you, Ben. I will always be your mom, always here for you, but I need this bit of space to unwind after looking after your father for years. It's not much to ask."

Ben glowered at his sibling. "And I suppose favourite son here put you up to all this, turned me against you, Mom. Admit it, he was always your favoured child. I never counted with you, did I?"

"Ben that's out of order," replied Jake. "You know Mom has always looked out for you and put up with your crazy ways. She's right, you need to take responsibility for your actions and man up."

As their voices rose, a warden approached signalling the end of the visit.

"You better go then, *my family,*" said Ben in a sarcastic tone. "Go off and enjoy yourselves and fuckin' abandon me here. And there I was thinking that you came today because you loved and missed me. How wrong could I be?"

Linda-Mae openly upset, attempted to calm him down. "No, Ben, we are not abandoning you. We will be here for you when you are released, please believe that, baby."

"Yeah, yeah, I hear you. Well I'm sure glad that Dad told *me* his secret and not you, Jake, he couldn't trust you with it."

"What secret? What are you talking about?" asked Jake.

"You'll find out soon enough," smirked the troubled prisoner as he was led away. He turned his head towards his bemused family and with a final remark said, "Read about it in his memoirs, guys."

On the drive home Jake and Linda-Mae tried to figure out what Ben meant by his closing remarks.

"What was that all about?"

"Jake, I have no idea, but you know your brother, he lets his imagination run riot at times. He's probably trying to wind us up. I hate to see him so messed up. Where did I go wrong? You were both brought up exactly in the same manner and turned out like night and day."

"Hey, Mom, don't beat yourself up over his mistakes. Ben made a choice to be difficult. He spent too much time with Dad and has been influenced by him; he put Dad on a pedestal and was taken in by his insistence that he was wrongly treated by the whole world it seemed, over his dismissal from politics."

"Always the wise one, Jake," smiled his mother as they turned into their driveway.

"Let's get serious about selling up. We need to organise so much stuff."

They began a frenzy of activity, packing boxes to be stored until their return, discarding items no longer required and generally downsizing.

"Mom, I've finished clearing Ben's room and packed everything away for storage. What's next?"

"Why don't you make a start on your father's library? The books can be packed in boxes; be careful with any personal papers and stuff that can be kept in a safe deposit box at the bank."

Linda-Mae returned to her chores happy in the knowledge that she had made the right decision to move from the place where she felt such unease. She was aware that she was humming a tune. *This house has been more of a refuge than a family home, far from normal life,* she mused. *I'm blessed to have such a level-headed son to see me through this darkness, and allow me to mourn for Ben, for that is what it feels like, a death... poor Ben, he is so messed up.* Her reverie was interrupted by a shout from Jake.

"Mom, you have to see this... I don't understand..."

Jake's hand was trembling as he handed a faded photograph to his mother, faded, yet clearly showing three people.

"Read the back, Mom."

Linda-Mae, studied the picture, looked at her son in total disbelief, shook her head and, with hands shaking uncontrollably, read the inscription on the back.

"Jake, do you know what this means?"

Brows furrowed and with her face as white as a sheet, she held onto the back of a chair to prevent herself from falling.

"Hell, Mom, if this is true then Dad has been living a lie all these years."

"Now we know what Ben was gloating about. His father shared this with him. Good God, Jake, what kind of man was he? I feel such a fool to have been taken in by him; not only me, but plenty of other folks have been duped by him. My parents welcomed him like a son and supported us when times were tough. Heck, they even gave us a home with them and financed us until we sorted our lives out. This is beyond belief."

She sat down, shocked to the core at what had been revealed, fearful of the ripple effect this would have on so many people.

"Have you come across that darn book he was writing? His memoirs? He would never share it; he said I would find out the contents soon enough."

"There's no sign of it so far, Mom. I think it might well be with a publisher… there's an e-mail here confirming that a manuscript has been received and will be attended to as instructed. Whatever that means. Do you want me to contact the publisher? Should we confront Ben with this?"

"Oh, Jake, I can't think straight. This has come as a shock. Let's leave it for the moment. Ben would only gloat at us, and I'm too upset to cope with his behaviour at present. I just want to get away now from this house and its memories. I was never at ease here. We can deal with all this when we come back from Europe. But, Jake, your dad knew all along! He damn well knew!"

"Don't get upset, Mom, it won't do any good. You're right, let's get away from here and try and forget all this," he said as he pointed to the photograph that Linda-Mae clutched in her hand, as if she wanted to crush the memory and erase it from her mind. She looked at it once more, turned it over and read in her husband's unmistakable handwriting, *'my daughter Lucy in the park with her nanny and another kid'*. The faded picture showed an unsuspecting Molly Kelly, housekeeper to Brenda Mears, pushing two little kids on a swing, one, her own daughter Nora, and the other, a child about four years of age, undeniably, Lucy Mears.

CHAPTER THIRTY-THREE

In New York the search continued for the homeless man who had abducted the four young adventurers. Staff manning surveillance cameras in the bustling bus hub in the Big Apple were alerted by their bosses to a request from NYPD to look for a suspect on the run.

"Another one?" commented Wayne Ickler, as he read the information handed to him. "Who is it now?"

His boss said, "We've an alert here, a BOLO has been put out for a homeless guy wanted in connection with abducting some kids and leaving them for dead. The kids' father was a retired Superintendent of CPD and we've to pull out all the stops to find this scumbag."

"Hey, I remember that," said Wayne. "It happened at the home of that crazy woman who abducted a young girl some years ago. I remember because my kid Judy was the same age as the missing kid. Didn't she die in a plane crash or something like that?"

"Yeah, you're right. I remember now, the girl was the daughter of some political guy who aspired to head to the White House as the next president. Anyhow, we have dates but no picture, only a sketch done by a police artist based on what the kids described. It's not ideal but it's better than nothing and it gives a good idea of height and weight. Get Stavros to help when he comes back from lunch. Here's all the information I've got. Do what you can with it."

The surveillance staff scoured footage caught on the network on the date in question. The bus station had been particularly busy that day as an impending storm forecast for later forced commuters to complete their journeys before the weather worsened.

"There's too much here," said Stavros. "How are we gonna get sight of a lone man who fits this description? This could be a wild goose chase."

"I'll move to the cameras that show people boarding, we might have some luck there," said Wayne who was well used to unproductive hours of searching.

After painstaking hours of scouring passengers joining bus queues, Wayne called out, "Stavros, come look at this. Could this be our guy?"

"It's possible," replied Stavros pulling up a chair beside his colleague. "Move to the next frame… hey, I think you've got something there. Can you bring it up a bit without losing definition?"

They called their boss for his opinion on the grainy picture.

"Can we bring it up a bit, get it a bit clearer?" he asked.

"We've tried that, sir, but we're losing clarity here," replied Wayne. "We could try a bit more, but we might lose even more definition."

"Let's get the investigating officers over here; maybe their lab guys could do something. From what I can see, this could well be our guy. I'll put money on it. Good show, guys; a job well done."

The lab technician worked on the faded image and produced a clear enough copy to cause a stir among the team.

"If this is our guy, then he boarded a bus to Boston. We have a breakthrough here, guys. Call Detective Bruce, he needs to see this."

Leo Bruce interrupted a meeting to take the call he had been hoping for.

"You've found him? Great, tell me more."

After listening to the lab technician, he put a call through to the chief of police in Boston, a man well known to him from their days when they were rookie cops before they each took up positions of authority and for whom he had the greatest respect.

"Hey, Phil. Leo Bruce here. How you doing, man?"

"Brucie, my old buddy. Good to hear from you. What you got for me? Not more work? You New Yorkers never manage without us Bostonians, do you?" He laughed as the two renewed acquaintances and chatted about family and work before getting to the crux of the call.

Phil Robb listened to the request, noted down the details and promised to get onto it asap. "I'll get a team onto this right now and get back at you. Fax through the info you have including the rough sketch and we'll take it from there."

Detective Robb's team put out a BOLO and asked specifically that the itinerant community be interviewed to locate the wanted man.

He addressed his crew. "If this guy's been living rough in this weather he may have taken shelter among the city's homeless. Take a walk to the wild side of town and talk to the itinerant community, show them the guy's mug shot but don't expect much response. We ain't too popular with some folks. It might be a problem; you know how suspicious they are of us. Grease a few palms if you have to, within limit. Check out refuge shelters and talk to all the homeless who deign to talk to you. Our guy is out there somewhere, let's go get him. Check the area around Newton bus hub to start with, then on to Cambridge. He probably got off at either of those stops. Also, check out airports and train hubs from CCTV cameras, get your teams onto it. There's a crazy guy out there, go get him."

The surveillance teams took on the onerous task of searching among thousands of commuters for someone who vaguely resembled the grainy image that had been faxed to them. They checked out CCTVs posted at the entrance and exits of bus depots, and finding nothing there, turned their attention to the busy hallways where their eyes skimmed over hundreds of people including a family group consisting of two parents and two young kids, the man carrying a suitcase, the woman pushing a stroller and heading towards the cab rank.

A hectic search began around the city in shelters for the homeless, the task being made difficult as extra temporary refuges had been set up to cope with the Boston winter and were now no longer operational. Scores of officers made enquiries at the established ones and, having no success there, were directed to various churches that had opened their doors to the homeless during the worst of the weather. At one such church a woman cleaning steps looked at the faded picture, adjusted her glasses, wiped her wet hands on her overall and studied it saying, "Mm, not much of a picture to go showing folks is it… mm… now, I was helping in the kitchen around that time… got to do your bit to help your fellow citizens, don't you, officer? Well, I ain't sure but he looks kinda familiar. Came in once or twice that I recall, quiet, well-mannered guy, not like some of them what turn up here demanding food… think they'd be grateful now and then, wouldn't you? Let me think… yes, sir, I'm sure he was here. Never spoke at all, just to say 'thank you, ma'am'…don't even get that from some of them homeless, but this guy… summat about him that made him stand out… a stranger, he sure was that… kept his self to his self, sir."

The chatty lady had no more information to impart and took herself back to her cleaning job attacking the steps with a frenzy as if eradicating the memory of the undesirables who did not appreciate what she, with her good will, did for them.

"I wouldn't like to cross her," laughed one cop as he made notes of their conversation.

"It looks as though our guy was in the area. Call it in to HQ, and check what they want us to do now."

Other officers had a similar response, most people commenting on how the faded picture didn't give enough clarity for identification. Success came at last when two rather frustrated cops called at the Salvation Army office and were met with a female officer who, while not recognising the picture, related the tale of the injured vagrant found in a pool of blood.

"It was quite a shock, officer, to see that poor man lying there in his own blood and close to death. They took him off to hospital, sir. That was four, five weeks ago. By the looks of him I guess the poor man might well have gone to his maker by now. I called 911 and the paramedics said it was touch and go for the poor man. He had been viciously attacked. It distresses me that human beings can treat each other like that. How do they sleep at night? Poor man."

This was the lead they had been hoping for. Earlier hospital enquiries had been unsuccessful, but there were still some other facilities to check out. At one trauma centre, they met with one of the team who had dealt with the unnamed patient, the John Doe of the unit, and verified that their patient was indeed the man in the sketch.

"It's a reasonable likeness to our John Doe," he said. "I wouldn't have been able to say that when he was first admitted, but now that the swelling on his head has subsided, yes, that's our John. We never did get a name for him. It distressed some of our nurses that no one knew his name or cared about him."

"Sir, we can give you a name and much more. He is Alex Bryson from the UK, a fugitive from justice for over a decade, he's been on the international wanted list, wanted for the murder of two USA citizens. He escaped from police custody in Scotland UK where the crime was committed, and fled to New York where he's been holed up until lately. He recently abducted four kids and left them for dead, and hasn't been seen since his hideout was found by NYPD, but we struck lucky with CCTV footage showing him boarding a bus to here in Boston. Other surveillance guys observed him on CCTV in Logan, they had a clear picture of him sitting in a coffee bar. Doctor, your patient is Alex Bryson, a criminal whom we have to apprehend and take into custody. We have a warrant for his arrest."

Another officer took up the story.

"Interpol has been searching for this international fugitive and, with help from law enforcement agencies including FBI and others, have named Alex Bryson as the person they were most anxious to locate and arrest, he being a long-time fugitive. It appears that the search is over now for this fugitive, and we are here to apprehend and arrest him."

"This is amazing. Let me call my boss, he's the senior consultant who dealt with John... Alex you say? Alex Bryson, mm? Well that's a new slant on things."

The consultant returned, shaking his head, still in disbelief at what he had heard from the officers.

"Mr Bromley is in surgery; he should be finishing fairly soon. Can we offer you coffee while you wait?"

Mr Bromley, senior neurologist, arrived shortly after and introduced himself to the officers.

"Sorry to keep you waiting, gentlemen. A tricky craniotomy took longer than planned… yes… tricky indeed."

He was an imposing figure, tall with thick silver hair, cut neatly to accentuate the shape of his face. He was impeccably dressed and gave the impression of having walked out of a page from a fashion magazine rather than from a hospital theatre. He listened intently to the account of the mysterious John Doe whom he had been treating for several weeks.

"I'm glad that at last we can put a name to the patient, but what a shock to learn of his background."

"Sir," said the officer in charge, "may we now see the patient? We have a warrant here to arrest him."

"Sorry, officer, my colleague didn't get around to telling you. Your man is no longer with us–"

"Oh," interrupted the officer, "are we too late? Has he died?"

"No, no," replied Mr Bromley with a shake of his head, "although he may as well be. He suffered a horrendous head trauma, we believe from an assault, and has never regained consciousness. He is being cared for now in one of the city's medical respite centres under Boston's health care for the homeless scheme, as there was nothing else we could do for him here. You will no doubt know that most rough sleepers who live on our streets are uninsured and tend to avoid shelters and the invasive questions that some paperwork fanatics seem keen to pursue, and, as a result, these people are high users of our emergency centres and pose a challenge to our health care system. The city has grants for facilities such as the one our patient was taken to. I must tell you that I doubt he will ever fully recover despite the care he is receiving and, as for being arrested and taken to court, that will never be possible, not in his present condition. His prognosis is grim. His brain has been irreparably damaged by a blood clot. We believe he had been left lying on the sidewalk for several hours, by which time there was severe compression on the brain. A sad case indeed. There are no family members that we know of to discuss his illness, and until we locate someone, he is being kept alive by machines. Regardless of these crimes that you tell me about, he is first and foremost a patient, and we must treat him as such. In effect, he is receiving palliative care."

The two officers looked at each other, disappointment showing in their faces, knowing that the criminal who was within their reach had now, through illness, evaded arrest yet again. They took their leave of the consultant who promised to alert staff at the respite centre of their impending visit.

"Don't expect too much," was the consultant's parting comment.

*

Back in the police vehicle, the senior officer, disappointed at what he had learned, sighed and said, "We've come this length with the enquiry and have hit a brick wall but hey, we need to go over there and check things out, best call it in."

"Yeah, we gotta visit the guy at the rehab centre. From what we hear it sure sounds like we're too late and the guy is brain dead. It's a bummer that we almost nailed him."

*

More voices… I want to open my eyes, why won't they open… I think they are open… are they? There's that voice again… 'Hey there, John, it's Sue here to check your vitals'… I feel someone touch my arm… I lift my hand to locate the voice… it won't lift… then a voice I've heard before… 'Billy here, John, to make you more comfortable'…I feel my body being moved this way and that way… I want to call out to the voice… then another voice, 'John, Greta here to change your feeding tube…' Who are these voices? Who is John… my name is not John… I am not John… why can't I speak out and tell them my real name… what is my name? I forget… my head pounds… I am so tired… sleep. More voices… different… not gentle… gruff voices… I try to open my eyes to see the voices… my head hurts… 'Alex Bryson, you are under arrest for unlawful abduction and imprisonment of Jack Carr, Tess Carr, Lucian Harvey and Poppy Harvey and for evading arrest'…Alex Bryson… yes that's my name… I am not John, I am Alex… who are these voices? Those names… do I know them? Do they know me? My head pounds as if it is going to explode… I am Alex… tired… sleepy.

*

Staff attending to Alex Bryson were astounded to learn that the gentle John whom they had been caring for, was in fact an escaped prisoner wanted in the UK for two heinous murders of US citizens more than a decade ago, and who had recently abducted four young people, drugged them and left them for dead. They now knew the identity of their patient.

"Are you sure?" asked a senior medic, his voice raised an octave or two in total disbelief.

"Such a gentle patient; poor guy, regardless of who he is or what he has done, he remains our patient and we have a duty of care for him until told otherwise. My staff have treated him with respect as we would any patient and we introduce ourselves when we tend to him in the hope that our voices become familiar and that he will respond to us."

Boston's chief of police, Phil Robb, arrived to back up his team and to see for himself the elusive Alex Bryson.

"I'll make calls to Detective Bruce of NYPD and Chief Officer Wynne in Chicago to let them know the search for the missing felon has come to a halt. There are so many others too, who need to know the outcome of this long search. Interpol will contact London and inform the guys there and their Scottish counterparts, I'll get someone on to letting the parents of those four kids know what's happened. Sure doesn't look like we can remove this guy to prison. He ain't goin' nowhere."

CHAPTER THIRTY-FOUR

Like a bush telegraph, word soon reached investigating officers that their search for the elusive escapee had finally ended. The news was greeted with relief from some quarters and anger from others who felt the atrocities of past crimes should not go unpunished.

Tony Harvey was one of the latter; his kids had been victims and he wanted someone punished for the trauma inflicted on his children, not to mention the emotional strain on himself and Gina. Carole Carr, always a calming influence on her former partner attempted to reason with him.

"Tony, our kids are safe, the danger is over and no other kid will suffer at the hands of that man. He will be forever locked inside his own body, a prisoner of a different kind, trapped in his own miserable frame. Sure, we want justice, it's in our blood as surely as it's been running through our veins, poured in there by years of dealing with injustice and lawbreakers, but, hey, the kids have put it behind them and have moved on with their lives. You and the rest of us parents need to move on too, don't let this anger and hatred eat you up, Tony. You are bigger than any wanted criminal."

Her wise words had the desired effect. Slowly, Tony Harvey let go of the hatred in his heart, perhaps not totally, but moved in the right direction.

The four young people, on hearing the news of their torturer, were more pragmatic in their acceptance of his fate.

"I guess he got what he deserved in the end," said Tess. "And I for one sure don't want to hear his name mentioned again. Life is too short and I've got my future to think of," she said adamantly.

"Yeah, sis, and would that future include the guy you hang out with? What's his name? Randall?" laughed her brother as he teased Tess until tears of laughter ran down her face.

"You've been snooping on me Jack Carr!"

"Just looking out for my kid sister!"

Lucian Harvey, probably the most sensitive of the quartet, accepted the news from his father with a shrug of his shoulders and a brief comment. "I guess he won't harm anyone else then."

Poppy, more vocal and exuberant like her father, at first felt cheated that the hobo had not been caught and jailed, but her shrewd mother managed to change her attitude.

"Sweetie, you can't go through life harbouring feelings like that, they eat you up inside. Let's be thankful that the man is being watched around the clock and will never leave that hospital bed. From what we understand he may not have long in this world, so let's leave his judgement to a higher authority."

Joe Bryson was given the news of his brother's whereabouts by the prison governor, an experienced and strict, but not unfeeling man, who was aware of the recent loss to Joe of his mother, and was sensitive to the prisoner's emotional state.

"I have news for you of your elder brother. Alex has been located in Boston, USA," he began.

"What?!" said Joe, his mouth wide open in astonishment. "America? Alex is in America? How the hell… excuse me, sir… how did he get there and how long has he been there? I can't get my head around this. I presume he's in prison somewhere, paying for his part in all this mess."

"He is in a worse kind of prison than you are, Joe. He had been living rough, was beaten up and left to die by the side of the road. The medics did all they could for him but he is in a permanent coma now, a prisoner trapped in his own body, a worse prison than that I can't imagine. Prognosis is not good. He is being kept alive by machine and, with no family able to discuss his treatment, things are looking grim for him. Sorry to bring you such news so soon after your loss."

Joe put his head in his hands trying to block out what he had just heard, his mind in turmoil, racing between relief that Alex had been found, despair at his plight, and underlying anger that once again he was alone in carrying the can for a crime perpetrated by him and his two brothers.

Alone in the privacy of his cell he vented his frustration by banging his fists on the rough wall until his knuckles bled and skin peeled from his hands. Family life as he had once known it had gone forever, and with it, any hope of seeing his elder brother, however fleetingly. The grief he felt at the recent loss of his mother surfaced once more and raw emotions came to the surface crushing his very soul like an iron bar squeezing the very breath from his body. *Bobby, Alex, Mum...* he cried out in despair as if by calling their names would somehow make them materialise and sooth his broken spirit.

He slept badly; his dreams were of dark days, of killings, of pit holes, of funerals. His brothers' faces appeared grotesque as if wearing zombie masks and mocking his incarceration. In his dream they danced around him as he fell deeper, deeper into a dark endless hole of pity. He was falling, falling, falling and as he tumbled into the abyss, his screams had wardens running to the normally placid prisoner. Joe was treated for his hand wounds in the hospital medical room; his physical wounds were easy to attend to, his emotional ones not so. The prison chaplain, who had been a source of comfort to him some months earlier, sat with him and listened to his gut-wrenching pouring out of grief, anger, frustration and hopelessness.

"Sir," began the tearful man, "I hated Alex for the way he abandoned Bobby and me, and I wanted him found and brought to justice, but now... now it's like another death... he won't recover from his beating and from what they tell me he will be attached to machines until someone makes a decision about pulling the plug. I'm scared that they might put that responsibility onto me. Chaplain, sir, how could I do that… how could I kill my brother? I couldn't do that to Alex, even if over the years I'd have happily strangled him."

"Joe, it's a difficult one. No one has the right to take another life. Euthanasia is constantly under debate, the pros and cons forum use situations like your brother to thrash out arguments, but you know, it's not until it touches home that the issue becomes serious. No one has asked you to make a decision and I doubt if they will and, given your situation here, I wouldn't like to guess what your rights are on this, if any. Let's not dwell on it; pray for your brother. The good Lord will be the one to decide when Alex's life is finished."

The pair talked at length, and after a period of calm, Joe was returned to his lonely existence in cell 45b to sit out the remainder of his prison sentence wishing that his brother Bobby had never encountered their foe Barry Jones in a London pub; Barry Jones, the man who attacked his mother so fiercely that she never recovered full health and who met his nemesis in a sunken pit hole at the hands of the brothers Bryson. *Was it worth it*? he thought, as he lay in his cell remembering and reliving the dark period in his life. *We should have left well alone.* He prayed that night as he had never done before, for his brothers, for Bobby, the vulnerable little brother who irritated the life out of him and for Alex, his hero, the brother he looked up to and idolised. *If only Bobby was here now to irritate me, and Alex to tell me tales of bravado for me to ape.*

*

News of the patient's identity did not impact on his care and treatment. Life for Alex went on as before.

Lots of people around me… voices, whispers, soft, gentle voices… someone wipes my lips… dry, dry… moist now… more whispers… there's a light… so bright that I want to shield my eyes… but… someone is waiting in the light… is that you, Mum? … Have you come for me, Mum? … I'm coming, Mum, coming home…

*

Joe was given the news of the demise of his brother Alex and knew then, that he, and he alone, would carry the burden of their evil deeds.

"Sorry to bring even more bad news," said the lawyer sent to impart the news to the troubled prisoner. "It seems that his heart gave out, they say his body was over-stressed and he simple passed away without ever regaining consciousness. Sorry for your loss."

CHAPTER THIRTY-FIVE

Linda-Mae Witherspoon, with her son Jake, arrived back from their time in Europe, landed at Chicago O'Hare and exited the concourse. There, they were stopped in their tracks by a newspaper headline that seemed to shout out at them, mocking them, enticing them and drawing them into its murky pit.

"Mom," said Jake who had noticed the headline while his mother was attending to her luggage. "Mom," he continued, "you have to see this."

They put their heads together as Jake held the news article that screamed out at them: *Memoirs of a Fallen Politician.*

"Oh no! His memoirs have been published and this crap newspaper is serialising it. Jake, who had control of this stuff? Who knows what your father has written?"

"Mom, I guess Ben had a hand in this. He knew more than he was prepared to tell us."

"As much as I hate it, we must buy the book; we need to know what was going on in your father's mind during those long years when he removed himself to that wretched library of his, and more or less banned me from entering. He sure didn't share any of this crap with me, apart from asking the date of our marriage. He seldom remembered our anniversaries."

"Yah, he asked me my date of birth. I thought that summed him up, not knowing his kids' birthdays."

Circulation of the 'Truth News Weekly' escalated over the weeks as word got around of the most startling disclosure from Ross S. Witherspoon's memoirs.

Tony Harvey, working at home, had a call from Ted Carr.

"Hey Tony, Carole is out for lunch with friends and they spotted something of interest in 'Truth News Weekly'. Tony, you need to read it."

"I never read that crap paper, they don't know what truth is. What's the score anyway, Ted?"

"Someone has published the memoirs of Ross Witherspoon; it's being serialised in the gutter press. Tony, they've dropped a bombshell. It's dynamite. He knew all along about Lucy; you have to read this for yourself."

"I'll call Gina, she's shopping with Poppy; she can pick up a copy. I can't believe what you have told me. You're saying he *knew* about Lucy's existence?"

"Looks like it, Tony. I'll get back at ya when the girls are home."

*

Abigail finished off an art lecture and returned to her own apartment where she kicked off her shoes, poured herself a drink and settled to chill out with some TV, relishing the peace and quiet before Ralph was due to join her. She flicked through channels searching for something to watch and was horrified to see the face of Lucy Mears fill her screen. She sat bolt upright, discarded her drink and listened, mouth wide open and brows scowling in fury at the news item. Shocked beyond belief at what she was hearing, she called her mom Gina, who, already alerted by Tony's call, was poring over the news article, gasping in disbelief as she silently read the astonishing revelation.

*

"Mom, what's wrong? You have gone very pale. Is it bad news?" asked Poppy.

"The worse possible, sweetie. Let's get home and Dad and I will discuss this with you. I don't want to talk about it now."

"Has someone died?"

"No, honey, it's not that. Let's wait until we are home."

*

Brenda Mears, relaxing at home, had a frantic call from Myra Hill, the chief executive of Mears Empire. She had been appointed by the board after Brenda retired and remained firm friends with her former employer.

"Brenda, turn on CNN right now. I'm coming over to you, you're gonna need someone with you, honey. See you in fifteen minutes."

*

If those involved in Lucy's abduction over a decade ago thought the horror and stress of the affair had diminished, they were soon jolted back to a world of confusion and disbelief, disbelief at the blatant lie that Ross S. Witherspoon had lived, anger at the hurt he now, even in death, inflicted on those who cared for, and about young Lucy. Her mother was bereft.

"Myra, I can't belief the callousness of the man. He *knew* about Lucy's birth yet he denied all knowledge of her existence when confronted at the hustings. He should have been given an Oscar for the way he carried it off, fooling everyone with his cold-blooded performance, and having people believe him to be a wronged father, and pointing the finger at me for concealing Lucy's birth from him. Oh the deceit! Myra, I can hardly take this in."

"Honey, we have to get hold of a copy of the book and read the darn thing. Leave it to me."

*

Linda-Mae Witherspoon sat in silence in the apartment that she had taken a lease on until such times as she found a suitable place to stay. She had asked Jake to leave her to read in private, to discover just what kind of man she had shared her life with. Hands shaking with trepidation, she began to read.

'My early years were spent with my paternal grandparents; my parents were in the military and chose to leave me in safe hands rather than have me move from place to place and disrupt my education. For that, I thank them. Living with my grandparents was idyllic; they spoiled me, indulged my every whim and spent time and money to ensure I had the best of

everything. My grandmother, a sweet lady, was a wonderful homemaker whose smile was infectious. She was petite but had a big heart that more than made up for her lack of height. Grandfather, more serious than his wife, was steeped in politics. He instilled in me a knowledge of the mysterious world of politics, and from him I found my niche in life. I wanted to enter politics, not the normal run-of-the-mill kind of politics, that I knew I would have to endure to reach my goal. I wanted, and was determined, to be at the top, and the top for me was Washington DC. I aimed to be the President of the United States of America. I focused my entire life on reaching my holy grail and was determined that nothing and no one would stand in my way. My grandfather died suddenly from a massive coronary. I found him sitting on the deck, newspaper open on his lap, his head down as if he was reading, but he had read his last. Grandmother and I struggled to come to terms with the loss of such a big man, big, not so much in stature, but in presence. His loss left a void in our lives and within six months of his death his beloved spouse joined him in the cold earth in the nearby churchyard. 'She died of a broken heart' the Pastor told the congregation, and how true it was. They had been childhood sweethearts and lived only for each other. My own parents returned for both funerals, but by now we were almost complete strangers; they were relieved to hear that I was heading to Washington DC and had been accepted at George Washington University and would not require them to be in my life. A generous inheritance from my grandparents would set me up for many years and help with future funding for my political dream. As I took my leave of my parents, a new chapter had begun in my life.

CHAPTER THIRTY-SIX

Myra Hill arrived at Brenda's home with copies of the memoirs. They sat together in silent reading, the only sound being an occasional sigh from Brenda. Myra, at times, looked up to gauge her friend's emotions ready to offer assistance should things become fraught. Brenda's knuckles were white as she gripped the offending book, her eyes seldom moved from the pages in front of her. At times she filled with tears, at times she gasped in anger at what she was reading.

I had no longer any need for my grandparents' house and arranged for decorators to move in to renovate the old building making it ready for a quick sale from which I made a sizable sum and, along with my inheritance from my grandfather's shrewd investment, became almost overnight, 'one of America's most eligible bachelors' to quote media reports. I took possession of an exquisite condo, my base from where, during my student days, I entertained a myriad of beautiful women with the sole aim of searching for a trophy wife, remembering my grandfather's advice that a successful politician required a stunning beauty by his side. I thought I had met such a person when I came across a student who dropped some books which I helped her retrieve. Brenda Mears was a stunning woman, her eyes lit up when she saw me approach and I often wondered if dropping her books had been a ploy to grab my attention.

Brenda gasped, drew a deep intake of breath and shouted, "The swine, the brute, how dare he say that! That is so untrue."

The memoirs of Ross S. Witherspoon continued.

My courtship with Brenda Mears lasted several months. I knew she was desperate to bag herself a good catch and often tried to seduce me, but I resisted. I had standards, even if she hadn't. She hinted at marriage and children, but I was not yet ready to commit to that as I wanted to have a firm foot on the political ladder before settling down; sure, marriage and children figured in my plans, but at a time that suited my career. That Mears woman continued to pursue me relentlessly and tricked me by claiming to be pregnant in the hope that I would propose to her. When I did not fall for her ruse, she threatened to abort my child, an action totally abhorrent to me and against my principals. We parted company. I had such a fear of my unborn child being denied a chance of life, that I had a good friend, my secretary Roc Shandon, arrange for surveillance and to supply me with regular reports. How delighted I was to hear that I had a daughter, whom I was told was named Lucy. Any attempt by me to contact my former lover and contribute to my child's upbringing was thwarted at every turn. I was distraught. I could have loved that child and guided her through life, had I been given the chance. I am a good father as my two sons will testify. My little Lucy was denied the right to know me and her brothers. When she was a tiny kid of about three or four years of age, I was alerted by my secretary to her routine with her nanny and the nanny's own kid. I discretely followed them to a park and, while they played, I managed to shoot a picture before a park attendant looked at me rather suspiciously. To this day I carry that picture in my wallet…

"Myra, the cheek of it, read this part here, oh the audacity of the man. This is a lie, a downright lie and shows the measure of the man that he arranges for this to be published after his death, when he can't be challenged or held to account."

Myra, startled by the outburst, jumped up and put her book down to attend to her friend whose anger was rife. Brenda's voice rose a few octaves in acute anger, her cheeks burning with fury as she waved her arms around as if attempting to let fly at her adversary. She threw the book down in disgust.

"I won't read any more of this tonight, but I intend to read the entire book and see what other fabrication has come from the poison pen of that man. How dare he write such foul lies?"

Such was the hurt felt by Brenda that she cut herself off from all but essential communication to concentrate on reading her former lover's book, taking note as she went along of parts that truly offended, and that she wanted to address. She had never felt such wrath, such indescribable bitterness and resentfulness towards anyone in her life, even at the height of her daughter's demise. The fact that she could not confront the writer raised her anxiety state to a new level. Sleep evaded her;

she mulled over in her tormented mind, phrase after phrase, sentence after sentence, until she felt her life had been taken over by Witherspoon's memoirs. *I will not allow you to destroy my life again,* she screamed in the night, as if her attacker were present in the room.

Having read as much as she could cope with of the vile book, she contacted her lawyer to discuss strategies for defending her good name. Clinton Whitlock had been her lawyer since she first joined the family firm of Mears Empire. He knew the calibre of the woman, her work ethos, her determination to succeed; he knew too the tragedy of the loss of her daughter and he knew that her good name had been defamed by the publication of those memoirs. She had asked him to read Ross S. Witherspoon's book and arrange a consultation with her when he had completed the task.

They met in his downtown office; he was not a man who consulted with clients in their homes, preferring to keep things as formal as possible. He was a true professional; his dress and deportment gave him an air of authority; his white hair, thick and neatly groomed never seemed to have a tress out of place, and the truly timeless eyeglass frame that perched on his nose suited the shape of his serious face. Clinton Whitlock should have retired several years ago but chose to continue to work until, as he told a colleague, he was forced through ill health to do so.

"I'm outraged at this," he said as he invited Brenda to sit down. "One falsehood after another. My dear lady, you must be distraught."

"I am devastated, Mr Whitlock. I am totally drained and I haven't slept properly since this trash was published."

"And trash it is, indeed. How clever was he to arrange for publication after his death when he can't be sued for libel; he and his family are untouchable. You can sue his estate as it is not immune from suits if there were any trusts set up *in vivos*. That, my dear lady, means set up outside the will and not included in the estate, then we can go down that road. Defamation cases are difficult to prove, and in my experience are dismissed for lack of proof. The onus is on you, the plaintiff to prove that your reputation has been damaged by the malice of what was published. Witherspoon's statements reflect negatively on your reputation as a person of some standing in the business community, and may harm too, your LMAMA academy. It could have a snowball effect on the reputation of your fine establishment."

Brenda sighed as she shook her head. "I'm not really interested in suing for financial gain; you know my circumstances Mr Whitlock. I have no need of Witherspoon money and would not touch a dime of it. What concerns me more is, as you say, the damage that has been done to my personal and business reputation, and the effect it could have on the academy just as we are establishing it as a centre of excellence. What hurts me more is that it has dragged my dear Lucy's memory into a murky world of untruths."

The kindly man thought how strong Brenda Mears was, and how challenging her life would become unless he could come up with some solution to ease the burden of pain that she obviously felt, but concealed well. He knew the old sayings, *mud sticks* and *there's no smoke without fire* and was aware that many people would wrongly judge his client and brand her as a shameful woman who deserved all that was thrown at her. He had given much thought as to how to repair the damage to her reputation.

Clinton Whitlock adjusted his glasses and looked sympathetically at the woman in front of him. Despite the knock she had received, she held herself up as the strong character he knew her to be, determined, honest and totally upfront. She had survived other traumatic times and he knew that she would rise like a phoenix from this latest attack on her integrity.

"I would like you to leave this with me a little longer while I ponder the best way to go forward. I'm thinking perhaps we should issue a statement and make use of publicity to denounce the defamation by Witherspoon, and involve other professional people to make statements about your integrity as a person. This won't get you an apology of course, but it may go some way to restore and protect your reputation. After all, you have spent a lifetime shaping your standing in the business world, and we must restore that. People who know you, my dear lady, have the utmost respect for you and will see these accusations for what they are, downright falsehoods."

As Brenda rose to leave she looked more relaxed. She trusted her lawyer completely and left his office in the knowledge that he would do his utmost to restore her honour.

CHAPTER THIRTY-SEVEN

TONY AND CAROLE MET TO discuss the vile revelations in the former politician's book. They were incensed at the knowledge that he had known about Lucy's existence.

"The effrontery of that man beggars belief," said an indignant Carole. "How did he carry off that deceit? He denied all knowledge of knowing that he had a daughter and told us he believed the pregnancy had been aborted. Now he blatantly writes that he followed her career and even carried a picture of Lucy as a child. Poor Brenda, he had written so much trash about the woman."

Tony stood up, paced the room, his temper almost exploding like fire crackers.

"So many people will believe these foul accusations. Only those of us who knew of Brenda's situation, and knew her true calibre, appreciate that he has destroyed the character of a good woman. Others who read this goddam crap will take it as gospel. Hey, we need to call her and offer our support."

Carole replied, "The guy was shrewd to the end, concealing this information until now for the sole purpose of making mischief and misery, not only for Brenda but for his poor wife and sons… how they must be suffering!"

Tony, back in unofficial detective mode said, "Who is this guy mentioned in the book? Roc Shandon? We've gotta find this guy if he is still alive and get his story. We owe it to Lucy."

"Yeah," replied Carole. "We have to track him. We'll start with political stuff going back to the heydays of Witherspoon as he moved up the career ladder. There must be records somewhere of the party's hustings and suchlike. We have the guy's name. Do you know anyone in the political world who could get us on track?"

"No one comes to mind, Carole, not at the moment, but hey, ask Ted, he might know some folk who could point us in the right direction. Get him on to it."

*

Ted, keen to be involved in his wife's latest project, spent time in the library going over some political papers that a former workmate suggested he look at.

Roc Shandon had known Witherspoon since college days when they met at George Washington University's induction day; they attended the same lectures and became firm friends. Both were engrossed in political life and, as Ross climbed the political ladder Roc was by his side as his mentor, secretary, trustee of his secrets, and custodian of the darker side of the aspiring politician. Roc shared his friend's apartment which became the focus, the strategy office, where plans were made and changed, speaking events arranged and fundraising organised as a priority in the building of Ross S. Witherspoon's future. It also became a place of respite for Witherspoon when he needed to be free of his family ties. There, he and Roc indulged in entertaining glamorous ladies, plying them with drugs and other illicit substances, while his unsuspecting wife believed him to be attending planning meetings. She was only required to be by his side when he needed a trophy wife to accompany him to events. This disclosure in the memoirs caused more grief to Linda-Mae who struggled daily to come to terms with the knowledge that her marriage had been a sham.

Witherspoon had employed an agent, Steve Wilkes, who oversaw the planning of hustings and kept in the background when such events took place. It was he who discovered, by employing a private detective, that his client was the father of Lucy Mears, and it was he who had spirited the politician and his wife from the hustings event when a news reporter revealed to the campaign faithful that their squeaky-clean candidate had concealed the fact that he was Lucy's father, and at a time when the child had been missing for several weeks.

In his memoirs, the politician wrote of this event:

The most political event of my life which, if successful, would have led me in the direction of my goal, the White House, was cruelly snatched from me when a reporter challenged me at question time. He asked if my family were excited at the prospect of perhaps living at the most prestigious of addresses. He caught me unaware; I was on a high with excitement. The evening had gone well. Steve Wilkes, my agent and campaign manager, had pulled out all the stops to make the event a gilt-edged spectacle where welcome dollars to fund the rest of my political journey cascaded in handfuls into the receptacles provided by my staff. The reporter stunned me, just as if he had thrown a knife through my torso. He publicly asked if my daughter, Lucy Mears, would be joining my family in the White House. My mind was in turmoil. I had to think on my feet. No one, apart from my good buddy Roc, my soulmate, knew my secret, and here was some crap reporter telling my assembled followers that I was the parent of Lucy Mears who at that time had been missing for months. The brash guy accused me of hiding Lucy to make political capital of finding her and discrediting her mother as the neglectful parent. I mumbled incoherently: everything I strove for was crumbling before my eyes. I was spewing sweat from every pore; my eyes nipped as I tried to wipe them with my clammy hand. Before I knew what was happening I was being whisked away by Steve via a back door to a waiting car. As he almost ran me out of the hall, I heard roars of 'he hasn't denied it… he hasn't denied it…' I had to endure the wrath of my wife who screamed obscenities at me. I had never seen her so mad as I tried to explain that I did not know about the pregnancy. There was no courage left in me to tell her the truth, and so I continued to live a lie, confiding only in Roc and later in my younger son as he grew into manhood. From that evening on my life became intolerable. I was forced to live like a condemned man in a lakeside chalet owned by my in-laws, whose coldness towards me was only marginally warmer than that of my wife. I could not face the world. Steve Wilkes had vanished from my life and any attempt by Roc to contact me was blocked at every try. I felt that prison would be considerably better than my almost solitary existence. I was becoming a recluse; conversations with my wife and her parents were mono-syllabic. It wasn't until several years later when we moved to Shelby County that I was able to resume my friendship with my lifelong friend Roc.

*

Ben Witherspoon, reading a copy of his father's book, gloated as he perused the pages of the work, knowing that he alone had been privy to its contents.

"Well, brother Jake, what ya make of Daddy boy now?" he spoke aloud as he read on.

It was my friend Roc Shandon who encouraged me to write my memoirs. 'Buddy,' he said, 'you have a wealth of experience to write about, hey, it could become a best seller in the political world, but you gotta put a bit of excitement into it, know what I mean? A bit about your personal life.'

'You mean, tell the truth?' I laughed as we began to write the outline of what I hoped would shock and stun my readers. 'Yeah, go for it, Ross', he told me, 'but don't mention 'us', that's gotta remain quiet.' I decided to come clean on my knowledge of Lucy's existence. That would sure shock her mother and go some way to avenge my feeling for the dame. You don't mess with Ross S. Witherspoon, I smiled, as I continued to write. Life has a habit, I have discovered, of pulling you up sharply to face mortality, like when attending a funeral of a colleague, or

someone younger, which I have done over the past few years. In the autumn of my days I had been feeling unusually tired and off-colour. My wife commented on my pallor, encouraged me to get outside more instead of living in my almost airless, and yes I have to confess, somewhat drab library, my haven for so long. I dismissed her concern and continued my reclusive life until I collapsed in a pool of blood and was found by my son Ben. Investigation and intrusive tests showed that I had succumbed to a debilitating illness. I was stunned to learn that prognosis was not good and that I was unlikely to see many more birthdays. My mind was in turmoil. I was in denial. Test results were not always reliable, I argued, and planned to ask for a second opinion. Slowly the reality of my situation overwhelmed me, and if it were not for my dutiful wife, I may have taken things into my own hands. Linda-Mae, my long-suffering and maligned spouse became my rock, ministering to me with a tenderness and love that I had disregarded for so many years, regarding her as surplus to requirements now that my political career had been so cruelly taken from me. Roc, my lifelong friend was devastated at the news, but, always the positive one, he spurred me on to complete the memoirs and leave a legacy for posterity. I spent time talking with my younger son; he was an easy kid with whom to converse, and I found myself telling him the contents of my book, my deepest secrets and my hatred of Brenda Mears. Should I have confided in one so young? He was outraged to hear of that woman and the damage she had done to my political career and depriving us of the pomp and ceremony of high living. Together we plotted revenge. I knew about her academy and suggested Ben enrol there and make mischief. We laughed together as we planned his onslaught. Given my present circumstances, I encouraged him to enrol as soon as possible and report to me when the deed was done. Little did I know that I would never see my beloved son again. News of his arrest was relayed to me as I lay waiting for my meeting with my maker; I could do nothing more to help him…

CHAPTER THIRTY-EIGHT

Jake and his mother had arranged to visit the rebellious young man in prison, and arrived at the appointed time only to be informed that Ben was refusing all visitors for the time being. The warden who spoke to them delivered a message from Ben. "He is refusing visitors at the moment, he said to tell you, it's because he is engrossed in a good book. He said you would know what he meant by that."

Jake was outraged. "He agreed to this visit; we've travelled here to speak with him on a serious family matter."

Linda-Mae was distressed at the snub from her youngest son and was prepared to plead with the warden to get him to change his mind, but Jake intervened.

"Sir, we're his family, his mom, and elder brother. We are on his approved visiting list," said an irate Jake, frustrated that Ben seemed to have the upper hand. "You guys tell us we have to keep family ties going," continued Jake. "How can we do that when you stop our visit?"

"I hear what you're saying," replied the warden. "But if the inmate refuses visits for whatever reason, there is nothing I can do about it. I can't drag him here against his will. Oh, and he said if you've brought anything for him, like candy bars, to give them to a warden on his block. Now, you need to write to the prisoner and request another visit."

Linda-Mae shook her head, crushed and defeated.

"Maybe we should do that Jake… write to Ben and ask for a visit."

"Mom, he's goading us, he wants us to react and beg for a visit… please don't fall for it… let things lie for the moment. Ben will need us before we need him, believe me, Mom. I know my brother."

"You're right, Jake. I'm over reacting, take me home I'm so distressed right now."

As they turned to leave, Jake picked up the bag of items he had for his brother, looked at them, and in disgust and threw them in a nearby trash can.

He drove home in silence; the only sound was from muted sobs from his mother who eventually fell asleep dreaming of kids behind bars jeering at her as she knelt on the ground, hands clasped as if in prayer, begging for clemency. At home she reluctantly read some more from her husband's book.

"Mom," protested Jake, "you don't need to read any more of that crap, it is only upsetting you."

"I need to read on, Jake. As uncomfortable as it is, I want to know what has been written about us. It may help me understand why Ben has turned his back on his family. There must be something in here that your father has concealed from us."

"You mean, apart from the shocking disclosure that he knew he had a daughter? Brenda Mears must feel as if she's been stabbed in the heart, poor lady. Have you ever met her, Mom?"

"No, honey, I never had any occasion to meet her, but, hey, I felt her pain when her daughter was killed, as any mother would."

She read on, fearful of what she might discover, but determined to learn what went on in the mind and life of her wayward husband.

After I disassociated myself from that Mears hussy, I concentrated on my political career with a vengeance, keeping in mind my need to find a truly acceptable woman to be my wife. A few women came and went in my life, none of them meeting my strict criteria, until I was introduced to a charming, rather dull, but very rich lady, Linda-Mae Sheringham whose father had contributed big bucks to the party. Potential was there for generous funding, so I wooed the lady and found her to be acceptable. She was presentable, charming and would fit the bill just fine. After a reasonable courtship, I proposed, and was of course, immediately accepted into the family. Who could resist me? Our wedding was a lavish affair, paid for by the doting parents, who must have feared that their daughter would be left on the shelf. I made the cursory offer to contribute to the nuptials, but the offer was swiftly and politely refused, as I had hoped it would be. We set up home in a more salubrious part of the city, more in keeping with my status in the world of politics. I kept possession of the penthouse condo where Roc was firmly established, and where I would find respite from my wife and her irritating parents. I was making a name for myself and came to the attention of those seeking to find a desirable candidate for future elections. I did the circuit of political events with my charming wife on my arm. Our son Jake, a morose child with whom I did not bond, spent his early days being cared for by his grandparents, and so keeping him out of my way during events. His mother, of course, whined at me to have him seen in public; 'We should portray a happy united family, Ross; voters love that kind of thing and it can only help in your career'. I didn't want the colicky child at my side, but did relent on a few occasions, holding him in my arms for photo shoots and handing him back to his adoring mother to exit stage left. Our second son Ben was an entirely different kid. He was chubby, giggled a lot and had a sweet angelic face that endeared him to me more than his ill-natured brother ever did. Ben spent many happy hours playing at my feet as I worked in my office. He was as amusing as he was happy, and as he grew our bond grew stronger. 'Some day, my son, we will have a chat about the political world, just like my grandpappy did with me. You and me, son, we could go places… hurry and grow up and join me in the crazy world of politics'.

Reading this, Linda-Mae, saddened at the description and neglect of her eldest son by his father, wiped a tear from her eye. *Poor Jake, he will be so hurt.* She was immensely proud of how Jake had turned out. He was a hard worker; his college degrees were excellent and set him off in the right direction on his chosen career. *His father never came to his graduation,* Linda-Mae reminded herself; *he told us he was unable to cancel an important meeting but would make it up to Jake. He never did.*

She closed the book, having read all she could cope with for one day and thought back to events in her life when she took as face value her ambitious husband's reasons when he was unable to be with his family. *Now I know that he didn't care about us, not me, not Jake, only Ben, and made excuse after excuse to avoid being with us. Oh, I've been taken for a fool.*

Had it not been for his mother, Jake Witherspoon would have disowned his brother and left for Europe. He had put his career on hold to see her settled in her new home and was determined to resume his career and forget his sibling. He was angry and desperately hurt by his father's revelations and personal comments about him. He considered changing his surname to that of his mother's, and ridding himself once and for all, from the shackles of being the son of Ross. S. Witherspoon.

"Mom, when you are settled in the new house, I plan to go back to Europe and have you visit regularly. I hate to leave you alone. I'd feel a heck of a lot easier in my mind if I thought you would stop trying to contact Ben. He hasn't answered any of your letters, has he? I guess he wants to break off contact with us. Let him wallow in his misery, Mom."

"Jake, I hear you, sweetie, but a mother/son bond can't be broken as easily as you think. He was my baby boy and I love him… I hate how he has turned out, but I'll never stop loving him and worrying about him. I guess I should hold back from visitation requests like you say, in the hope that he will want me to come visit sometime in the future when the furore over your father's book has subsided. Jake, I'm going to make a fresh start, change my name back to Sheringham and move on with my life. Yeah, honey, I sure will visit you in Europe when I'm settled. Now, you need to move on too. I truly appreciate what you've done for me and how you carried me through the days of that sickening read. I'm so glad my parents are no longer around to witness this revolting book. Jake, you and I are free, sweetie, to get on with our lives… you have my blessing to pack up and head off as soon as you like."

CHAPTER THIRTY-NINE

Reluctant at first to contact Brenda Mears, Tony consulted Carole on the wisdom of doing so.

"Part of me wants to leave the lady in peace to come to terms with the betrayal of that evil man, yet, now that Ted's friend has come up with an address for Witherspoon's secretary, who is bound to know what was going on in his mind, we need to take this forward. Over to you, wise one…"

"Hey Tony, I've been sitting on this one trying to do the right thing. She's sure bound to be suffering and may appreciate our support now that we have located Witherspoon's friend. From what we've gleaned, they were lifelong friends from college days. The guy, Roc Shandon, is in the background of every picture, of every political event: the quiet man. He still lives in Witherspoon's condo in DC. It was bequeathed to him in recognition of his loyal friendship. That real estate is worth a few bucks."

"We have to remember that we ain't cops now," laughed Tony, "like you keep telling me, but what the heck, let's see if Brenda will be agreeable to seeing her favourite law enforcers once more and take it from there. You make the call, partner."

"Hey, Tony, you ain't my boss, but as usual I get the messy bits to do. I'll get back at you."

*

Brenda, surprised at the call from Carole, was not averse to a visit from the duo who had been part of her life for over a decade; at times they riled her by what she saw as their intrusion into her private life, especially when they coerced her into revealing the name of Lucy's father, at times comforting her in her darkest moments and now, now, she regarded them as genuine caring people who struggled as she did, with the aftermath of Lucy's demise. She was aware too, of their recent experience of having their kids abducted, and empathised with them, feeling their pain and prayed at that time that the outcome for the retired officers would be very different from her own.

Over coffee in her comfortable penthouse condo, Brenda related her conversation with her lawyer, Clinton Whitlock.

"The guy is right, Brenda. There doesn't seem any point in pursuing a defamation suit that is likely to be thrown out, but I wholly agree with him that you need to put out a statement refuting the allegations that he has made against you," said Tony as he sipped sweet coffee.

Carole took up the conversation. "That is why we are here, to let you know we have located Roc Shandon who seems to have been the right-hand man behind Witherspoon's memoirs. He must have inside information about the vile man that you could perhaps use... I'm thinking if we can get a confession of sorts from him, it would go a long way to support your statement."

"Yeah," replied Brenda, "but you guys are no longer cops."

She smiled as she watched Tony's face change from animation to despondency.

"Tony forgets he's no longer with law enforcement," laughed Carole. "I have to remind him quite regularly that he ain't a cop."

They laughed at Tony's discomfort, past animosity and suspicion confined to the trash, the trio comfortable now in each other's company.

"Sure, I'm retired but I'll never stop being a detective. If there's a bad guy out there, I want him where he belongs, behind bars. You're right, Brenda, we're no longer cops but we do have buddies who are. So, what's your take on this?"

"Go ahead please, contact your cop friends and bring me the guy's confession."

*

Roc Shandon lived a rather sedate life since the death of his friend Ross. He had been pleasantly surprised when the latter informed him that he intended to leave the upmarket condo to him, expecting that it would be passed on to the eldest son, Jake.

"Hell no, Roc," Witherspoon had told him. "That kid means nothing to me. I'm his biological father, nothing else. I never warmed to the brat. No, Roc, I plan for this place to be yours, you've been Roc by name and rock by nature. Anyway, buddy, you gotta remember that neither Linda-Mae nor my boys, not even Ben, know of this place, and we've sure had our fun here. It's been my refuge in times of stress as they say in the good book."

"Well, if you insist, my friend," replied Roc. "I sure do appreciate your kind gesture."

"Yeah, and so we're sure of things, I've arranged for the royalties of my book to go to Ben. If it takes off as we hope it will, that kid will be a rich catch for someone. When he's finished that session in LMAMA academy, I intend to talk with him and explain the ins and outs of my will."

*

Roc, tidying some paperwork, was interrupted by a call from the concierge of his apartment stating that some detectives were there and wished for a few moments of his time.

"Sure, send them up."

Roc invited the detectives into his apartment, completely unaware of the reason for their visit. He was relaxed, knowing he had done nothing to warrant a visit from the authorities and was intrigued to find out what they had to say.

"Can I offer you guys some coffee?" he asked pleasantly.

"No thanks, sir, if you don't mind we'll get down to business."

"Sure, officers, I'm intrigued."

"Nice pad you have here, sir," said one officer glancing around at the place that his salary could never look at. "Have you lived here long?"

"Yeah, since my student days at GW. It actually belonged to a good friend of mine who sadly passed away recently and bequeathed it to me."

"Quite a bequest, sir. You must have been real good friends."

"Ross was the best buddy anyone could ask for."

"That would be Ross Witherspoon, the former politician?" enquired the second officer.

"Yes, sir, a fine man, much maligned by media slurs, but he rose above it, took it on the chin."

"Sir, that's who we've come to talk to you about. You are aware of course that he published his memoirs since your name features in it?"

"Sure, officer. I helped him finish it off when he got sick. Is there a problem?"

"Only a possibility of a defamation suit against his estate, and I might add, it could include your cosy pad here."

Roc Shandon paled, he withdrew a handkerchief from his pocket and wiped his brow.

"Um, sorry officer, you've lost me there… what… what do you mean? A defamation suit?"

The senior detective, not a man to be messed with, continued. "It seems that your real good buddy fabricated a good section of his book and perjured himself when he wrote about certain people, in other words he lied, and these innocent folks, one in particular, ain't too happy at what he said. He's written falsehoods against them, upset them and destroyed their reputation. A clear case of defamation, sir. How much input did you have in this book? What was your contribution?"

Roc stood up, walked towards the window and gazed out at the scene below as if seeking inspiration. He turned to the officers, shook his head and said in an almost inaudible high-pitched voice:

"I mainly typed it up for him; he would dictate and I typed."

"Like a secretary, then?" asked the junior officer relishing the man's discomfort.

"Yeah, that's what I am... was... Ross's secretary."

"Didn't you question what you were asked to write? Didn't you think you were aiding and abetting a pack of lies?"

"Certainly not. I typed what he dictated. I didn't know that he wasn't telling me anything but the truth. Hell, I've known him for most of my life. He's an honest man... was... I have to say."

"So you didn't question anything or think anything odd about his narrative?" asked the senior officer of the flustered man.

"I had no reason to question anything, officer. Look, do I need a lawyer? I don't like where this line of questioning is going."

"Sir, if you think you need a lawyer, then go get yourself a good one. We won't take up any more of your time. Here's my details, get your brief to contact me if he needs any information."

Roc Shandon showed the officers out, poured himself a stiff drink and collapsed onto a chair; he was visibly shaken by the encounter and totally bemused at what had been said. *Surely they must be wrong?* he thought as he pressed the number for his lawyer. He spent a restless night going over in his head his sessions with Ross when they worked on the memoirs. As if he had a light bulb moment, he sat bolt upright as a memory invaded his mind and would not leave him. He recalled one occasion, or was it more, when Ross laughed as he said: *'Roc, my friend, there's a bit of exaggeration in this work of art; it sure as hell will stir things up when that Mears dame and my wife get hold of the book'.* Roc sweated. He had the beginning of a migraine. He felt miserable. *Oh no, don't let it be that I let myself be party to some kind of vendetta,* he thought as he tried to recall what else may have been included in the book that would cause deep offense, enough it seems to warrant a court case, and if what those officers hinted at was correct would mean he might lose his precious apartment. The two officers, well-known to both Tony and Carole, contacted them to unofficially relate their interview with Roc Shandon.

"He seemed genuinely stunned, Tony. At first it was hard to decide if he was a good actor and covering up for his best buddy, but as time went on I felt the guy was telling the truth. He believed every word that came out of the mouth of Witherspoon. It was as if the scales had fallen from his eyes and he realised he'd been taken in hook, line and sinker. He's gonna call his lawyer but, hey, I don't think we'll have any problem getting this guy to make a statement which will go a long way to helping Brenda."

"So we wait for his lawyer to call? Bring it on. The sooner Brenda can put this behind her, the better."

CHAPTER FORTY

The more Linda-Mae, now Sheringham, thought about her obnoxious husband and his harsh writing, the more determined she became to rise above it and somehow clear her name and that of her son Jake. Several months had passed since she last set eyes on Ben. She had ceased writing to him, leaving him to wallow in his loneliness in the correction facility. She had left a forwarding address with the prison authorities but not with her son. *If Ben wants to contact me he will have to make the effort and speak to the governor,* she thought to herself as she sifted through yet more boxes that had remained unopened since her move to the new house. She took a walk later in the day to collect mail and to clear her head. She was surprised to recognise Ben's handwriting on one of the envelopes. She called in at a coffee shop, settled herself with a welcome latte and began reading:

'Mom, why did you stop writing me? Okay, I guess you're mad at me but you could have written. I had to ask the governor for your address, it sure wasn't easy as the guy hates me. I see you've moved hundreds of miles from me, and what's

this Sheringham name change about? What happened to our family name? There weren't nothing wrong with Witherspoon. But hey I guess my brother put you up to all this, change of name and move to the East. Well, I ain't gonna change my name for no one. I'm proud of my name. I was gonna ask you to resume your visitation rights, but what the heck, if you're so far away, well I guess you won't come see me. Mom, I miss you and want to see you, please come. I promise I won't be mean like last time you and Jake asked to visit, but I sure was mad at you telling me you were moving away. I want to talk with you. That's all for now, Mom, your loving son, Benjamin Simon Witherspoon'.

Linda-Mae wiped a tear from the corner of her eye, returned the letter to its envelope and stuffed it unceremoniously into her pocket. *Well, I'll be damned,* she thought as she returned home to update Jake.

Linda-Mae did not reply to Ben's letter for several weeks until she felt emotionally able to make the journey and face whatever her young son had to say to her. She felt, as Jake did, that Ben was hiding something of immense importance. She made the long journey alone, aware that the visit could be a disaster depending on Ben's frame of mind. As her airplane touched down, she sighed so deeply that the passenger seated beside her, mistaking her nervousness for fear of flying, patted her arm saying, "We're down now, ma'am, we've landed safely." Linda-Mae smiled her thanks, collected her carry-on bag and exited the plane.

Before visiting Ben, she checked into a hotel, freshened up and ate a light snack. She had collected a few things for him and hoped that this time, she would be able to hand them directly to him.

At the correction centre she met with Ben and was stunned at his appearance. He had aged considerably and looked as if he carried the troubles of the world on his young shoulders.

"Hi, Mom," he almost whispered the greeting, his voice wavering as he spoke.

Tears streamed down his face as he sat opposite her.

"Mom, I've missed you so much. I'm sorry I was mean to you. I guess it was all too much for me, Dad dying and all that, and being locked up in this place. I'm glad you came back, I thought I'd lost you forever and that you hated me."

Linda-Mae's heart went out to her troubled son, all past anger abated as she looked at the vulnerable young man in front of her.

"Ben, sweetie, I've never hated you, sure I've been disappointed with you at times, but hate, no, that's too strong a word. You'll always be my baby and I'll always love you… I might not love what you do, but I'll be here for you when you are released."

Ben relaxed and he and Linda-Mae conversed for some time before she brought up the thorny subject of the memoirs.

"Honey, I want to talk with you about your father's book. You do know, don't you, that he has hurt me deeply, me and Jake, and I'm sure a few other people, by his harsh words. I feel I never knew him, perhaps I never ever had and he's not here to explain himself.

Ben, sweetie, what do you know about what your father wrote?"

The young man hesitated. *This could go two ways,* he thought; *do I gloat at Mom or do I come clean*? Looking at his crestfallen mother whom he knew he loved and was loved by in return, his stony heart melted, and with remorse, he chose the latter course.

Linda-Mae taking his hesitation as a refusal to answer, quietly said, "Ben, help me here, please. I need to know what you knew… Ben?"

"Mom, I'm struggling with this. I've been carrying it like a millstone around my neck for so long, I'm confused, Mom. I loved Dad and loved that he favoured me against Jake and that he confided things in me, but, well, he's gone now and I need to come clean… Mom, don't be mad at me at what I'm gonna tell you…"

"Honey, just get things off your chest, you know I won't stop loving you, but Ben, I want to know everything."

Ben took a deep breath as if summoning courage from the depth of his being and began his confession. He maintained eye contact with his mother as if it were of immense importance to him that he could read her reaction.

"Mom, Dad told me things but made me promise never to reveal to anyone what he was to tell me. Mom, I was real happy and proud that he chose to confide in me, I guess it went to my head. Hey, I was only a kid. He told me that he knew all along that he had a daughter Lucy, he'd gotten a private detective or someone to keep him in the loop about the kid and knew her whereabouts and that she had a real talent for music. He showed me a picture of her when she was about four years of age. He even managed to sit in on part of one of her concerts, but didn't hang around in case he would be spotted. When she went missing he was real worried, but couldn't come clean, so he just followed the media reports about her. He was sad when she was killed and regretted that he'd never met her. Mom, he told me that he hated the kid's mother, Brenda Mears, for getting pregnant just when he was launching out on his career but begged her not to abort but she told him she had, so he said. Now I don't know what to believe."

Linda-Mae raised her eyes, sighed some and smiled at Ben to encourage him to offload. He continued:

"Mom, he hated the woman so much that he wanted revenge so he got me enrolled in her LMAMA place where I was to study art and do damage to the place. He said when I'd done that, he wanted to talk some more and tell me stuff. He said he'd been feeling sick but I wasn't to worry. It wasn't serious or anything bad. Hell, Mom, I was so crazily besotted with him I'd have done anything he asked of me. Well, you know the rest, I slashed a portrait of Lucy and tried to smash the windows of her shrine place, but the glass was extra tough. I thought I'd gotten away with it as Dad got me false student papers, but the cops were everywhere and, well here I am paying the price… and I never got to see Dad again or tell him I'd done what he asked. I guess I needed his approval. Mom, I'm so sorry."

Linda-Mae remained silent as she held her son's hand. She kept her thoughts to herself: *how could that selfish man use his own son for such an evil deed? Poor Ben, how he craved his father's love.* Eventually she spoke quietly to the young man seated in front of her waiting for her reaction, waiting for her judgement, waiting for her acceptance of him.

"Thank you, Ben, for your honesty. I want you to know I appreciate what you have told me, I need to take what you said on board and do some serious thinking. I'll write to you, sweetie, as soon as I get home and hey, it won't be long until you're out of here so keep that thought in mind."

"But, Mom, there's more. I have to tell you that Dad told me that Jake was not my full brother, that you had him by another man and he, Dad, stood by you. He said he never warmed to Jake and that I was to remember that he was only my half-brother and that I was his one and only son. Mom, is that true? Did you have an affair with someone?"

It took all her strength of will not to scream, *No, No, No,* at her bewildered child. She had to handle him with care, his vulnerability was clear, he was confused and looked to her for answers. Taking a deep, painful breath, she held both his hands in hers, looked into his tear-filled eyes and said, "Ben, sweetie, look at me, Ben, look into my eyes as I do yours. Ben, honey, that was total fabrication on the part of your father. There was never any man in my life but your father, both you and Jake are his and my children. There was never any affair, never. Do you believe me, Ben?"

Ben nodded his head, his unkempt hair falling over his eyes and momentarily shielding his gaze from his mother. He found it difficult to speak.

"Mom, I'm confused. I don't understand why Dad said what he did."

"Neither do I, sweetie. I think he spent so much of his life living a lie that he could no longer separate truth from falsehood. Ben, he has gone now and has taken his reasons for hurting us with him to the grave. We will never figure out what made him tick. We need to move on, you, me and Jake, we must build bridges, not walls that shut each other out. Honey, when you are out of here, we'll take a vacation, somewhere special and get to know each other again. Would you be willing to do that, Ben? Jake needs to get to know his kid brother."

Ben, still overcome with gut-wrenching emotions, could only wipe his eyes with his sleeve and nod his acceptance to the woman he knew loved him unconditionally.

Her flight home gave Linda-Mae time to reflect on what she had heard. She had no doubt that Ben had told her the truth and hoped that he would be a better person for it. Deeply angered at the betrayal by the man she had loved and given her life to, she was shocked at how he had used his vulnerable son to commit a serious felony resulting in the boy being jailed. She was furious at the blatant untruth about a non-existent affair resulting in Jake being fathered by someone else. *How could he do that to his own flesh and blood? I'm grateful at least that he didn't include such degrading remarks in his book. Poor Jake has suffered enough*. She closed her eyes to shut out the horrors, the hurt, the betrayal from the man she gave her life too, but sleep evaded her.

Once home, she mulled over the things her son had told her, and tried to find a way to move on with their lives. Ben was due to be released from jail in a few months and she wanted to clear her mind of negative thoughts and be a positive influence in his young life. To do this, she had to bring Jake on board and knew that might be difficult for her older boy to accept. Somehow or other she had to bridge the emotional gap between the brothers and help them bond.

A long skype conversation took place between Linda-Mae and young Jake. It was not easy to reveal what Ben had told her about the circumstances of Jake's birth. She wondered why Ross never warmed to the child, and would never know the answer to that question. Jake listened in silence as his mother related the events of her visit to Ben. The level-headed young man shook his head in disgust, and reassured his mother that he too would be willing to help his brother reconnect with him and help them all move forward as a family of three. He suggested a trip to Switzerland, a neutral country the concept of which was not lost on his mother, where he hoped the Alpine air and change of scene would benefit them all. He offered to make arrangements for the extended trip and promised to have everything in place for Ben's release from prison, leaving his mother free to pursue other matters.

CHAPTER FORTY-ONE

Linda-Mae Sheringham and Brenda Mears had never met. They each suffered in their own way from knowing Ross S. Witherspoon and were each victim of his cruel revelations. As Linda-Mae mulled over the horrors of Ben's confession she felt compelled to contact the other maligned woman.

Brenda took a call from her lawyer, Clinton Whitlock saying that the lawyer representing the Witherspoons had been in touch with an interesting proposition.

"Witherspoon's widow has requested a face to face meeting with you to discuss something of mutual interest. From the little I gleaned, it may well be to your advantage to meet with her on neutral territory. Would you like some time to think about your response and call me when you have made a decision?" Brenda was intrigued as to what the meeting would reveal, and after some deliberation agreed to meet Linda-Mae Sheringham, as she was led to believe the lady now called herself.

"I've nothing to lose and may have something to gain," she told Mr Whitlock as he arranged the meeting.

The rendezvous took place in a hotel midway between Chicago and Florida Keys. Both women were understandably nervous at the prospect of what lay ahead. Brenda paced her hotel room like a caged lion ready to pounce on its prey. She had redone her make-up to perfection and constantly studied herself in the mirror. She dressed conservatively in a smart pants suit, wore the minimum of jewellery and, satisfied with her appearance, rode the elevator to the venue. Her stomach turned somersaults as she entered the 'Rose Lounge'. She was approached by the maître d who welcomed her and led her to a private area where a tall, elegant woman rose to meet her. Brenda had no time to take in the appearance of Linda-Mae and was swiftly seated and handed a wine list.

"Ladies, if you would like to choose your drink, I'll have it brought immediately, and leave you to enjoy your afternoon."

They selected their drinks and sat facing each other, both nervous, anxious, uncomfortable and slightly in awe of the other. Brenda broke the ice. "Thank you for having the courage to arrange this meeting. I gave it some consideration before I accepted, but thought, what the heck, we're grown women, we have something in common, albeit unpleasant, so let's talk."

Linda-Mae visibly relaxed; her smile was genuine and welcoming and put her companion at ease. "I wondered if I were doing the right thing by you. I didn't want to stir up memories but when your lawyer told mine that you were considering putting out a media statement, I though, hey, I have to talk to this lady."

The two relaxed, chatted for a time about life in general and then got to the crux of the matter that had brought them together.

"My husband," began Linda-Mae, "was a deceitful man to write what he did about us. You must be so hurt by his lies, as I am and my son Jake. How that man could go to his maker knowing the devastation his words would have. Pure falsehood. His entire life was a lie; he used me for his political career and nothing else. I now know that the man I loved and married and gave my life to, never loved me. He loved only himself."

Brenda admired her honesty and warmed to the victim who shared her repulsion of the man. The two talked for some time and were comfortable in each other's presence, each empathizing with the other. They spoke at length of Lucy and shed shared tears; of Ben's destruction of the portrait and his confession concerning his father, of Jake's hurt and of their own charged emotions.

Linda-Mae said, "And to think I was so scared to meet you!"

Brenda said, "Exactly my sentiments too. I almost called off but hey, I am so glad we've met."

"I guess my husband never envisaged the two wronged women in his life being together over lunch," laughed Linda-Mae, uninhibited now by the presence of the formidable former president of Mears Empire. She told Brenda of her difficulty with her younger son and how she hoped a proposed vacation to Switzerland would help them to turn a corner in their fraught lives.

"Despite the reason for your son enrolling in the academy," commented Brenda, "it's worth knowing that he did show potential as an artist; perhaps you could encourage him to pursue art as a means of sorting his life out."

They concluded their fruitful time together with an agreement that they would each talk to their lawyers with a view to issuing a joint media statement.

"From what I hear, a long-time friend of our mutual adversary is willing to make a statement about the untruths he was asked to type during the writing of the despicable memoirs. It will give credence to our own statement. We'll face the world together," commented Brenda in positive mood as she took leave of her new friend.

A kindred spirit, she thought, as she returned home to ponder the next stage of restoring her, and Linda-Mae's, reputation.

CHAPTER FORTY-TWO

Several months on from the successful meeting of the two maligned women, a statement appeared in several newspapers and was picked up by media throughout their home state, and beyond. It condemned the published memoirs of Ross S. Witherspoon, detailing and exposing the lies and revelations within it, as figments of a disturbed and spurned, disgraced politician's imagination. The statement, released jointly through the lawyers of Brenda Mears and Linda-Mae Sheringham, led to the voluntary withdrawal of the book from several bookstores, and, with a guarantee by the publishers that no more books would be released by them, meant that those burdened by the damaging innuendos were exonerated and free now to continue with their blameless lives with heads held high.

"An end to a sordid chapter," remarked Carole as she read the media statement.

"Yeah," replied Tony as they relaxed with their respective spouses in Carole's comfortable sitting room, "but will the hurt ever go away?"

"I'm sure it must fester deep inside, despite the media input," said Carole. "But, knowing Brenda's strength of character, that lady will cope and face the world head-on."

Tony continued, "That guy, Roc Shandon, was one lucky guy to get off so lightly. I'm sure as hell certain that he knew more than he told us. He gave enough info to condemn Witherspoon and save his own bacon, but I have a niggling feeling that there was much more lurking there."

"Sure, Tony," said Carole. "But he wanted to keep his precious condo, so he couldn't say too much in case he incriminated himself and ended up in court, party to a defamation case."

"Now, you guys, listen up," said Ted with a laugh, "don't get any ideas of pursuing this...you have retired... finished with all that... okay, dudes?"

"As if we would," whispered Carole, knowing fine well that given the opportunity, she and Tony would relish investigating the guy further.

Tony looked across at Gina who threw him a look that spoke volumes, as if to say, *don't even think of it.*

"No problem, guys," said Tony with a sigh. "We'll leave well alone."

"And, honey," said Gina. "We'll have other things on our mind now that Abigail and Ralph have announced their engagement. We have a wedding to plan and it's going to be a day fit for our princess. Poppy is so excited at the prospect of being chief bridesmaid and getting to help organise the pre-wedding activities and bridal shower. We'll never get her to come down to earth."

Carole took up the theme. "I *love* weddings, it's so exciting to help a couple set off on their lifetime journey together. We have fingers crossed that Jack's romance with Sue will blossom. She's adorable and we love her very much. And, Tess seems keen on her boyfriend, Randall. We've yet to meet him but from what she says, he's 'the one'."

Carole and Gina, engrossed in wedding fever, did not notice that their spouses had snuck out to the den.

"We'll have nothing but wedding talk from now on," laughed Tony as he accepted a beer from Ted. "I must say though, that I was touched when Abbie asked me to walk her down the aisle. However, I've persuaded her that honour should go to her mom, after all, Gina brought her up and it's only right that she takes her place by her daughter's side. It took a bit to persuade them both, but they see the wisdom in it, and I'll be there with her at the top table. Lucian will be head usher, he's a bit anxious about it, but we'll talk him through procedure. He still needs reassurance and can be quite morose at times."

"Sounds like you guys will be so busy over the next few months that you won't have time to think of detective work. Seriously, Tony, I want Carole to forget all that stuff and concentrate on the kids. The scare we had with them has focused our priorities onto family life. I never want to take my kids for granted again."

*

In a Swiss resort, two brothers finished their mountain hike and sat together admiring the visage in front of them.

"Stunning scenery, isn't it Jake? I've never seen anything like it, ever. After prison, this is heaven, the air is so clear, I feel I'm breathing properly for the first time in years. I wish I could capture this forever."

"You could, you know. You could do just that. Paint it. Ben, you have to believe it when we tell you that you have an artistic eye, you have real talent, little brother."

Ben looked fondly at his older brother. He felt a warm glow from the words *little brother* knowing they were sincere and heartfelt. The brothers had talked long into the night, opened their hearts, dealt with their demons and emerged as brothers, bonded together with strong glue, determined that nothing and no one would stand in the way of them journeying through life together. Ben told of the horror of his imprisonment, the loneliness, his shame, the fear, the boredom and the feeling that he had lost the love of his family forever.

"We've all been to hell and back," reassured Jake. "But, hey, we're going to put it all behind us and move on with our lives... no turning back... no going to a dark place in your mind... right, dude?"

"Right, big brother," replied a smiling Ben as he playfully slapped his brother's arm.

Linda-Mae Sheringham, sitting in the sun relaxing with a book, looked up at the sound of familiar laughter. Her heart was filled with love as she watched the two young men who meant everything to her exit the nearby cable car that had brought them from their mountain hike. Life had taken on a joy that she embraced wholeheartedly, experiencing a freedom and contentment that had evaded her all her days. As her sons hugged her she felt she would explode with happiness.

"Mom," said Jake, "Ben has some news for you, we've had a long discussion."

"Yeah, we have. Mom, I want to study art, seriously this time. I want to go to college and paint landscapes. This place is an inspiration."

"Ben, I'm so pleased to hear that, and you know I'll fund your time at college and support you all the way."

"Thanks, Mom, but my rich brother here," he said, pushing his brother down on the snow, "this dude here, who can't keep his balance in the snow, has offered to help fund me and take me to Paris with him to watch Parisian artists at work at the Left Bank and visit the Louvre on the Right Bank, Mom, it's so exciting!"

As they escorted their mother to their hotel, Ben held her hand and whispered, "Mom, I'm going to apologise to the folks at LMAMA. I'll compose a letter; will you check it over for me?"

Linda-Mae, squeezed her son's hand and replied, "Of course, Ben, of course I will."

She offered a silent prayer of thanks that her world was once more on a steady path, a path through life where Ben would thrive with the help of his brother.

*

BRENDA, VISITING ABIGAIL AND RALPH to offer congratulations, sat, as was her way, in Lucy's room, the glass now fully repaired after Ben's attack and talked to the spirit of her lost child. She folded a well-written letter and placed it on a table there.

"This apology is meant for you, baby."

She sat by the baby grand piano, fingering the keys and imagined she could hear her daughter playing the instrument. She let her mind recall past years: the highs and lows, the joys, regrets, sorrows and now, the contentment she felt within her soul.

"Maybe now, Lucy, we can rid ourselves of the legacy of Anna Leci."

∞

ABOUT THE AUTHOR

Terry H. Watson qualified in D.C. E. and Dip.Sp.Ed. from Notre Dame College, Glasgow and Bearsden, and obtained a B.A. degree from Open University Scotland.

A retired special needs teacher, Terry began her writing career in 2014.

THE LECI LEGACY is the final part of a mystery thriller trilogy.

Terry has also written a compilation of short stories, *A TALE OR TWO AND A FEW MORE* and a children's book, *THE CLOCK THAT LOST ITS TICK, AND OTHER TALES.*

She is presently working on a mystery novel, *A CASE FOR JULIE.*

Terry lives in Scotland with her husband Drew and can be contacted via

Website: www.terryhwatson.com

Twitter: @TerryHWatson1

e-mail: Terryhwatson@yahoo.co.uk